playing
with
fire

D0752571

playing with fire

kayla perrin

HARLEQUIN® MIRA®

Recycling programs
for this product may
not exist in your area.

ISBN-13: 978-0-7783-1498-1

PLAYING WITH FIRE

For questions and comments about the quality of this book, please contact us at CustomerService@Harlequin.com.

Printed in U.S.A.

First printing: August 2013
10 9 8 7 6 5 4 3 2 1

1

"Wow, I can't believe what I'm hearing. You're blowing me off tonight—for *a man?*"

Zienna Thomas heard a smile in her friend Alexis's voice, which made her feel a lot less guilty for canceling their dinner plans last minute.

"I know, and I'm sorry." Not since she was in her twenties had Zienna canceled on a friend for a guy. "It's just that Nicholas said he really needed to see me tonight. I'm on my way there now. Something about how he created the best new dish for his restaurant and he wants me to try it before he loses his inspiration. You know Nicholas. When he gets excited, he's like a dog with a bone. I couldn't tell him no."

"Maybe not, but you could tell him that your best friend has taste buds, too...."

"I could have," Zienna agreed. "But he's at the new restaurant, testing out the facilities before the grand opening, and he's sensitive about only one person trying—"

"I'm just giving you a hard time," Alexis interrupted her. "I know how Nicholas is. If he wants only you to sample some-thing, he'll be mad if I show up wanting a plate."

"Ain't that the truth." A soft smile touched Zienna's lips as she thought of Nicholas's quirks. He was set in his ways when it came to how he did business, and in the five months she had been dating him, he had deemed her his food tester. And he wanted only one person to give him an unbiased opinion on his creations before presenting them to the public.

"Plus," Zienna went on, "I kind of get the sense…" Her voice trailed off. The thought that had occurred to her sud-denly seemed foolish.

"Sense that what?" Alexis prompted.

"I don't know. Kind of the way he was stressing that I had to meet him *tonight,* that tomorrow wouldn't do… He men-tioned a few days ago that a best friend of his was coming back to town. I'm not sure why, but I wouldn't be surprised if he wants me to meet him tonight."

"Wow, so this is really getting serious," Alexis all but sang.

"I don't know." Zienna's stomach tickled at the thought. "Maybe. But if his friend does drop by, it's not like he's in-troducing me to his parents or anything."

"But a best friend—that's just as critical. He obviously likes you."

Zienna's heart swelled. "I know. And I like him, too."

"I did good, didn't I?" Alexis asked, and Zienna could pic-ture the huge smile on her face.

"Yes, you did good." It was Alexis who'd met Nicholas at his restaurant, and struck up a conversation with him with the sole purpose of introducing him to Zienna. "Things are going better than I ever expected."

"Go have fun with your man. I won't hold it against you that you're blowing me off. Don't worry about me, wasting away on my sofa…."

"Look at the bright side. You can finally catch up on the latest season of *Criminal Minds* that you've got stored on your PVR."

"Ouch. No sympathy at all."

"There are worse ways to spend an evening than watching Shemar Moore."

"This is true. Now if only I could get him to come to Chicago, help me nurse my broken heart."

Zienna didn't bother to comment as she maneuvered her car into the parking lot of Reflections on the Bay, the restaurant her boyfriend was about to launch. Alexis's own relationship of two years had recently ended, but she was the one who'd crushed Elliott's heart by calling off their short engagement. According to Alexis, Elliott was a great guy, but something vital was missing from their relationship. Getting engaged had made her realize that she couldn't settle for a guy who was only good enough.

"Look, Alex, I just got to the restaurant. So I'll talk to you later, okay?"

"Sure," Alexis replied. Then, hurriedly, "Hey, if Nicholas's friend does show up and he's sexy, give him my number."

"Whatever." Zienna laughed. "You're supposed to be wasting away on the sofa, remember?"

"Actually, you're supposed to be encouraging me to jump into bed with a random stranger so that I get over Elliott."

"Talk to you, Alex," Zienna said.

"Fill me in later!"

Zienna ended the call and shook her head. Alexis had always been talking about finding someone new—even before she'd finally dumped Elliott. Someone who didn't know her might wonder what more she could want in a guy. She'd been in a serious relationship for two years, and unlike a lot of other women involved with men that long, she had secured an engagement ring. But once she'd gotten engaged, she had done a one-eighty with her emotions, saying that Elliott was too safe, too predictable…and for that reason, ultimately boring. And the last thing Alexis wanted was to marry a guy who didn't excite her.

While Zienna didn't necessarily agree that her friend should have dumped Elliott, she understood only too well her sentiments. Zienna had once been crazy about a guy who was sexy as hell, with an edge that never failed to electrify her. But Wendell didn't want to get married—ever—and had moved away four years ago. Since then, Zienna had come to realize that part of the thrill with him had been the chase. The way he'd kept her on her toes by never completely giving her his heart.

She had had to work for his time and affection, which had been exhilarating and fun. And the prize—superhot sex—had always been worth her efforts. The men she'd dated after Wendell had been dull and hadn't challenged her. Not to mention that they couldn't compare in the bedroom.

But finally, Zienna had met Nicholas, and he was different than the duds she'd dated in the past. Though he'd made his attraction to her completely clear, so she wasn't challenged in that regard, Zienna didn't find herself getting bored with him. Maybe it was because she'd grown up and could appreciate a man who was willing to hand her his heart on a platter, instead of play games.

Games only led to pain.

Zienna had been crazy about Wendell, but ultimately devastated by him. Yet foolishly, even as the years passed, she had often hoped he would return. Tell her he'd made a mistake by leaving her. How insane was that?

Thankfully, she was older and wiser now. In her midthirties and definitely more mature, she had come to realize that she'd never really had a relationship with Wendell at all. Oh, he had given her great loving, which had left her craving more of him. But he had never promised her tomorrow, not with words, anyway. Zienna had been dumb enough to believe their incredible sexual connection meant he must have loved her.

People said that time healed all wounds, and it was in the last year that she had finally started to let go of the residual feelings she'd had for Wendell. Which, she knew, was the main reason she hadn't been interested in the other guys she'd dated—she'd still carried a torch for a man who hadn't returned her feelings. But once she'd been able to put Wendell in her rearview mirror, she had been willing to open up her heart to someone new.

That person was Nicholas. They'd been dating for only five months, but Zienna was really into him.

And it felt good.

She lowered the car's visor and checked the mirror to make sure she still looked as presentable as she had before she'd gotten behind the wheel of her Hyundai Sonata. Located north of Chicago's downtown core near the Belmont Yacht Club, Reflections on the Bay was the sister property to Reflections, a restaurant Nicholas had been running for eight years. He had wanted a location that overlooked Lake Michigan, so was elated when he'd been able to get this property. The fact that it had a parking lot for guests, unlike the location in the theater district by the Loop, was another bonus.

Satisfied that she looked good, Zienna exited her car. Turning, she faced the lake, which was a spectacular sight at night, with the moon's rays dancing on the ripples. The tables for the patio had already arrived, and she had no doubt that the outdoor seating area would be a preferred spot for many customers in summer.

She grinned. The place was coming along nicely. The sign bearing the establishment's name was now illuminated, glowing orangey-red just like its sister location. The doors were set to open in a couple weeks, on May 4. Zienna couldn't help feeling a sense of pride for Nicholas.

His car was the only other vehicle in the parking lot. That meant she'd been wrong about her suspicion that he wanted to introduce her to his friend.

She opened the door to the restaurant and stepped inside. Unlike at Nicholas's first restaurant, Reflections, where the lights would be dimmed to create ambience for the diners, the lights here were fully up. This restaurant was almost identical to its sister establishment in terms of decor, with the exception of some of the lighting fixtures and framed photographs on the wall. All the photos here and at Nicholas's other location were black-and-white, and reflected moments in Chicago's history—hence the name.

"Hello?" Zienna called out. A delectable aroma of some sort of fish wafted to her nose, and her stomach grumbled in response. Nicholas must be in the kitchen. She couldn't wait to sample his new dish.

As she walked through the extensive bar area, she thought back to the first time he had brought her to Reflections, five months ago. He had given her the whole romantic treatment with the just the two of them there—the lights down low, candles on the table, and soft music playing through the sound system. It had been an incredible date. She'd quickly realized the huge benefit of dating a chef.

"Baby?" Zienna said.

Just then, Nicholas came out from kitchen area, his eyes meeting hers. And in that nanosecond, she took in his entire appearance and couldn't stop the jolt of heat. Dressed in black slacks and a black shirt open at the collar, his six-foot-three frame couldn't have been sexier. The white apron tied around his waist made him all the more appealing.

Seeing her, his handsome face lit up with a grin. He had the kind of earnest smile that brightened his eyes and could make a girl melt. That was the feature that had drawn Zienna in, but she was a woman who lusted over a hot guy just like anybody else, and loved Nicholas's lean and muscular frame, and his tight behind. With his shirt off, his golden-brown skin was flawless but for a dark circular birthmark over his heart. With his washboard abs and honed physique, he could have easily graced the cover of a sports magazine. He'd played football and basketball in college, and still had the body of an athlete.

Zienna had seen a college picture of him with long dread-locks, something she could hardly have imagined, given that his hair was currently cropped short and his face clean-shaven. It was a look he preferred now, claiming it was more profes-sional.

"There you are," Zienna said.

"Look at you." His eyes swept over her from head to toe. "Wow."

"This old thing?" she teased. She knew the black sheath dress and strappy four-inch heels she'd put on made her look like a knockout.

"You're not supposed to come in here wearing something I want to take off of you...."

Zienna giggled as he hugged her. "I figured I should dress to impress. No point acting like an old married couple already."

"I'm not gonna complain." Nicholas eased back. "Damn, girl. That dress fits you like a second skin." His eyes settled on her ample cleavage, his favorite part of her body.

"You'd better stop looking at me like that," she warned him in a low voice. "Unless you want to christen this place again." Which was exactly what she'd hoped for when she'd dressed earlier. Placing her hands on his chest, she leaned in close. "Because you are looking pretty hot yourself. I always was a sucker for a guy dressed to the nines…and wearing an apron."

Which truly was a turn-on. Nicholas knew how to cook, and had regaled her palate with mouthwatering entrées and scrumptious desserts.

"There'll be no christening tonight," Nicholas said. He placed his hands on her shoulders and squeezed gently.

"No?" Zienna pouted a little. They had done it on the counter in the kitchen, and both had reflected afterward that a booth would have been the smarter choice. "You sure I can't lure you over to a booth in the back?"

"Sorry, not tonight. Because in addition to me wanting you to try my latest dish, I have someone I'd like you to meet."

"Oh?" Zienna glanced around curiously.

"I told him to show up for eight, but he called about twenty minutes ago, said he'd be about ten minutes late. Which means any second now he should be walking through the door."

"Way to spoil a girl's anticipation." She again pouted play-fully as she crossed her arms over her chest. "I was kind of hoping for round two." Their coupling in the kitchen had been out of the ordinary, and highly exciting for Zienna, who wished that Nicholas would be a little more spontane-ous when it came to sex.

"Rain check?"

"Of course." A beat passed. "At least I have time to do this." Zienna tipped up on her toes, and Nicholas immedi-ately encircled her waist with his strong hands and lowered his lips to meet hers.

Warmth spread through her entire body as they kissed, the only sound being their heavy breathing.

And then the door chimes sang, and Zienna quickly pulled

her lips from her man's. Meeting Nicholas's eyes, she suppressed a giggle.

"I can come back," said a deep voice from behind her.

"My man," Nicholas said, another grin exploding on his face. He released Zienna and stepped past her.

She surreptitiously dabbed at her mouth to remove any moisture. Then, smiling sheepishly, she turned to meet Nicholas's friend.

And as her eyes landed on the familiar face, her smile went flat a moment before her stomach bottomed out.

2

"Nick."

"Wendell!"

Zienna watched in shock as her new lover and old lover embraced. In four years she hadn't seen this man, and now here he was, like an apparition come to life.

When the friends separated, Nicholas walked back over to her and slipped an arm around her waist. He pulled her close. "Wendell, this is Zienna. Zienna, this is one of my best buddies. At least he *was*—until he followed some girl to Texas and didn't come back."

Nicholas chuckled, but Zienna could hardly breathe. She glanced up at Wendell, saw that he was staring at her with an amiable expression. Damn, he looked even better than she'd remembered.

"Well, don't just stand there," Nicholas said. "Say hello."

Wendell extended a hand. "Hello, Zienna." He paused. *"Again."*

Oh, lord, Zienna thought, her heart thundering. Wendell

had done what she hadn't expected and certainly didn't want—made it clear that the two of them had a past. What was he thinking?

Nicholas looked from Wendell to her with a curious expression. "Again?"

"Zienna and I used to know each other," Wendell explained, his gaze locked on hers.

She widened her eyes at him slightly, the only way she could think of to tell him *not* to spill the beans on just how well they'd once been acquainted.

"Remember when I tore my rotator cuff?" Finally, Wendell turned his attention to Nicholas. "Zienna was the kinesiologist who helped me get back to optimum performance."

"You're kidding!" Nicholas chuckled.

"She was one of the team's athletic therapists," Wendell went on.

Nicholas looked at her. "You never told me you worked with the Bears."

"It was a long time ago," Zienna said. She still felt regret over how she'd left a cushy job with Chicago's pro football team because she hadn't wanted the conflict of interest once she'd started seeing Wendell. Only for him to ultimately leave her. That was the reason she'd never mentioned her previous job to Nicholas or anyone else.

"You weren't with our team long before you left and joined the group of physiotherapists at—what was it called? Back in Motion?" Wendell said.

Because of you! Zienna didn't say it out loud.

"You certainly remember a lot about her," Nicholas commented.

Zienna threw a glance at him, and saw what she feared—suspicion in his eyes.

"That's because I continued to work with her at the clinic,"

Wendell explained smoothly. "I'd become accustomed to her technique, and liked the way she challenged me."

"Her technique? Is that all?" Nicholas sounded skeptical.

Zienna opened her mouth to speak, but Wendell did before she could. "It was four and a half years ago, man."

Though he had evaded the question, his comment seemed enough for Nicholas, who nodded, saying, "Ahh. Right. That's when you were crazy over Pam."

Zienna's stomach clenched. *Pam? Who the hell was Pam?* Four and a half years ago, Wendell had been giving her the best sex of her life.

"Pam?" Zienna all but croaked.

"His girlfriend," Nicholas said.

Zienna's head swam. How could this be true? Wendell had told her he was single when they'd gotten involved. And she could still remember his final words to her.

I'm not ready to settle down. I'm sorry.

And then he'd left town.

"Is Pam the one who went to Texas?" Zienna asked, trying her best to keep her voice neutral. It was one thing to see your ex again under these circumstances, but to learn that he'd lied to you years ago, and not be able to react accordingly…well, this was excruciating.

"Yeah," Nicholas answered. "Pam. The swimsuit model." He clamped a hand on Wendell's shoulder. "My man Wendell. Always chasing the hottest women. I'm surprised he didn't come on to you."

"A real playboy, I bet," Zienna said, an edge to her voice. "The type of man who never settles down."

Wendell met her gaze, and Zienna couldn't help narrowing her eyes in a little glare…the most emotion she could allow herself under the circumstances. Besides, the fact that he had lied to her in the past didn't matter now. He was firmly in her rearview mirror. Nicholas was her future.

To emphasize that point, she ensnared Nicholas's waist with both hands and rested her head against his shoulder.

"He was the consummate playboy—until he got involved with Pam," Nicholas clarified. "I've never seen this guy get all nuts for a woman until he met her."

"Stop exaggerating," Wendell said, but his eyes were still on Zienna's. "It wasn't like that."

"You follow a woman to Texas, it's got to be serious," Zienna commented. "You put a ring on her finger, too? Of course, you must have." She quickly assessed his left hand, saw that it was ring-free. "But it appears you're already divorced— unless you don't believe in wearing a wedding band. Or perhaps you never stopped your playboy ways, even after saying I Do."

Nicholas chuckled. "Easy, Zee."

Had she been too harsh? "I'm just… You're the one who said he was a player."

"I didn't marry her," Wendell stressed. To Zienna, it sounded as if he was trying to make a point for her sake.

Whatever, asshole, she thought.

Then she placed a hand on Nicholas's cheek, turned his head so that he was facing her, and eased up to plant her lips on his.

The kiss started as a peck, but even as Nicholas began to pull back, Zienna held his head in place and continued kissing him, adding tongue.

After several seconds, he finally broke the kiss. "Down, girl," he said, grinning. He glanced at Wendell, "See why I wanted you to meet her?"

"She's gorgeous," his friend agreed. "I always thought she'd be a great catch for someone. I'm glad it's you, Nick. You both look happy."

"We are." Nicholas kissed her on the temple. "Now, I hope

you're both hungry. Because I can't wait for your opinion on my latest dish."

Nicholas hurried off to the kitchen, leaving Zienna and Wendell alone.

She could her hear her heart pounding in her ears. Her chest ached with each heavy breath.

She glanced over her shoulder.

"It's safe," Wendell said. "He's gone."

She whipped her head around. "*Safe?* What's that supposed to mean?"

Wendell said nothing, just let his eyes roam over her body top to bottom, pausing on her cleavage, then stopping as he regarded her feet.

"Damn," he muttered.

"You're not seriously—" Zienna clamped her mouth shut, abruptly stopping her words.

"Checking you out?" Wendell supplied, reading her thoughts. "You're a beautiful woman. I never could help but notice you."

"But I wasn't a swimsuit model," she retorted. "Was that the problem?"

Before he could reply, she turned sharply and walked up to the bar. She didn't want him to answer her question. Good grief, what was she doing? Acting as if the past had any bearing on this moment? Who cared if Wendell had run off with a harem of women? He didn't matter to her now.

She heard his footfalls as he approached her. "I think we need to sit down sometime and talk. About everything."

Zienna faced him, guffawing. "For what purpose?"

"So I can explain."

"Are you out of your mind?" She was seething now.

"I think I was…four years ago."

Zienna opened her mouth, but Wendell's response left her speechless. And, God help her, he actually sounded contrite.

"I'd really like to talk to you at some point," Wendell went on. "Clear the air."

And though nothing he said now should matter to her even one iota, Zienna's stomach fluttered at the idea that he wanted to make amends on some level.

Good Lord, what is wrong with me?

In a split second, the answer came to her. It was the memory of their explosive times in the bedroom…memories that had plagued her for years. That was why she was suddenly flustered around this man she should despise with every fiber of her being.

Remembering her hatred for him enabled her to speak once again. "We're not meeting to talk about anything. For goodness sake, I'm dating your best friend."

Wendell edged a little closer. "Is it serious?"

Her eyes bulged. He truly had lost his marbles. "You are— We are *not* talking about this."

"Talking about what?"

At the sound of Nicholas's voice, both of them turned in his direction. Blood rushed to Zienna's head, and she thought she might pass out.

How much had he heard?

Stepping coolly away from the bar, Wendell said, "I was prying. Asking how you met, when you started dating."

Nicholas made a face, as though that answer didn't quite make sense to him. "Oh. It kind of sounded like Zienna was upset."

"That's because…" Wendell shrugged sheepishly. "Well, I asked her how long it was before you guys ended up in bed."

Nicholas rolled his eyes as he set two glasses on the bar in front of them. "Zee, pay my friend no mind. He always was motivated by his dick."

"Shocking," Zienna said in a tone of feigned disbelief.

"My bad." Wendell held up both hands. "I'm just used to the days when Nick and I had no secrets between us."

"Those days are over." Nicholas's tone was jovial, but there was something about how his eyes flickered that made Zienna think there was more to the comment.

"I call this Island Sunset," Nicholas went on, pushing the drinks forward. "Mango, pineapple and coconut rum."

Wendell sipped it. "Nice."

"And I'll be right back with the main course."

Zienna felt Wendell's eyes on her, but didn't dare look his way as Nicholas disappeared into the kitchen. Thankfully, he returned quickly, carrying two steaming plates.

He was beaming as he placed the entrées on the bar. "And in keeping with the island theme, this is my Jamaican fried snapper on a bed of vegetables steamed in a spicy vinegar sauce."

"Looks amazing," Zienna said. "And it smells even better."

"You think so?" Nicholas asked. "To be authentic, I've kept the whole fish intact instead of using filets. I don't know how the guests will feel about that, but when I've traveled to Jamaica and Costa Rica, that's how they serve snapper."

"Looks good to me, man," Wendell said.

Zienna cut a morsel of the fish with her fork and brought it to her mouth. "Ooh, spicy," she said after a moment.

"Too spicy?" Nicholas asked, regarding her with concern.

She shook her head as she continued to chew. "No. It's delicious. Very flavorful, and just the right amount of spice."

"She's right," Wendell concurred. "Loving the spice. But you know I've always loved heat."

Zienna paused as she was about to swallow, unable to stop the thought that Wendell's comment had been a loaded one.

"So I should add this to the menu?" Nicholas asked.

Zienna nodded. "I think it's great."

He smiled. "Good. I can always decide to use filets if that's the feedback I get. Good, good. I'm glad you two like it."

"I'll bet you created a dessert to go with this. Something with pineapple or coconut. And lots of whipped cream," Wendell stated.

At his comment, Zienna angled her head slightly toward him, and wasn't surprised to find that he was looking at her. Because she knew, just knew, that mention of whipped cream had been for her benefit.

"Mango cheesecake," Nicholas told him.

Suddenly, Zienna slipped off her bar stool. "You know what, sweetie—I'm gonna head home."

"What?" Nicholas asked. "You just got here."

"I've had a long day. I should really get some rest. Your friend's back in town. Spend some time with him."

"Don't leave on my account," Wendell said.

Zienna ignored him and picked up her purse. "Will you walk me out, babe?"

"You sure you have to leave?" Nicholas asked.

"I really should. I feel a headache coming on." And she shot a glance at Wendell.

As they moved toward the exit, Nicholas placed a hand on the small of her back. "You okay?"

"Yeah, I'm fine."

When they were through the front door, he turned her in his arms so that she was facing him. "Is it Wendell?"

"No. No, of course not." Zienna stroked his cheek. "I'm just tired, babe."

"Why don't you go to my place, get into bed and rest until I get there?" He lowered his voice. "If I can't have more of you right now, I at least want your body next to mine tonight."

"That I can do," Zienna told him. She smiled. "And, yes, maybe a couple hours of rest and some aspirin will do me a world of good."

She headed to her car with one goal in mind. When Nicholas got home, she was going to do him good.

Do him until she rid herself of the memory of Wendell altogether.

3

"Pick up, pick up," Zienna said into her cell phone as she sat in her car, anxious to speak to Alexis. She'd called her friend the moment she'd left Nicholas's restaurant the night before, desperate to reach her, but her series of calls had all gone to voice mail.

Even though Zienna had put every ounce of her energy into making love to Nicholas, and should have been tired, once he had fallen asleep beside her she had instead lain awake, the evening replaying in her mind.

I'd really like to talk to you at some point. Clear the air.

At a quarter to five, Zienna had slipped out of Nicholas's bed and gotten dressed. She had hoped he wouldn't wake, but he had.

"Go back to sleep," Zienna had whispered. "I'm heading into the office early, and there are some things I have to do at home first." She gave him a peck on the cheek. "I'll talk to you later."

Once she'd left Nicholas's house, she rushed to her car and

immediately tried calling Alexis again. Ever since they'd become friends in second grade, Zienna had been sharing everything with Alexis, the good and the bad. And Alexis had forever earned her trust when she'd punched the class bully in the face for throwing a rock at Zienna's forehead in third grade. That incident had sealed their status as best friends for life.

Now, Zienna groaned in frustration when she heard her friend's cheerful voice begin her short message again. Where on earth could she be at this hour?

Undeterred, Zienna promptly disconnected, then called the number once more. She would redial one hundred times if that's how long it took to reach her.

Three rings later, a groggy-sounding Alexis finally answered the phone. "This had better be good."

"I need to come over," Zienna said without preamble.

"Now?"

"Yes, now. I'm going out of my mind, Alex."

"Shit, Zee—it's five-fourteen in the morning."

"Which is why you know it's got to be urgent. I called you hours ago, you didn't answer."

"I ended up going out for a drink with that guy I was telling you about, the one I met online. I forgot my phone at home."

Zienna had pulled up to the curb on a street a few over from Nicholas's house, waiting to reach Alexis. Now that they were talking, she started her car. "I have to tell you what happened. I'm kind of freaking out."

"Okay." Alexis didn't sound happy, but Zienna knew she wouldn't abandon her in her hour of need.

Sure, Zienna could wait until the work day was over and see her friend then. But she'd already had to wait hours, since leaving the restaurant and going to Nicholas's place. Making love to her man had done nothing to alleviate her stress. And the way her heart was still beating rapidly, Zienna knew that she had to see Alexis now and share with her what had transpired.

"I'll see you soon," she said. "Want me to grab coffee or something?"

"No. I'm going back to bed once you leave."

Zienna ended the call and began to navigate her way through the Lincoln Park neighborhood, where Nicholas lived, toward the West Loop, where Alexis made her home in a trendy loft. It was a vibrant and artistic area, with chic cafés and restaurants, and several warehouses that had been converted to loft-style condominiums.

As Zienna continued to drive, she wondered why she was so torn up over seeing Wendell again. Seriously, she shouldn't be this frazzled.

"You got the shock of your life," she told herself. "That's why you're freaked out."

But damn, what were the chances? She had had the hottest sex of her life with Wendell, and it turned out that he was Nicholas's best friend? Could this situation be any worse?

The traffic was light at this hour, and Zienna made it to Alexis's loft within twenty minutes. She parked her car at an available meter and then called her friend's number.

"I'm downstairs," she told her when they connected.

Zienna hurried out of the car and up the steps of the building. Moments later, the front door opened. Alexis faced her with one hand perched on her hip. She looked none too pleased.

"You know I hate you right now." She flashed her the evil eye.

Zienna breezed into the condo foyer, her heels clicking on the marble floor. "Wendell's back in town."

"What?"

Zienna didn't answer, instead walking the short distance

to Alexis's unit. Her friend scurried into the loft behind her and closed the door.

"Wendell called you?" she asked, then rubbed her eyes with balled fists. "I can see why you were surprised, but girl, it's not even six in the morning—"

Zienna's throat felt tight as she sauntered across the living room toward the floor-to-ceiling windows that overlooked the street. She glanced outside, and wondered how the world could look the same when it had undeniably changed.

Inhaling deeply, she moved to the nearby armchair and gripped the back of it. "Remember I told you that I suspected that Nicholas wanted to introduce me to his friend tonight? Well, I was right. Wendell's the friend. *Wendell.* He's Nicholas's best friend."

A beat passed. And as Zienna's words registered, Alexis's jaw dropped. Then her eyes bulged. "Oh, my God. You're saying you *saw* Wendell last night—*with Nicholas?*"

"Yes." Zienna rounded the leather armchair and plopped onto it.

"Holy shit." Alexis crossed her arms over her chest. "Does Nicholas *know?*" She went to the sofa across from Zienna and sat on the arm. "What did Wendell say?"

"Nicholas doesn't know, but Wendell— Fuck, he told Nicholas he knew me years ago. That I was the kinesiologist he worked with when he was playing for the Bears."

"Okay," Alexis began slowly. "That's not so bad, right? I mean, there's no reason not to say you knew each other."

"Except for the fact that Nicholas looked suspicious."

"He did?"

"Yeah, and he made an offhand remark about being surprised Wendell never hit on me. And then it gets better. All this time I thought Wendell didn't want to commit to anyone…well, it turns out he did want to commit. Only to someone else. Some swimsuit model named Pam."

Alexis looked as confused as Zienna had been hours earlier, so she took her time and filled her in on exactly what she'd learned.

"Damn." Her friend made a face. "The bastard was friggin' cheating on you. Or cheating on Pam, it seems."

"No matter how you slice it, he was fucking around."

"Wow," Alexis said. "At first I was pissed that you woke me up, but damn, I get it now. Bloody hell."

Zienna didn't smirk the way she normally did when her friend used her latest British curse. Instead she said, "Bloody hell is right. I just about died when Wendell walked through the door." *Looking even sexier than he did four years ago…*

"I can imagine. It took you years to get over him."

Hearing her friend say those words gave Zienna pause. Because with that statement, she had summed up what Zienna's big issue was with Wendell's reappearance. It had been incredibly hard to shake him from her system, and though she was getting close with Nicholas, there was definitely a part of her that feared seeing Wendell again was going to erase all the progress she'd made.

And there was an even bigger issue. "What do I do?" she asked. "Nicholas knows that Wendell and I used to work together, but do I tell him about our relationship? Or do I say nothing at all? And if I tell him, is he going to be okay about it, understand that Wendell and I were over a long time ago? Or is it going to cause undue grief? I have no clue what to do."

Alexis was silent as she contemplated Zienna's dilemma. After a moment she said, "I think you tell him. Tell him before Wendell does."

Zienna's eyes bulged. "You think Wendell will tell him?"

"Maybe not intentionally, but there's no guarantee he won't let it slip."

"Oh, God." Zienna groaned. "Are you sure? I just… Telling him could open a whole can of worms. Create an issue for him and Wendell, for one thing. And maybe even cause him to feel insecure. You remember how iffy Nicholas was during the first couple of months we were dating. He liked me, but didn't entirely trust that I was into him."

"I remember. He couldn't understand why someone as beautiful as you would be single."

"And I'd said the same to him. He's gorgeous, successful…. Things are finally easy between us. And now this."

"Maybe you shouldn't say anything, then."

Zienna paused. "But if I don't tell him, and Wendell does—"

"It's going to be much worse," Alexis finished for her. "Nicholas is a big boy. He knows you weren't born yesterday. So what if you dated Wendell years ago? He can't hold that against you."

"True." She was silent a moment. "But I don't think Wendell would tell him. I mean, what has he got to gain from something like that? They're best friends. And if not best friends, at least very good friends. Wendell has to know better than to open his mouth."

"I still think you should tell him," Alexis said. "There are too many variables."

Zienna drew in a deep breath. "And it kind of gets worse."

Alexis eyed her warily. "What do you mean by that?"

She shrugged. "I don't know. Maybe it's nothing. It's just… I'm not sure what Wendell wants."

"You're totally confusing me."

Zienna was confused, too, which was part of her problem. It was one thing to find out that Wendell was Nicholas's best friend. But what he'd said to her had undeniably added to her anxiety. "Wendell asked me if my relationship with Nicholas was serious. And then…then he said that he wanted to get together to talk, clear the air."

"Shut up."

"What am I supposed to make of that? That he wants to pick things up where we left off? Or did he just not know what else to say? Maybe he feels bad because of how he ended things with me—and the fact that I just learned he was a cheater."

"You're not gonna do it, right? You're not going to meet with him to talk?"

"No," Zienna said emphatically. "Definitely not. I don't want to talk to him. I want nothing to do with him." She paused. "But…I'd be lying if I said there wasn't a small part of me that wouldn't mind hearing what he has to say. If for no other reason than to give him a piece of my mind when he's finished. Because that's what I wanted to do when I saw him last night. I wanted to scream and yell and slap him, and tell him what an asshole he is. All that crap about not wanting to get married and not wanting to hurt me, when he was really seeing someone else. But I couldn't react. I had to pretend as though him coming into the restaurant hadn't affected me one bit."

"Zienna…" Alexis's tone held a hint of caution.

"What? I'm not stupid. I'm over Wendell. But that doesn't mean I'm not mad at him."

"Unless you want to flirt with danger, then you need to drop it and stay away from him, period. And maybe what you've just said is the biggest reason why you need to tell Nicholas about your history with Wendell. Tell him the truth, and he'll make sure the two of you stay apart."

"Don't misunderstand me," Zienna said. "I'm just telling you what would be nice—in a perfect world."

Alexis made a face as she regarded her. "It took you a long time to get over Wendell."

"And I am. I am over him." She sighed softly. Alexis knew her too well. "Maybe you're right. Nothing good will come of me giving him a piece of my mind. In fact, the best revenge will be him seeing that I'm happy. That I've moved on. And perhaps the fact that it's with his best friend is even better."

Alexis continued to regard her with a narrowed gaze, and Zienna could see the wheels churning in her mind. "What?"

"Just be careful. Come clean with Nicholas, because it's not like you did anything wrong. But come clean so there's no issue that can come back to bite you. And unless you still want something with Wendell, I'd stay away from him."

"You're right," Zienna said. At least regarding her advice to stay away from Wendell. But she wasn't so sure about telling Nicholas that she and his friend had once been lovers.

For the time being, Zienna had done the most important thing, and that was to get this troubling news off her chest. Speaking with Alexis had allowed her to think clearly, and now that she had, she was starting to realize that her past with Wendell would be an issue only if she made it one. Because certainly Wendell wouldn't say anything to hurt his friend, would he? Not when he knew how much Nicholas liked her.

As she left Alexis's apartment so that her friend could get another hour of sleep before getting up for work, Zienna felt a lot better. No, she wouldn't say anything to Nicholas. Their relationship was going well, and she couldn't see Wendell doing anything to jeopardize that.

So if he wasn't going to say anything about their past involvement, there was no reason for her to. She had stressed over Wendell's reappearance for several hours, but it was suddenly apparent that she had done so needlessly.

Because the fact that he was back in town wasn't going to affect her relationship with Nicholas.

Not at all.

4

Zienna finished reading the medical questionnaire her newest patient, who was sitting on the examining bed, had filled out, describing the pain he was experiencing. Before he'd arrived for his appointment she had studied the files that had come from his physician—over two cups of very strong coffee, since she needed the caffeine to help her stay awake after her largely sleepless night.

"So, let me sum up what I understand from what you've told me and what I've read in your file," she said as she placed the clipboard on her desk, then moved to stand in front of him. "You've been dealing with pain in your right elbow for nearly two years, which you attribute to your work as a machinist."

Ed, a heavyset man in his mid-forties, nodded. "Yep."

"And despite various therapies, you're still suffering pain."

"Yeah. And now my doc has suggested surgery, but I don't want to do that. Not yet, anyway."

"Which is why you're here." Zienna smiled pleasantly. "I'm very glad you contacted our clinic. Even though you had disappointing results with other doctors, you're going to be quite happy with your decision to put off having surgery."

"You sound really sure about that."

"There's a saying—he who treats the site of pain is lost. So let me ask you, have you ever had any problems with your left knee?"

Ed's chubby cheeks puckered with his frown. "My left knee?"

"Kinesiologists believe in holistic treatment, which is based on the interconnectedness of the entire body. What I see time and again is that the area where a person suffers pain is often not the source of the pain. It's something called interlimb neural coupling, which is a fancy way of saying that the limbs are connected in terms of functionality. So hearing your symptoms with your right elbow, I wouldn't be surprised to learn that you've had issues with your left knee."

Zienna regarded Ed, and saw in his eyes when his brain connected the dots. "I did. I injured my left knee years ago when cycling. I still feel pain there from time to time."

She couldn't help smiling. "Excellent."

"Excellent?" he echoed, looking confused.

"Sorry," she said. "It's just…well, I love my job, and I especially love when I'm able to help someone who feels all hope is lost. Just last month I had a patient come here with a torn ligament in his shoulder, and he, too, believed he would have to have surgery. Once I was able to diagnose the true source of his shoulder problems—which were actually connected to problems in his opposite ankle—within a couple of sessions he was pain-free."

Ed looked skeptical.

"It's the magic of kinesiology." Zienna had treated patients whose issues were emotional, with their stress manifested as pain in their body. In her practice, she dealt with a person's physical, emotional, mental and spiritual well-being as a way to effectively care for their problems.

"I won't begin treatment until you've had all the tests we require here at the clinic, but I feel very confident that I can successfully eliminate the pain in your elbow."

Now Ed smiled. "If you can save me from surgery, I'll be forever in your debt."

At that moment, the wall phone rang. Zienna turned to look at it, knowing that for the receptionist to have put a call through to her in the examining room, it had to be important.

"Excuse me a moment, Ed."

She crossed the room to the phone and lifted the receiver. "Hello?"

"Hey, babe."

At the sound of Nicholas's voice, Zienna frowned slightly. Why was he calling her on this line?

"Hey," she said in a lowered voice. "What's up?"

"Just concerned about you. The way you left this morning… it didn't feel right. I called your cell, but you didn't answer."

"Right."

"You okay?"

"Um-hmm. Yep. But, um, can I call you back in a little bit? I'm with a client right now."

"Oh, okay. No problem. I just wanted to hear your voice. Make sure you're all right."

"Excellent," she said, hoping for Ed's sake to sound professional.

"I get it. You can't talk. But let's do something tonight."

"Sure. You'll give me the details in a bit?"

"Yeah, I'll call you later."

Zienna was inwardly beaming as she replaced the receiver. It was a nice feeling, knowing that Nicholas was worried about her. He was a great guy, and for the first time in a long time she was in a happy relationship. She still got butterflies when she talked to him, something that hadn't lasted with the men she'd dated in the more recent past.

"If you go out to reception, Jamie will take care of booking the tests we require, which are all done in-house. You should be able to see me again by next week."

"Great. Thanks so much."

Zienna saw Ed out of the examining room, but her mind was on Nicholas and what she'd discussed with Alexis that morning. Hearing Nicholas's voice, she felt better about her decision not to tell him of her past with Wendell. Doing so might hurt him, and she didn't want to jeopardize what they had.

"Um, hey."

Zienna turned, and was surprised to see Ed standing in the doorway. "Yes?"

"I just wanted to say that not only are you beautiful, you're incredibly smart. I'm glad my friend referred me to this clinic."

"Oh." Zienna hadn't expected that. "Why, thank you."

Ed offered a bashful smile, then a little wave.

As he disappeared again, Zienna made a face, confused by what had just happened. Was Ed simply being nice, or was he a little bit smitten?

It wouldn't be the first time a client had become enamored with her. She was attractive and liked to smile, something that won over many men. The way she saw it, having male clientele develop a crush on her was a bit of an occupational hazard.

As she sat at the desk, her mind ventured back to when she'd met Wendell five years ago. And the crush that had turned into something more.

As one of the four athletic therapists for the Chicago Bears, she had seen him during practices, and then when the NFL season had started. He'd been thirty-two at the time, almost considered a senior when it came to professional sports, but he still had the kind of skill that put some of the younger players to shame. His talent as a wide receiver kept him in the starting position on the team's roster.

Zienna hadn't personally engaged with him until the tackle that had injured his left shoulder. And pretty much instantly, the professional demeanor between them had changed.

He had torn the rotator cuff, and weeks of physiotherapy with the team's head athletic therapist followed. Once his shoulder had stabilized, he'd begun work with Zienna to further help with his healing and regain optimum strength.

The spark between them had been immediate that first day she'd met with him one on one. Perhaps it was the way he'd looked at her with those beautiful hazel eyes...a heated look that had melted her professional resolve almost instantly.

Zienna knew it was about more than the look he'd given her, because right from the start she had noticed him. Of all the players on the team, Wendell was the one who stood out to her. Of course, she never would have approached him in a personal way. She'd valued her fairly new position with the Chicago Bears too much to do that.

Wendell, on the other hand, had no such qualms. He'd asked her out the day of their second session.

Everything about him had made Zienna want to forget all about being professional, but she knew better than to accept his offer, and had politely turned him down. Undeterred, Wendell had proudly told her, when they got together for his third exercise session, that he'd made reservations for the two of them to have dinner the following Saturday night at Michael Jordan's Steak House. It hadn't been a question.

He had known her answer without having to ask.

And Zienna, turned on by his confidence, had been unable to deny him.

The dinner had been wonderful, enhanced by a personal exchange with Michael Jordan, who'd been in that night. Zienna wasn't surprised to learn that Wendell and Michael knew each other, but she did feel extraspecial when the basketball legend sat at their table and chatted with them for a few minutes.

It wasn't just the top-of-the-line champagne that had Zienna forgetting her own moral code after dinner and agreeing to go back to Wendell's place for a nightcap. It was her lust for him. From the moment she'd agreed to have dinner with him, she'd known that the sex would be inevitable.

What she didn't expect was just how amazing he was in bed. Or on the sofa, in the shower...

Zienna felt the stirring of desire, and it snapped her out of her trip down memory lane. Made her realize where she was, and what had just happened.

Good Lord, what was wrong with her? She was thinking about Wendell to the point where she was getting aroused?

She stood, paced the floor. And all she could think of was what Alexis had said last night. *It took you years to get over Wendell.*

That comment had allowed her to acknowledge her fear that seeing Wendell would erase all the progress she'd made. Damn it, was that already happening? Were thoughts of him going to invade her mind at regular intervals again?

"No," she said aloud. She wouldn't let them.

She was going to see Nicholas later, the man she loved. The man who could be her everything.

Unlike Wendell.

He'd never been hers. Learning he'd followed someone else to Texas—when he'd told her that he wasn't ready to settle down—was the most bitter part of all.

Oh, he had wanted to commit—just not to her. When

he'd left her, Zienna had stupidly told herself that Wendell had been afraid of their intense connection, intimidated by it. That he didn't know how to handle his feelings for her. And she'd fully expected him to return.

It had been a fairy tale concocted out of total bull to make herself feel better.

That thought helped her purge the unsettling sexual memories of Wendell from her mind. He was the last man on the planet she should be thinking of.

Zienna got her cell phone and sent Nicholas a text: Can't wait for tonight.

And to make the night extraspecial, she would stop by a lingerie shop on the way home and pick up something very skimpy—for Nicholas's eyes only.

5

Nicholas didn't call back. But he did send a text to tell Zienna where they would dine. And she wasn't surprised when he said he'd made reservations at Café Tagine in the West Loop for Mediterranean fare, as it was one of the few places he enjoyed eating other than his own restaurant. The highlight of the dining experience—if you were there at the right time— was the belly dancing performance.

Zienna sent him a text back to ask if she should meet him there or if he would pick her up. She wasn't one of those women who expected to be picked up for every date. She had her own car, her own career, and she could take care of herself. A few guys she'd dated had told her that she was too independent. But after years of providing for herself, she wasn't about to pass over the reins to a man.

Not yet, anyway.

When her cell phone trilled, Zienna lifted it from the bathroom counter and looked at the screen.

I'll pick you up.

She grinned. It would be better this way. Because being beside him in the front seat, she could get a little frisky.

Sample a little of the heat of what was to come.

At 7:30, Zienna's cell phone rang. Even before she looked to see if Nicholas was the one calling her, she hurried to the window of her second floor condo, which looked down on North Kingsbury Street, and saw Nicholas's car. He was nothing if not punctual.

She then ran to pick up her phone, which was on her dining room table. "Hey, you."

"I'm downstairs."

"I know, I just saw you. I'm on my way."

She gathered her clutch purse and headed to the door, where she stopped to give herself one last glance in the hall mirror. She was wearing a red dress with a plunging neckline that went to the base of her cleavage. It was an outfit that revealed what Nicholas had termed her "great boobage." The dress hugged her waist, then flared slightly over her hips. It was a sexy yet classically feminine outfit.

Beneath the dress, she was also wearing red—a lacy red thong adorned with a tiny white bow at the front, and a matching bra with little bows on the straps. A grin played on her lips. She knew she looked absolutely amazing in the ensemble, and she knew that Nicholas would go nuts when he saw her without her dress later.

Zienna made her way downstairs. Ever the gentleman, Nicholas got out of his black Infiniti SUV to meet her as she headed down the short walkway toward him.

"Wow." He whistled, then reached out and fingered a strand of her long, flat-ironed black hair. It was a look that suited her well.

"Gimme a kiss," she told him, and took him by the jacket lapel and pulled him close. He kissed her on the lips, a peck that lasted a few seconds.

Zienna pouted a little when he eased back. "That's all?"

"I don't want to ruin your lipstick."

"Okay then," she said, giving him a you're-missing-out look. He hurried to the door and opened it for her. As Zienna sat, she deliberately pulled her dress up on her thigh, allowing him a glimpse of her bare legs.

"Damn," he uttered.

Then he got into the vehicle beside her and gave her a wink before driving off. Zienna frowned slightly. She had hoped... Well, she'd hoped for at least a little grope in the car before Nicholas turned his attention to the road.

She couldn't have looked more seductive. Her makeup was perfect, the deep auburn shadow on her eyes meant to accentuate the red in her outfit. And she was wearing a pair of four-inch Louboutin leopard print pumps. Even her purse matched—leopard print with red at the edges. Not to mention that she'd changed her toe polish after work to make it a cherry red.

Nicholas had always told her that he loved her in red, and she'd been hoping for a more carnal reaction from him.

She offered him a smile. When he grinned back at her, she took his hand and lifted it to her breasts.

"Easy, babe," he said. "I don't want to get to the restaurant with a throbbing erection."

Zienna kissed his hand, then released it, inwardly disappointed.

Nicholas was gorgeous and ambitious and a gentleman... but sometimes she wished he'd be a bit more spontaneous. She wouldn't mind if they got a little hot and bothered in the car and missed dinner altogether. But she knew that wasn't something Nicholas would do, because he'd already made reservations for the night.

Sex before dinner wasn't in the plans.

"You really look great tonight," he said to her. "Smoking."

"Thank you, baby."

He must have picked up on her disappointment, because he said, "You're not upset, are you?"

"Upset? Why?"

"Because…" Now he reached for her leg, trailing his fingers along her exposed thigh.

Zienna glanced at him, wondering if he was going to do something out of character.

"You think I don't want to touch you?" he asked. "Quite frankly, I'm tempted to forget dinner and do you right here."

Now Zienna beamed. Nicholas had come to a stop, so she eased her body across the front seat and kissed him. This time he didn't pull away, and they continued until a horn blared from the car behind them.

Both of them giggled, and Nicholas began to drive again.

"And so you know," Zienna began, "this is that lipstick that's guaranteed not to smudge off. During dinner, or kissing…"

"Ah. Well, good to know."

"I'm happy to forgo dinner…well, at least in a restaurant. Because I definitely want to eat something else."

Lust was already consuming her, and she wanted nothing more than to get naked with him. Have wild sex tonight, unlike the pleasant sex they'd had the night before.

Nicholas's groan was low and throaty. "What did I tell you?"

His eyes went downward to his lap. Zienna followed his

gaze and saw the evidence of his desire for her straining against his black dress pants.

"Then let's turn around."

"You know we have reservations for tonight. And I always hate when people skip out on reservations."

"I know...."

"Plus I have a surprise for you."

Now her eyes lit up. "You do?"

He wriggled his eyebrows. "Yep. Besides, I love the idea of wanting you so badly during dinner that I can hardly stand it. It will make it that much better when we finally get home."

He had a point. And maybe the sex would be even hotter after sitting through dinner for a couple hours.

She could wait.

Nicholas turned on the car stereo, and the sound of smooth R&B began to play. Zienna looked out the window as he continued to drive, wondering what the surprise was.

She liked what he'd said about keeping the sexual tension between them going through dinner. Maybe they could even do something a little risqué, like have sex in the backseat of his car. Something they had never done.

She was falling in love with Nicholas, she knew. But while he satisfied her sexually, she kind of wished he was a bit more...

Well, wild.

Typically, when they got it on, it was at his place and in his bed. He'd never specifically said that he didn't want to dirty the leather sofas, but Zienna had to assume that was his issue, because even when they got hot while on a sofa, he always made sure to lead them to the bedroom before they got naked.

It wasn't a big issue, but Zienna would enjoy a bit of variety.

At Café Tagine, Nicholas left his car with the valet, took

Zienna's hand and headed inside. The moment guests entered the door, they felt as if they'd stepped into Morocco. Lively berber music floated from the sound system. The hostess, a gorgeous woman with olive skin and long, dark hair, greeted them with a bright smile. She was dressed in a jeweled black halter and a long, flared gold skirt adorned with a top layer of strips of black beaded material.

"I have a reservation," Nicholas announced. "For Aubrey."

"Ah, yes," the hostess said. "Follow me."

Zienna loved the architecture and ambience of Café Tagine. There were archways designed to look like the top of a temple. Delicate gauzy swags in bright reds and oranges divided the seating areas.

She was grinning as she peeked past the privacy swags and saw various diners. Earlier, she had hoped to simply forgo dinner and do Nicholas, but now she was happy that they were here. She really loved the romance and elegance of this place.

The hostess stopped, then gestured for them to enter the draped-off area that housed their table. Zienna stepped in first—and then stumbled in her four-inch heels, toppling sideways.

"Whoa," Nicholas said, instantly reaching for her before she hit the floor. He pulled her upright against his hard body. "I gotcha."

Zienna's heart began to pound erratically. This couldn't be happening.

Wendell was sitting at their table!

"Are you okay?" the hostess asked.

"Fine." Zienna brushed a strand of hair from her face.

"You know I love heels on you," Nicholas began, "but dang, they're dangerous."

The hostess put the menus on the table. "Ghita, your server, will be with you shortly."

When the woman had walked away, Zienna faced Nicholas. "Wendell…" Her heart was racing in her chest. "He—he's eating with us?" she murmured quietly.

"Yeah." But there was a question in Nicholas's voice. He continued on to Wendell, who stood to greet them. Nicholas shook his friend's hand, then asked, "Where's your date?"

"She couldn't make it. Sorry."

"Date?" Zienna's throat went dry.

"Hello, Zienna."

She didn't respond to him, but instead turned to Nicholas. "You didn't mention we were having dinner with anyone."

"That was the surprise. Wendell was supposed to be joining us for dinner with his girlfriend."

Zienna was aware that her breathing was coming in painful gasps, and wondered why the idea of him joining them at the restaurant should even bother her.

"Not really a girlfriend," Wendell explained. "A friend with potential. But she couldn't make it, and I didn't want you to have to cancel. I figured the three of us could have a nice dinner instead."

"Of course, man," Nicholas said.

"Especially since Zienna had to leave early last night," Wendell went on. "Feeling any better?"

Her eyes went to his. She couldn't be certain, but she thought she saw a hint of self-satisfaction. Clearly, he knew that she'd made up an excuse to flee yesterday.

"Yes," she told him stiffly. "Much better, thank you."

Nicholas pulled out a chair for her, and Zienna sat, a feeling of dread spreading through her. It was one thing to try to put all thoughts and memories of Wendell behind her, but how could she do that if she had to see him at every turn?

"You were right, Nick," Wendell said. "This place is awesome."

"It opened up after you left town. Last-minute reservations can be hard to come by, but I know the manager, and he always leaves at least one table open in case special guests come by. Usually celebrities, city officials, that sort of thing. So he gave me the table. And in time for the eight o'clock belly dancing show."

"Lucky us," Wendell commented.

Lucky? Right about now, Zienna would have considered being thrown into a dungeon a luckier stroke of fate.

Nicholas sat beside her, with Wendell sitting across the table from them. No matter where she sat, she wouldn't be far enough away from the man she had vowed to forget.

She let him and Nicholas talk while she pretended to study a menu she already knew too well.

Ghita came to the table a few minutes later. She was dressed similarly to the hostess, except her outfit was in pink highlighted with silver, and she was just as gorgeous.

"Good evening."

Zienna couldn't help herself…she watched Wendell. Watched how his face lit up as he regarded this beautiful woman.

Shit, what was wrong with her? Why did she care?

Because it was so obvious now. Obvious that Wendell only had eyes for pretty faces and sexy bodies.

"Can we get a bottle of La Dame Blanche?" Nicholas said to Ghita. "Then we could all use a few more minutes before deciding."

"Absolutely."

When Ghita turned to leave, Zienna once again looked

at Wendell, certain she would find him ogling the waitress's behind.

Instead, she saw him watching her.

She quickly pulled her gaze away and returned it to her menu. She was well aware that her pulse had picked up speed.

There was silence for several moments as they checked out the menu, then Nicholas suddenly said, "Hey, Youssef!" He pushed his chair back and stood to greet the manager. "How're you doing, man?"

Nicholas and Youssef pumped hands, smiles on their faces. "You remember Zienna," Nicholas said, gesturing to her.

"Of course." Youssef took her hand in his. "You get more beautiful each time I see you."

"Thank you."

"And this is one of my best friends, Wendell Creighton. He used to play for the Chicago Bears."

Wendell stood to shake Youssef's hand.

Zienna tuned everything out as they chatted for about a minute, but her hearing kicked in again when Nicholas said, "I'll be back in a few minutes, babe."

She looked up at him in alarm. "Where are you going?"

"Youssef wants to show me something in the kitchen."

"I won't keep him long," the manager promised.

And then they were off.

The silence that followed was profound, with Zienna not daring to look in Wendell's direction.

He finally broke it, saying, "You're not going to look at me?"

Zienna drew in a sharp breath. "Why are you here?"

Wendell gave her a confused look. "Nick invited me out."

"You know what I mean. Why are you... You know it's not a good idea for us to be hanging out together."

"What am I supposed to say? Hey, Nick—don't invite me out because I used to sleep with your girl and she might be uncomfortable around me?"

Zienna said nothing. She knew he had a point.

"You want me to tell him, I will."

She remained silent.

"So now you've got nothing to say?"

"I don't like this. It can't be comfortable for you, either. Figure out a reason to say no to us getting together, that's all I'm saying."

Ghita arrived with the wine and poured some for Wendell to taste. He nodded to indicate it was fine, and Ghita filled the three glasses.

Once the waitress was gone, Wendell turned his attention to Zienna. He stared, and she felt as though she were on the hot seat. "Zienna," he said after a moment. "What are you so afraid of?"

But before she could answer, she saw Wendell's gaze jerk upward. She looked up, surprised to see Nicholas standing there.

He smiled at both of them, reclaimed his seat and then took Zienna's hand in his. "I think Youssef has a little crush on you. He remembers the appetizer you love, and he's sending it to the table, complimentary."

"Oh." Zienna forced a little chuckle. "Well, isn't that sweet of him?"

"Youssef's a great guy," Nicholas went on, speaking to Wendell. "He came to the States for school, planning to go into medicine. But he dropped out because opening a restaurant was really his passion. He told me how his family was upset, thought he would fail. Three years later, this place is a huge success."

"That's why I always say go after what you want," Wendell commented.

The way you went after me, Zienna thought. *Simply wanting another notch on your belt?*

"Excellent," Nicholas said. "The wine's here." He lifted his glass. "I'd like to make a toast." Zienna and Wendell lifted their glasses. "To Wendell being back in town. And for him agreeing to manage my new restaurant."

Nicholas and Wendell clinked glasses, but Zienna merely gaped at them. "What?" she asked.

Nicholas faced her, looking excited. "That was my real surprise. The news that Wendell has agreed to manage the new location."

"Yep," Wendell concurred.

Zienna didn't get to say anything, because at that moment, Youssef arrived at their table carrying a platter of beef Bourgogne, a mix of sirloin and tenderloin tips roasted with onions, carrots, celery and mushrooms and served over a bed of garlic mashed potatoes.

"Enjoy," he said, placing it before them.

Somehow, Zienna made it through dinner. It helped that the belly dancing show distracted her and prevented them from engaging in conversation during that time. But she hardly ate her dessert, *brûlée royale,* which she typically enjoyed.

Nicholas rubbed her leg. "You okay, babe? You've been a bit quiet."

"I'm fine," she lied.

A beat passed, then Wendell spoke. "I think I know what's wrong."

"You do?" Nicholas asked, sounding confused.

"Nick, there's something I should tell you. *We* should tell you."

Zienna's heart spasmed. *No!* she thought. *Please, no...*

"We?" Nicholas asked. "As in you and Zienna?"

"Nicholas, let's just call it a night," Zienna suddenly said. "I know I wasn't the best company this evening, but it's just because I'm overtired."

But Nicholas wasn't looking at her. He was gazing at Wendell. "What is it, man?"

Now Wendell looked at Zienna. And to her horror, she saw resolve in his eyes.

"Do you want to tell him, Zienna, or shall I?"

6

"What's this about?" Nicholas asked.

"Nothing," Zienna lied.

"The cat's pretty much out of the bag now," Wendell said.

"One of you tell me." Nicholas looked from his friend to her with curiosity. In an effort to imply that she had no idea what Wendell was going to say, Zienna shrugged. Then she tried, ever so subtly with a look, to give Wendell the hint that he should keep his big mouth shut.

"It's been bugging me ever since I came back and learned that you and Zienna were an item," Wendell said, not getting the point—but more likely, not caring. Why was he doing this to her?

"Now I'm really curious," Nicholas said.

"I figured Zienna would have said something to you by now, but I'm guessing she didn't. Otherwise, I'm sure you would have brought it up with me."

Zienna wanted to jump across the table and claw Wendell's eyes out. For the life of her, she couldn't understand his motivation.

"Don't keep me in suspense," Nicholas said, his tone light-hearted.

"Wendell," Zienna said sharply. "What are you doing?"

"We need to tell him."

Sickened, she realized there was nothing she could do to stop him. Which would be futile at this point anyway, since Nicholas could likely figure out what the deal was.

Wendell cleared his throat before continuing. "Years ago, when Zienna began working as my therapist, we…we were involved."

A wave of sensations, hot and cold and dizzying at the same time, swept over Zienna. Good Lord, what had he just done?

For a nanosecond, Nicholas didn't react. Then the slight, curious grin on his face went flat. "What?"

"It was a long time ago," Wendell said. "And obviously it doesn't have any bearing on the present. But there's clearly been a bit of tension during dinner—no doubt because of this secret. And now that I'm going to be managing your new restaurant…I realized that we needed to lay this out on the table, then bury it."

Zienna's skin was growing hot, her face flushed.

"Something like this has a tendency to come out at some point, which would only seem more suspicious the longer we wait," Wendell explained.

"Right," Nicholas said, his tone not revealing how he was feeling about what he'd just heard.

But it hadn't escaped Zienna that he had released her hand.

"It wasn't a serious relationship. Zienna and I had an off-and-on thing for about six months."

It wasn't a serious relationship… Hearing Wendell say the words made her want to slap him. After how crazy she had been about him, to hear him say that their relationship hadn't been serious hurt like hell.

More than it should.

"But Pam?" Nicholas said, narrowing his eyes in confusion. "When you hurt your shoulder, you were dating Pam."

"I know, I wasn't perfect." Wendell faced Zienna. "I'd been with Pam since college," he said, as though that was supposed to make his betrayal forgivable. "What can I say? Temptation got the better of me."

Zienna guffawed and jerked her eyes from his.

"Wow," Nicholas said, and when she looked at him, she saw that he was shaking his head in disbelief.

"I was just the fuck buddy," she said, her voice overly sweet. "No need to worry."

Ghita arrived with the bill at that moment. She seemed to sense the tension, and quietly slipped the check onto the table before turning away.

"Like I said," Wendell went on, speaking to Nicholas. "You're my friend. I didn't want to keep this secret from you, especially when it's not like there's anything going on between us now."

A few seconds passed. The glum mood at their table was accentuated by the happy laughter that came from people nearby.

Nicholas suddenly turned to Zienna. "How serious was this relationship for you?"

"What?"

"Wendell said that you were just a fling. Of course, his heart was with Pam. I don't agree with what he did—and he knew I wouldn't, which is why he never told me about you years ago." Nicholas paused. "But what about you?"

Zienna frowned as she regarded him, her heart thundering in her ears. "You heard Wendell. It wasn't a serious relationship."

"Why didn't you tell me?" Nicholas asked her. "Why didn't you tell me yesterday at my place?"

Her lips parted, but much like an accused person sitting on the witness stand, she felt stunned and disoriented, and didn't know what to say.

Finally, she said, "I do not want to do this. Not here. You want to talk about this, I'm more than happy to leave now, and we can do that." And then she faced Wendell. "What were you trying to do, dropping a bomb like that without any warning? We'd just had a nice dinner. This was not the time nor the place."

"You wanted him to keep me in the dark?" Nicholas accused.

Zienna stood, flustered. She didn't like Nicholas's tone, even if she could understand his shock. Because suddenly, she was the bad guy, when she hadn't done anything wrong.

"Sit down," Nicholas said to her.

"No. No, I don't think I will." She spun around, pausing only to say, "And don't follow me. I swear."

She made it several steps before she heard her name. *Wendell.* As if he had the right to even speak to her right now.

"Zienna," he said again.

She glanced over her shoulder. He was standing just outside the curtains that gave their table privacy. Knowing that Nicholas wasn't able to see her, she gave Wendell the finger and then stormed off.

She was almost at the exit when her heel slipped on something. And unlike earlier, when Nicholas had been there to catch her, this time she went down on her knee.

Zienna heard the collective gasp of nearby patrons, a group of five who were standing in the entranceway.

"Oh my goodness!" The hostess rushed over and offered her an arm to help her up. Zienna took it, not facing the woman.

She got to her feet unsteadily, tears filling her eyes. As she extended her leg, pain shot through her knee. She winced.

"Zee—"

Zienna looked up at Nicholas, who was suddenly beside her, gazing at her with concern. Wendell stood about a foot behind him. In the distance, she saw a concerned-looking Youssef heading toward them.

Zienna swatted Nicholas's arm away and walked off.

The cool night air washed over her when she stepped outside. She wished she could be like Dorothy in *The Wizard of Oz* and simply click her heels together to make a quick getaway.

"Come on, baby," she heard Nicholas say. "I was just surprised."

Anger consuming her, she faced him. "You're treating me as though I was cheating on you. For God's sake, you just introduced me to Wendell last night. Of course I wanted to tell you. But I was trying to figure out the best way to do it. And it's not like the relationship mattered," she added, the words tasting bitter on her tongue.

"Come back inside," Nicholas said. "Finish your dessert."

"After I've been humiliated in front of everyone?"

She hobbled to the street and threw her arm up to flag a passing cab. As the taxi came to a stop, she was already digging her phone out of her clutch.

Alexis didn't live far from here. Zienna could go to her place.

"Where are you going?" Nicholas asked.

"You're so good at figuring things out. I don't need to spell it out for you."

"Come on," Wendell said. "It's done now."

Zienna turned to glare at him as she pulled open the taxi

door. It was the only thing she could do. And she hoped that her eyes conveyed just how much she hated him.

Then she got into the taxi, slumping into the backseat. She felt crushed.

If only she'd driven herself here tonight. She had dressed to the nines for her man, bought special lingerie.

All gone to waste.

"Eight-fifty West Adams," she told the driver, giving him Alexis's address. When the cab made a U-turn, she glanced out the window, saw Nicholas throw up his hands in frustration.

As she expected, a few seconds later her iPhone rang. She saw Nicholas's photo pop up on her screen, and she quickly pressed the icon to reject the call.

Zienna knew how this was going to play out. No matter what he said, he wouldn't be able to handle the fact that his best friend had once had a relationship with her, meaningful or not. The fact that she'd slept with Wendell was the hurdle she and Nicholas wouldn't be able to overcome.

It was that man code, much like the female code, in that respect. You didn't date someone your best friend had been involved with.

Zienna's iPhone made a little musical sound, and she glanced at the screen to see that Nicholas had sent her a text message.

Come back. Let's talk.

She didn't bother responding.

Craning her neck for one last look as the taxi drove away from Café Tagine, Zienna saw both Nicholas and Wendell still standing on the street.

God only knew what they were saying.

"You know what, take me to the Near North Side instead. Kingsbury." Last night, Alexis had told her that she needed to come clean with Nicholas. And Zienna wasn't in the mood to hear any I-told-you-sos.

She just wanted to be alone.

She eased her head back and closed her eyes. Why had Wendell spilled the beans to Nicholas? Without even a heads-up to her beforehand? What was his game plan?

And that's when a fleeting thought came to her, one that was no doubt ridiculous.

The thought that Wendell had brought up his past with her because he'd deliberately wanted to sabotage her relationship with Nicholas.

7

Zienna was asleep in bed when she heard the door buzzer going off several times in rapid succession. She had barely drifted off before she'd been jarred awake by the loud, annoying noise.

Her eyelids heavy, she lifted her head to glance at the clock: 2:21 a.m.

Good Lord, she thought, plopping her head back down. It was Nicholas. It had to be.

He'd called her several times since she'd abandoned him at the restaurant, and had left her at least six text messages. But she hadn't responded, and had ultimately turned the phone off.

She wasn't ready to talk to him about her relationship with Wendell. Not after his reaction at the restaurant.

The buzzer sounded again. Zienna didn't get up.

If she were honest with herself, she knew that a big part of why she wasn't ready to talk to Nicholas was because it would require telling the absolute truth. And the last thing she wanted to do was confess to him that her feelings for Wendell had been stronger than she'd let on.

It wasn't that it mattered anymore, because it didn't. It was how Nicholas would deal with the knowledge.

She certainly couldn't deny that seeing Wendell again had left her reeling. No matter what she said, Nicholas would be smart enough to figure out the truth. And Zienna could only imagine that he would conclude Wendell was a threat on some level.

Nicholas was tall, dark, handsome and successful—but an ex-past girlfriend had devastated him when she'd had an affair. It was the reason he had put Zienna through the ringer in the beginning. Not in a way she hadn't been able to handle, because she knew what it was like to have your guard up. But she'd had to work extra hard to put his mind at ease and assure him she was the faithful sort.

They'd gotten to a happy place…and now Wendell had threatened everything.

The buzzer sounded again. Clearly, Nicholas wasn't going away.

Zienna rolled over, wondering if she should continue to ignore him. If only she knew his frame of mind… If he regretted what had transpired over dinner was one thing. If he still felt she had betrayed him, that was another thing altogether.

It was too late and she was too tired to rehash the argument. The last thing she wanted was to fight about Wendell—not when he had so easily pointed out that she hadn't mattered to him in the least.

She'd been an easy lay. That was all.

Zienna glanced at the clock: 2:27 a.m. The buzzer hadn't gone off for a few minutes, and she wondered if Nicholas had finally decided to leave. Snuggling against her pillow, she figured it was just as well.

Not more than ten seconds later, the knocking started.

Finally, Zienna threw off the covers. She slipped into a robe and made her way to the door. There was no doubt that Nicholas wouldn't go away until she answered.

She looked through the peephole, and there he stood, his expression dour. She grinned a little, suddenly glad he was here. Of course he wouldn't be here if he was mad at her. Obviously he was here because he, like she, hadn't been able to sleep with how things had ended between them.

But Zienna didn't open the door immediately, letting him suffer a little bit longer. He'd hurt her, and she wasn't going to let him off that easily.

"How'd you get in?" she called through the door.

"I followed someone in through the front door."

"What do you want?"

"Are you going to let me in?"

"Why should I?"

"I'm sorry. I was just shocked. But I talked to Wendell, and everything's cool."

"Everything might be cool for the two of you."

"Let me in, Zee," Nicholas pleaded. "Come on."

Inhaling a deep breath, Zienna unlocked the door and took a step backward. Saying nothing, she pulled it wide, allowing him to enter.

He looked wary, his expression uncertain. "I'm sorry," he said without preamble.

Zienna walked the short distance to her living room and took a seat on the armchair, where Nicholas couldn't sit beside her.

He dropped to his haunches in front of her, the look in his eyes making it clear that he truly regretted having freaked out. He delicately rubbed her right knee. "How's your knee?"

"I'll live."

Several seconds passed in silence. Nicholas was looking at her, she knew, but she wasn't meeting his gaze.

"You've got nothing to say?" he finally asked.

"Seems to me you and Wendell have it all figured out."

"I didn't dream Wendell would tell me he used to sleep with you. That was the last thing I was expecting tonight."

You and me both. "It was a long time ago."

"I reacted badly. I admit it."

"You didn't even want to have a decent discussion about it. You just acted like I'd screwed around on you."

"No," Nicholas said firmly. "I didn't. But I acknowledge that I didn't handle the news in the most mature fashion. I was caught off guard, and yes, I get that you were, too. But now that Wendell's investing in my business, I don't blame him for wanting to get this whole deal into the open."

"Why should you blame him when you can blame me?"

"Zee..."

They stared at each other for a long beat, neither saying anything. Zienna was the one to speak first. "So...now what?"

"I told you I was sorry, didn't I? I talked to Wendell and he assured me that your relationship wasn't serious. Nothing like what you and I have together."

"So Wendell drops his bombshell, and yet he's the one to reassure you when I can't? How do you think that makes me feel?"

"What do you mean?"

"When I told you the relationship meant nothing, you got mad at me. You weren't hearing it."

"We never got to have a real discussion." He quickly held up a hand. "Not after my knee-jerk reaction. That's why I called you all night. That's why I'm here."

"You remember what you said to me, right? You had no

problem believing that I meant nothing to Wendell, but you didn't seem to believe that he meant nothing to me."

"I came to apologize," Nicholas said, sounding a little exasperated. He stood and turned toward the window that faced the river. "But it seems to me you want to keep fighting. I can't help wondering why."

Well, that hadn't gone the way Zienna had hoped. She stood and wrapped her arms around her torso. "I'd like to go back to bed."

Nicholas spun around and stalked toward her, and she actually reeled backward as he reached her. Then he placed both his hands on her shoulders.

"I got upset, yes. But it's not so simple." He paused. "When I heard..." He expelled a sharp breath. "The truth is, Wendell's my best friend, but we've always competed. This isn't the first time we ended up dating the same girl."

Zienna narrowed her eyes in question, but said nothing.

"Some of the best of friends have the biggest rivalries, even if they love each other. You and Wendell...it brought me back to our college days. In a way, my reaction wasn't even about you."

"Really?" she asked disbelievingly.

"Yes. The point is, it's over now."

Suddenly, Zienna was hit with a disturbing thought. "How do I know that you didn't already know about me and Wendell? You two were always competing, maybe you got involved with me because you knew he was coming back to town. What better way to one-up your friend than to be dating the girl he used to sleep with?"

"It's not like that."

"Isn't it? You question my loyalty, but maybe I'm the one with reason to question yours."

"Enough," Nicholas said. Both his hands went to her face.

"Enough." He brought his lips down on hers, ever so softly. "Enough."

He eased back and pinned her with a gaze that was now filled with lust. Taking her hand in his, he forced it to his groin. "I am really tired of fighting."

He was rock hard.

"This is our first real fight, isn't it?" He trailed the fingers that were on her face down her neck, to the opening of her robe, dipping them between her breasts. "I'm ready to make up."

Zienna said nothing, but her breathing became shallower.

Nicholas's hand slipped lower, parting her robe a little more, but not fully. "This is what I was looking forward to. From the moment I picked you up and saw you looking so incredible."

Zienna's lips parted. But all that escaped was a wisp of air.

"Are you going to tell me you don't want this?" Nicholas asked, his voice low and sultry.

She could, but she would be lying. She'd been turned on the moment she started getting dressed for dinner hours ago, anticipating what was to come. Wendell's appearance and bombshell had thrown her plans for one hell of a hot night down the toilet.

"I'm still mad at you," she told him. But she was also aroused. Her chest was heaving from a mixture of anger and lust. And all she could think was that makeup sex was just about the best sex there was.

"You won't be mad for long."

His words were a promise.

And with that, he loosened the knot on her silk robe and let the folds fall apart. As his eyes traveled downward, taking in the sight of her, he groaned with pleasure.

She was still wearing the lacy bra and thong she'd bought

earlier. Just seeing the look of desire in Nicholas's eyes had her forgetting all the unpleasantness of the evening.

He reached for her, pressing his warm palm against her belly. His fingertips stroked her skin before venturing a little lower, toward her thong. "Did you expect me to show up?" he asked, his warm breath fanning her face. "Is that why you're wearing this?"

This was the way Zienna had hoped to end the night. She pressed her body against his hand, and Nicholas slipped his fingers into her panties. When he stroked her, a carnal sound of pleasure pushed past her lips.

Nicholas put his free arm around her waist and pulled her against him with force. Then his mouth came down on hers and he began to kiss her ferociously.

Heat consumed her. They shared a hungry, urgent kiss, the kind they hadn't had in a while. Their relationship had become comfortable, and their kisses these days were more sweet and emotional than wild. The passion between them was generated by knowing that what they were doing was more than simply having sex.

But now, as he kissed her, he slipped his hands into her hair and tugged, creating a little pain.

Zienna made a purring sound. She liked it.

Nicholas drew her bottom lip into his mouth and sucked on it before grazing it with his teeth. Then he plunged his tongue into her mouth again, tangling it with hers.

His hands found her bra, and he none too gently shoved the lace covering her breasts downward, over the large mounds. The Nicholas of yesterday would have taken his time removing the delicate fabric.

"Are you still mad now?" His lips trailed her jawline, and teased her skin there while his fingers squeezed her nipples.

In response, Zienna gasped.

Nicholas's mouth made its way to one of her nipples. He flicked his tongue around the tip before pulling it into his mouth.

"What about now?" he asked. "Still mad at me?"

"No," Zienna rasped. "No, baby."

He grinned, then took her other nipple into his mouth and suckled it until she was moaning.

Although lust had taken over her body, somewhere her senses kicked in. "The windows," she said. "The blinds aren't closed."

Her breast was still in his mouth as he turned toward the window. "You're right," he said around her hardened peak. And then, obviously not caring if someone from the next building might be looking in on them right now, he laved the erect tip with his tongue.

Not with the tender, soft flicks of his normal style, but with fervor, as though he was trying to brand her as his.

He moved his mouth to her other breast and teased her with the same intense determination.

Zienna didn't have the strength to stop him. The sensations were too electrifying. He sank his teeth into her nipple, again creating a mix of pleasure and pain. Then he moved his mouth to her other breast and drew it so deeply into his mouth, it was as though he wanted to swallow it.

"I want to do you right here, and I don't care who sees." He flicked his finger over the nipple he was currently torturing. "Almost," he added, grinning up at her.

Zienna hadn't encountered this Nicholas before, but she liked him. Liked him enough that she could make love to him right here, any onlookers be damned.

"Nicholas, baby, what's gotten into you?"

"You." He lowered himself to his knees and kissed her stomach.

He pulled at the sides of her thong, so hard it snapped. Zienna gasped as the elastic waistband stung her skin. But the next moment she moaned, when Nicholas's fingers found her sweet spot.

"You're wet."

"Nicholas…" He wasn't really going to do her right here, was he?

"Yes," he said with resolve, seeming to have heard her silent question. He stroked her nub. "I can't wait."

But he was smart enough to angle her body so that her back was to the window. And then he swept his tongue over her most sensitive spot.

"Oh, God…" she moaned.

His fingers and tongue moved faster, heightening her pleasure. Her eyelids fluttering shut, she gripped his shoulders. She was caught up in rapture, mesmerized by this carnal side of Nicholas she had never seen.

He tantalized her as though his only goal was to please her. He used his tongue, his teeth and his fingers, until she was coming, coming hard. Then he scooped her into his arms and carried her to the bedroom.

Weak from her orgasm, she let Nicholas take off the rest of her clothes. Then he positioned her on her knees and entered her from behind with a blinding thrust.

Zienna cried out, arching her back.

He gave it to her hard, his thrusts relentless. "Oh, my God, Nicholas. Ohhh…"

"Tell me you love me," he said.

"I love you," she managed to reply, with a breathless sigh.

"Tell me I'm all you need."

"You're all I need, baby. You're all I need."

"No one can give it to you better than I can. Ain't that right, babe?"

Even in the midst of her pleasure, the comment gave Zienna

pause. What was he going on about, needing to hear that he could rock her world sexually? This wasn't like him.

He slipped his arms around her waist and drew her upward so that her back was against his front, while he was still inside her. He pressed his lips to her ear. "Tell me no one can give it to you like I can. Tell me."

"No one…only you, baby."

He kissed her, sucking on her lips and her tongue, his lust for her on overdrive.

And as he continued to make love to her, Zienna couldn't help thinking that he was doing her harder than ever before to erase any feelings that she might still have for Wendell.

8

When Zienna's eyes opened, she found Nicholas looking down at her, smiling. He was lying beside her on the bed, but perched on his elbow so that his face was above hers.

"Good morning, baby."

"Morning," she said.

"How're you feeling?"

A slow grin formed on her face. "Amazing. Definitely sore in a lot of places, but amazing." She stroked his cheek and added in a playful tone, "What got into you last night?"

"You mean The Slayer?"

Now Zienna giggled. "Is that what you call it?"

"Yes. But I only let him out sometimes." He gave her a tender kiss, one that lingered. It was sweet and full of meaning—not burning with the carnal need of the night before.

"I am sorry about last night," he told her when he pulled back.

"It's forgotten."

"Damn." He gazed beyond her to her bedside clock. "It's already after seven."

"Ugh. I don't want to get up."

"I hear that." He trailed a finger along her neck bone. "And I take all the blame. I barely let you get any sleep. But I wanted to give you the night of your life."

"That you did, baby."

"Cappuccino?" Nicholas asked.

"Yes, please."

He got out of bed, slipped into his briefs, then exited the bedroom. Minutes later, he returned with a steaming mug of cappuccino for her. On her birthday last month, he'd given her one of those fancy coffeemakers that brewed coffee and made espresso and cappuccino. Zienna had yet to figure out how to operate it.

"Thanks, sweetie," she said, sitting up to accept the mug from him.

"I have to get going. I'm off to the new restaurant before I head into Reflections."

"One more week," Zienna said, smiling.

Nicholas began to put on his pants. "I know. One week until the big grand opening."

"Are you nervous?"

"I'd be lying if I said I wasn't. But mostly, I'm excited."

"So," Zienna began, then paused. "What exactly is Wendell going to be doing for you?" She wasn't sure if she should mention him, but the issue had been resolved last night, hadn't it? There was no doubt she would be seeing Wendell in the future, and certainly she should be able to ask a question about him.

Nicholas shrugged into his dress shirt. "For starters, he's one of my primary investors in the new restaurant. And he's also going to be a manager."

"Does he have experience doing that?" Zienna asked.

"Yep. He bought a small restaurant in Dallas, but it didn't do well. That's how the idea about him working with me started. Now that his football career is over, he's ready to find something else to do with the rest of his life."

"Oh. Does that mean he's given up on his dream of coaching?"

"Coaching?" Nicholas asked.

"Um, yeah. He used to mention that…say that he would one day become a coach." She shrugged. "Of course, that was a long time ago. What do I know?"

Now dressed, Nicholas approached her, leaned down, and kissed her on the lips. "It's okay for you to mention Wendell," he said softly. "You don't have to feel awkward thinking about him. Okay?"

Zienna nodded. "Okay."

"I'll see you later, babe."

"For round two?" Zienna suggested, giving him a wink.

"You want more of The Slayer, do you?"

"Oh, absolutely."

Nicholas kissed her again. "Then I'll definitely see you later."

Zienna went to work bone tired, but with a smile on her face. The night with Nicholas had been incredible. Make-up sex always was, wasn't it? But he had surprised her with his carnal hunger. Last night had been about love, but with a healthy dose of lust.

And Zienna had enjoyed every moment of it. Tender, meaningful sex was wonderful…but it was nice to know at times that your man just plain craved you.

The lust factor had been off the charts, but Nicholas's stamina had also surprised Zienna. He had thrilled her for hours, in several different positions.

Zienna called Alexis on the way to work, and filled her in on what had happened last night at the restaurant. How Wendell had spilled the beans about their past relationship, which had led to the fight with Nicholas.

"I told you that you should've mentioned it to Nicholas first," Alexis said. "This wouldn't have happened if you'd taken my advice."

"I certainly didn't expect Wendell to drop the bomb at the restaurant, right after a lovely dinner," Zienna said in her own defense. Then she smirked, remembering her intensely hot night. The fight had been worth it, just for the make-up sex. "But, strangely," she went on, "it was better this way."

"So you leave the restaurant pissed off, and it was better that way?"

"Yes," Zienna said. "Because Nicholas and I had our first real fight. Which led to the best sex of our relationship. Our make-up sex was off the charts."

Alexis squealed. "Seriously?"

"He was like a different man. He came to my door at two-thirty in the morning. And he wasn't leaving until he had me. Made me his." Zienna lowered her voice, as if someone was in the backseat of her car and could overhear her. "I was so turned on, I was going to let him do me in the living room… with the blinds open."

"Wait—what?"

"We were arguing for a bit in the living room. And then… well, then he began to seduce me. I pointed out that the blinds were open, but that didn't stop him. I have no clue if someone caught the first part of the action."

"Nicholas?" Alexis asked, her tone rife with disbelief.

"I know. He was totally different. He said he couldn't wait

to have me, not even to move to the bedroom. And then…
well, a lot happened before we made it to the bed."

"Nicholas, an exhibitionist. Who knew?"

"It was a whole new side of him, and I loved it." Zienna's
body throbbed, remembering the illicit nature of their foreplay. She had never thought herself an exhibitionist, either—
at least not these days—but the excitement level had been a
huge turn-on.

"Now that's what I'm talking about," Alexis said. "Because for a while there, I was starting to think that Nicholas
was like Elliott."

"Meaning?"

"Just that—"

"You dumped Elliott. When did I ever give you the im-
pression that I was going to dump Nicholas?"

"You didn't…and I'm not saying that you would."

"Nicholas is a nice guy. And he's into me. I'm happy."

"Meaning I should have been happy with Elliott?"

"It's not up to me to tell you who's good for you."

"I know I had a great guy. Elliott was into me, would
never cheat on me. But you know how I felt. I started to miss
the excitement of a guy who wanted you so badly, he would
take you…anytime, any place. Within reason, of course. It's
not just men who want partners with a bit of freak in them."

Zienna pondered the comment. Maybe Alexis was right.
Because she definitely wanted more of The Slayer, and the
loving he had given her the night before.

But was comfortable sex a reason to dump someone? "All
I know is that I've got a good guy. The fact that he can give
it to me like a bad boy is a perk."

"If Elliott could have done that, things would be different."

"So you dumped him solely because of the sex?" Alexis had

complained that he no longer excited her, but Zienna figured it was about more than just his performance in the bedroom.

"In part, I guess." Her friend sounded conflicted. "I just… I needed something more. Something he wasn't giving me."

"You did what you had to do," Zienna said. She loved Alexis, but when it came to relationships, she didn't know what her friend was looking for.

"I'm sorry," Alexis said. "I'm just testy. Elliott's mother came by last night. She wanted to know what was wrong with her son. I kept telling her that there was nothing wrong with him, that he would make someone very happy one day."

"Which she didn't understand," she supplied.

"No."

"Of course not."

"All I could tell her was that he just wasn't right for me. She was crushed."

"Well," Zienna began, "that's understandable. She grew to love you, same as Elliott did."

Alexis expelled a breath. "I know. It just makes it hard. I've made my decision and want to move on."

For someone who had resolved to move on, she didn't sound happy. But Zienna said all that she could say. "I know."

"No more about me and Elliott," Alexis stated with resolve. "I'm so glad that your first fight with Nicholas led to one seriously hot night."

"I'm already thinking of ways to cause our next fight," Zienna said with a laugh. "Because that sex was *hot*."

"I love it."

"All right, Alex, I'm gonna have to run," Zienna told her. "I'm driving into the parking lot."

"And I'm about to head out the door. Talk to you later. Maybe we can go for a drink tonight."

"Maybe…but no promises. I might be seeing Nicholas again."

"Now you're making me jealous!"

"See ya."

"Later."

Zienna ended the call. And as she headed into the clinic, the smile was still on her face. She was certain it would last all day.

Days like today, Zienna was glad that the Back in Motion clinic had a cafeteria on-site, one that served a variety of healthy sandwiches, salads and beverages. She was too tired to pick up lunch somewhere else, so took the opportunity to eat a turkey wrap in her office, drink more coffee and take a twenty-minute nap.

The ringing office phone woke her up. She jerked her head up from her desk and looked at the time: 1:01 p.m.

Zienna snatched up the receiver. "Zienna Thomas."

"Oh, good. You are in." It was Jamie, one of the clinic's secretaries. "I didn't see you come back into the office."

"I took a short lunch. What's up?"

"You have an emergency appointment. Sorry. I told him that he needed to make an appointment for a later time, but he's apparently in excruciating pain. And since you didn't have a patient after lunch… He asked for you specifically, by the way. His file is outside of examination room one. Sorry."

Zienna had planned to review a few patient files and plan some strength-building exercises for a local marathon runner before her two-o'clock appointment. But the staff knew she didn't believe in turning away a patient in need. "It's okay, Jamie. I'm on my way."

She freshened up by combing her hair and applying more lipstick. Deciding that she looked presentable, she exited her office and headed to the examining room, where she lifted the file from the holder outside the door, glancing at the name. She almost dropped it as though her fingers had been scorched.

Wendell Creighton.

"Oh, my God," she muttered.

Her stomach began to twist. What was he doing? Why was he here?

Zienna couldn't very well run away screaming. She had to face him.

Maybe he had come in to apologize, after the way he'd so senselessly told Nicholas about the two of them at dinner. He certainly owed her an apology.

When she heard someone walking down the hallway, she drew in a deep breath and opened the examination room and stepped inside, her eyes on the file, all businesslike.

"Wendell," she said, her voice flat when she looked at him. "This is a surprise."

He was sitting on the examining bed, appearing comfortable and not the least bit in pain. "I wanted to talk to you."

"Perhaps that's something you should have done before last night," Zienna retorted, giving him a pointed look.

"I know. You're absolutely right."

She sighed. "Why did you do it? How could you…out of the blue like that?"

"Why?" Wendell shrugged. "For one thing, you would hardly look at me. I figured that Nicholas at some point was going to wonder why. It made me realize that everything was too awkward, and we needed to get it out of the way. Clear the air so that it wouldn't come up later and be a bigger issue."

"So that was your motive?" Zienna asked, knowing she sounded skeptical. "To clear the air?"

"Of course it was."

Something about the way Wendell looked at her, with that familiar, intense gaze, made her doubt his sincerity.

"You should have given me a heads-up."

"I told you I wanted to talk to you. You refused."

"So you were punishing me?"

He narrowed his eyes. "Punishing you? I just told you why I did it. And I talked to Nick afterward, made sure everything would be cool for the two of you."

"How sweet."

Zienna turned around. Her heart was beating too fast. She didn't like this. Didn't like being in a room alone with Wendell.

"You looked good last night," he said in a low voice. "Real good."

Turning back, she gaped at him. "And you're telling me this why?"

"Just stating the truth. That's not a crime, is it?"

"Yes. Yes it is. At least, it should be." She summoned her anger, because that would get her through the next few minutes. "Fuck, Wendell. Do you really think I want anything to do with you? I was nothing to you, remember?"

"What else was I supposed to say to Nick?"

"So you were lying?" Zienna asked, and for some reason, her pulse picked up speed.

"Of course I was lying."

"You were pretty convincing. But then, you always were a convincing liar."

She looked away, hardly able to stomach the sight of him. "Ouch."

Zienna faced him again. "You know the shoe fits. Don't pretend you weren't lying to me when we were involved."

"You don't know everything," Wendell said, and he sounded… Zienna couldn't be sure. Unhappy? Serious? "Sit down with me," he went on. "Let me explain."

Zienna had spent years trying to get over Wendell. The last

thing she wanted was to spend more time with him. "You were involved with someone else. There's nothing to explain. It is what it is."

"So every time I see you with Nicholas, you're going to scowl at me?" He held her gaze. "I don't want there to be any awkwardness between us. If we could just—"

His words stopped abruptly when his cell phone rang. He reached into his pocket and took out his iPhone, looked at the screen and put it to his ear. "Hey, man. What's up?"

Zienna watched him as he spoke. And for the first time since seeing him again, she allowed herself to fully check him out. He was wearing a pair of faded jeans, cowboy boots and a white dress shirt that was open at the collar. Around his neck was a gold necklace with a charm in the shape of a cross. That was new. Was Wendell a born-again Christian or something?

Her eyes went lower, to his muscular thighs. God, his body had been an absolute fantasy—and it still was. Those thighs, that butt...

His incredible sexual prowess.

She jerked her eyes upward. Wendell had shaved his head, and a goatee framed his full, sexy lips. He was a little leaner than he'd been years ago, which made sense, since he was no longer playing football. At six foot four, he had the kind of athletic body that commanded attention and could pull off lean or bulky muscle.

"For sure," she heard him say when she tuned back in. "All right, I'll be there for the delivery. Yep, see you soon."

"Who was that?" Zienna had a sneaking suspicion that Nicholas had been on the other end of line.

"That was your boyfriend."

"Your best friend," she retorted, as though trying to score her own point in a tennis match.

"Yep. My best friend. And he really seems to like you."

"Good. Because the feeling is mutual." She paused. "Did you tell him you were here?"

"As you said, he's my best friend. He might understand that we had a relationship before, but the fact that I'm here right now... I don't know about that."

"What's your game?"

"Nothing. Just... I just wanted some time to talk to you." And then, despite the fact that she was wearing a pair of black slacks and a long-sleeved blouse, Wendell's eyes roamed over her, as though she was wearing the skimpiest of lingerie.

In a flash, a memory entered her head, of the time he had sent a gift to her office, a beautiful pink camisole. In the accompanying note, he'd asked her to wear it when they got together later. And after dinner, he'd taken her to Erie Park, near her home, and had asked her to model the lingerie for him. Zienna had been timid at first, unsure, but Wendell's heated kisses had warmed her to the idea. Beside the children's playground, which was deserted after dark, she modeled the lingerie. And then, Wendell had taken her beneath the playground structure and made love to her. Zienna, who had never done anything so wild, had savored the experience. The idea that they could have been caught added an extra thrill.

Coming back to the present, she looked at Wendell and saw that he was regarding her with a little smile.

"When shall we get together?" he asked. He was being the presumptuous man he'd been five years ago, a tactic that had worked for him then.

But Zienna wasn't as stupid as she'd been years ago. Wendell had given her a painful lesson in loving a liar, and she wasn't going to make the same mistake twice.

"We won't," she said, and it felt good to reject him. Felt good to see his smug look falter. "There's nothing for us to say to each other that hasn't already been said. I wish you luck with your new lady friend and with everything else you're doing in your life. And I'll be happy to see you when I'm with Nicholas. But privately, like this? Please don't do it again. We can be friendly, Wendell, but we can't ever be friends."

And with that, Zienna went to the door and opened it wide—her not so subtle hint that the appointment was over.

9

For the next few days, Zienna didn't see Nicholas, as he was busy getting his new restaurant ready for the grand opening. He'd told her that she could drop by Reflections on the Bay to pay him a visit, but she'd countered that her appearance would only be a distraction. Besides, going to the restaurant would no doubt mean she would run into Wendell, and she definitely didn't want to see him.

And Alexis needed her now. The visit from Elliott's mother had put her in the dumps, and Alexis needed a pick me up. Which was why on this Saturday night, instead of even thinking of scheduling some late-night time with her man, Zienna was at Alexis's condo, the two of them getting ready for a night on the town.

"Wow," Zienna said when she saw the dress Alexis had forced her body into. It was black, hugged every curve and barely covered her ass.

"You like?" Alexis asked, doing a twirl.

The neckline plunged, and her friend's breasts looked like

large grapefruit. "I thought we were just going out for some fun. You're dressed like you plan to hook up with someone."

"Too much?"

"Most people break up and go out and drown their sorrows in chocolate cake. They don't get dressed to the nines and go to a club with a dress that screams fuck me."

"Of course they do." Alexis giggled. "Where have you been—living under a rock?"

Zienna turned back to the bathroom mirror, where she assessed the state of her hair. It was more limp than she liked. "As long as you know what you're doing. I don't want you to make a mistake you can't live with."

Alexis joined her at the mirror. "I love that you worry about me. But it's time. I need to get back out on the dating scene."

Zienna wasn't Alexis's mother, and wasn't going to act as if she were, but she was a tad bit worried about her friend. Once, Alexis had lamented the fact that there seemed to be no good men in the world, as if that was all she wanted. Then she'd found one, but a little over two years later, she'd gotten bored with him.

"Have you heard from Elliott?" Zienna figured her hair looked as good as it was going to, and moved on to applying her makeup.

"He called. I told him not to phone me ever again. I wasn't impressed by that stunt with his mother."

"You think he put her up to it?"

"He says he didn't, but I'm sure he did." Alexis finished applying liner, then faced Zienna. "I turn thirty-five in two months. I think that's why I said yes to Elliott's proposal. You know I was unsure about him."

Zienna did. Alexis had always expressed the sentiment that someone better was out there for her.

Her friend turned back to the mirror. "I wanted to be married by age thirty, and it didn't happen. I guess I figured Elliott was my shot at happiness. But I felt anxious about planning our wedding, and it hit me. I can't just get married because the clock is ticking. I have to be certain that it'll last forever."

"You have to be happy," Zienna said. "And you have to be sure."

"Exactly."

A short while later, they were ready. They went downstairs to get into the cab they'd called for. There was no point driving to the club, as parking spots were hard to find and lot parking would be pricey. Not to mention the fact that this way, they could both drink and not worry about a designated driver.

The club they picked was in the West Loop, not too far a drive from Alexis's loft. The cab dropped them off shortly after ten-thirty, and the line was already long.

Zienna knew one of the bouncers, however. He'd been a client of hers. So she went right up to him and he greeted her with a huge smile and a hug.

"Hey, Zee. Wow, you look great."

"Thank you, Keith."

He let out a low whistle when he checked out Alexis. "Damn, girl. You're out to do some damage?"

"I broke up with Elliott," she explained.

"Ah." Keith lifted the velvet rope to let them gain access. "Go easy on the guys, Alex."

They entered the busy establishment, which was filled with tons of women dressed more like Alexis than Zienna—tight, short outfits and high heels. Clearly, Alexis wasn't the only one trying to find Mr. Right in the wrong place.

"This club is rocking," Alexis commented. "I'm so glad we came out. It's been too long."

Zienna and Alexis didn't typically hit night spots like this, not these days. They preferred to hang in lounges with good music and good food.

Alexis scanned the room. "And am I wrong, or are the men looking especially *fine?*"

"Alexis, let's just keep this night about having fun. I don't want to see you make a rash decision."

"You mean jumping into bed with someone new? It's hardly a rash decision. You of all people know that I've had questions about Elliott for at least a year."

"Yes…but maybe not the right questions."

"What's gotten into you?" Alexis asked her. "You used to understand my reservation about marrying a guy who was great but dull."

"On some level, yes." She hadn't discouraged Alexis from taking the time she needed to figure out what would make her happy. "But you know what? This week has thrown me a curve ball, and made it clear that the alternative to the nice guy are guys like Wendell. Guaranteed to break your heart."

"So that's the problem. You've got Wendell on the brain."

"I can't believe he came to my office. Extending an olive branch after trying to ruin my relationship with Nicholas."

"Have you heard from him again?"

"No. Thank God. I'm sure he and Nicholas are slaving away at the new restaurant. I'm already dreading the grand opening on Thursday. I don't want to be anywhere near Wendell."

The two friends headed for the bar. Alexis settled herself on one of the high stools and crossed her legs, exposing almost the full length of her thighs, and feet clad in strappy red stilettos. Obviously, she was hoping to attract attention.

"What do you want?" she asked. "I'm buying."

"I'll have a glass of wine. White."

"Actually, why don't we have margaritas? It feels more fun."

"Yeah! That reminds me of our trip to the Bahamas at Christmas."

"Where it was far too cold to go into the water—"

"—but never too cold to drink!" Zienna grinned as she finished Alexis's statement. That had been their running joke for their five days in what they'd hoped would have been a sultry hot paradise. The Caribbean islands had been unusually chilly last December, and sadly, the cute bathing suits they'd excitedly purchased for the trip hadn't gotten any use.

Alexis placed the order for two frozen margaritas, and then faced Zienna. "Do you really think Wendell was trying to ruin your relationship by telling Nicholas about the two of you?"

"I don't know. But it certainly seems like he was trying to cause trouble."

"Hmm. Interesting."

"Why?" Zienna asked.

"If you think he was trying to cause trouble, you must have considered this. Do you think he's jealous?"

"He made it perfectly clear that I never meant anything to him. And even if I thought he was lying for Nicholas's benefit, how do you explain Pam?" Zienna shook her head. "No, clearly I was the other woman. Nicholas said something about them always having competed in college, so maybe that's what it was about."

Alexis made a face. "Nicholas said they used to compete?"

"Yeah, but it didn't sound serious. Obviously, it couldn't be, if the two of them are still best friends. I guess just typical rivalry stuff...like sports."

"And women." Alexis gave her a pointed look.

"I guess. I suppose it was all just for fun, friendly competition to figure out who was the better man. Men—who can understand them?"

The bartender pushed the drinks across the bar toward

them, and Alexis paid him. Then she raised her glass, and Zienna followed suit. "To the two of us never competing over guys...or anything else."

"I'll drink to that." She sipped the margarita, which was refreshing. Easing back against the bar, she let the beat of the lively Beyoncé tune get her in the mood to have fun. It was nice being at a dance club, instead of going out to dinner as they typically would.

The dance floor was packed, so Zienna didn't mind staying right where she was, especially considering she wasn't trying to find a guy to dance with. Her gaze wandered...and then narrowed when she thought she saw a familiar face.

No! It couldn't be. Not again.

Whipping her head back toward Alexis, she muttered, "Oh my God!"

"What?" Alexis asked.

"He's here," she said in a panicked voice, hunching over the counter to make herself less visible.

"Who?"

Was her friend dense? There was only one man who could cause such a reaction in her. "Wendell! Wendell's *here!*"

Alexis quickly started to survey the bar.

"Don't," Zienna told her. "I don't want him to see us."

"Ohh. There he is."

Zienna turned again, and her heart slammed against her chest when she saw he was with a busty, scantily clad girl with hair that went all the way down her back. Probably extensions, and definitely fake boobs.

Was that the woman with potential? That slutty-looking chick?

"Nothing to worry about," Alexis told her. "He's here with a date."

As though it were that easy. Just being in the same room

with Wendell had Zienna feeling smothered. This was too much for her. She needed to get out of here.

"I want to go somewhere else."

"We just got here," Alexis complained. "And the music's hot."

"We'll find great music somewhere else."

"You know this is the only club I like in the West Loop. And this is about me, remember? Taking my mind off my misery…"

"You're don't seem to be in much misery—and you can get your mind off your problems anywhere. Just not here, fifty feet away from Wendell."

Alexis reluctantly slid off the bar stool. "Fine. If that's how you want it."

"I would prefer it."

"Why are you running scared, anyway? Your relationship ended years ago." And as if something suddenly dawned on Alexis, her eyes widened. "Oh, my God. You're not over him."

"Of course I'm over him. And if I wasn't before, I certainly am now. He was never in love with me. I was the other woman, remember?"

"Yes…and now you're dating his best friend." Alexis's tone said she didn't understand what the problem was.

"I just don't like seeing him. Would you want to run into someone you'd broken up with practically every time you left the house? For God's sake, it's been three times this week."

"I hear you," Alexis said, a little smirk on her face. "And if you want to leave, I won't question it. But I do remember what you always said to me about Wendell and the sex."

"That is something I want to forget," Zienna said, annoyed.

"Maybe you're not so unlike me, after all."

"What's that supposed to mean?"

"Maybe there's a part of you that's still attracted to him." She raised an eyebrow.

Zienna gaped at Alexis. "You are impossible. Why would you even say that to me? You may have broken up with Elliott, but I'm perfectly happy with Nicholas."

More than a little perturbed, Zienna started to push through the crowd with determination. Thankfully, the front doors were in the opposite direction from where Wendell was currently mingling. As she reached the exit, she was certain he hadn't seen her.

"Maybe we could go to that jazz bar—" She turned, but her friend was no longer behind her.

Zienna searched the crowd frantically, wondering where Alexis had run off to in a minute and thirty seconds. And then she saw her. A guy about six feet tall was holding her by the elbow. This mystery man had clearly waited to make his move.

Zienna marched back toward Alexis. And then her heart began to beat rapidly as she saw Wendell heading toward her.

Without his date.

10

"Are you following me?" Wendell asked, a smile gracing his face as he reached her. He had the decency to chuckle, making it clear he was joking.

Still, Zienna didn't appreciate his humorous comment, because she didn't find it funny in the least.

"Why would I ever follow you?"

"I was kidding."

"Obviously. It just wasn't very funny."

"Wow, that look on your face. Is that how it's always going to be between us now?"

"Didn't I see you in here with some woman with giant boobs and hair down to the floor?"

"So you noticed me." One of his eyebrows shot up.

"Everybody noticed you and that girl you were with."

"You sound a little jealous."

"You're insane," Zienna told him.

"A guy can hope, can't he?"

A beat passed, and Zienna blinked when his words registered. "Pardon me?"

"I'm not gonna lie. I'd be flattered if you were a little jealous."

"Are you playing some sort of game? Did you forget that I'm dating Nicholas?"

"How could I forget that?" Wendell pinned her with a look. "Doesn't mean I have to like it."

Zienna's heart began to accelerate. But she didn't dare ask him what he meant.

"Forget it," he said. "Forget I said that."

"Why are you here, anyway? Aren't you supposed to be with Nicholas at the new restaurant?"

"He's got it under control."

Zienna made a face. Wendell working with Nicholas was no doubt a bad idea.

At that moment, the woman with the boobs and long hair who looked as if she had undergone numerous surgeries in order to resemble some sort of Barbie doll, appeared and slipped her arm through Wendell's. "There you are, baby," she purred.

"See ya," Zienna said, and turned. She made her way back toward Alexis, who was still with the guy who'd been holding her arm.

"Alexis, I'm ready."

Her friend pouted. "Actually, Zienna, I changed my mind. I don't want to leave. This is Brock. He's a fireman." Alexis gave her a look she knew too well, one that silently begged her to stay.

Zienna glanced over her shoulder to where she had left Wendell and his bimbo girlfriend. They were no longer there.

Then she thought about Alexis's question. Why was she

running away just because Wendell had shown up? She wasn't afraid of him.

In fact, she could call Nicholas, have him meet her here.

"All right." She forced a smile. "I won't take you away from Brock."

A slower song began to play, and Brock took Alexis by the hand and led her onto the dance floor. Zienna found her way to the bar, where she took the one available seat facing the floor, and watched her friend dance. Alexis's smile was bright and her hands wandered over Brock's wide shoulders.

She certainly looked happy. Alexis had been right when she'd said that getting out would do her a world of good.

Moments later, Zienna couldn't stop her eyes from wandering in Wendell's direction, when she spotted him with the bimbo. They weren't on the dance floor, but close to it, and his date was gyrating her body like a seasoned stripper, giving not just him, but everyone in the immediate vicinity a show.

Turning away from the raunchy performance, Zienna called Nicholas. She put the phone next to one ear and a finger in the other one in order to hear above the music.

"Hey, sweetie," she said when he answered. "How's your night going?"

"Busy. Where are you?"

"I'm out with Alexis, but I miss you."

"Huh?"

"I'm at Wet… You know, that club? I'm with Alexis," Zienna said, speaking louder. "But she's met some guy, and I'm here, bored. Why don't you come meet me?"

"I'm having a hard time hearing you."

"Hold on." Zienna crossed the club to the restrooms, where the pounding pulse of the music was no longer a distraction. "I was saying that Alexis has met someone, and I'm here by myself. I know you've put in a long day. Why don't you come join me?"

"Ah, babe, I don't know. I'm tired."

"Come on," Zienna said in a softer voice. "And guess what—I saw Wendell."

"You did?" There was an odd note in Nicholas's voice.

"Yes." Zienna had hoped that the mention of his friend would inspire him to come to the bar. "I thought he'd be working late with you tonight."

"He wanted to check out early. It's all good. I was overseeing some last-minute paperwork, and he didn't need to be around for that."

"Oh. Well, looks like he's here with his new girlfriend. I'm guessing she's the one who was supposed to come to dinner. And if that's her, I'm so glad I did not have to share a table with her."

"Why?"

"Because she looks…fake. Porn-star fake. Wendell is so clearly driven by the superficial." Which made it all the more baffling that he'd ever dated her.

"All right. I haven't been out to a club in a while. I'll come join you."

"Great, sweetie."

"I'll text you when I get there."

That text came forty-five minutes later, and Zienna was relieved. She'd had to turn down men who'd been hitting on her and offering to buy her drinks. With Alexis on the dance floor, Zienna felt foolish, sitting in a club by herself.

So she smiled hugely when she saw Nicholas approaching her at the bar. Alexis had come back a few times for more drinks, but other than that, she and her new friend seemed to be inseparable. They were working up a sweat on the dance floor, and Zienna had even seen them sharing some pretty hot kisses. It wasn't like Alexis—at least not a sober Alexis.

Zienna hadn't seen Wendell in a while, but the club was large, with two levels. And it wasn't as if she was keeping tabs on him, anyway.

The moment Nicholas got to her, she reached for his arm and pulled him toward her, planting a kiss on his lips that lingered longer than it should have in a public place. But in this crowd, she fit right in with that kind of public display of affection.

"I missed you," she told him. "It's been a few days."

"I missed you, too." He placed a hand on her thigh. "Where's Alexis?"

Zienna indicated the dance floor with a jerk of her head. "She's dancing. She all but forgot I exist. I've been sitting here bored out of my mind, waiting for you to get here."

"And Wendell?"

Zienna shrugged. "I don't know. Maybe he left. Or he's upstairs. I haven't seen him in a while."

"You talk to him?"

"We said hello."

"And that's it?"

"Yes," she answered, narrowing her eyes. "Why? Shouldn't I have spoken to him?"

"No, of course not. I'm just asking."

"Good." Zienna placed her arms around Nicholas's waist. "Because you know you're my guy."

She stood, leaned into him and planted another kiss on his lips. It was the kind of kiss best left for the bedroom, but she was sure none of the patrons here would care.

"I hope you're not too tired for later," she said into his ear as she smoothed her hand over his stomach. She wanted another amazing night of hot sex with him.

He pulled back and looked down at her. "So, of all the spots in Chicago, Wendell ended up here?"

"This is a pretty popular spot."

Nicholas nodded, but he pursed his lips, as though something was on his mind.

"What are you saying?" Zienna asked after a moment. "That he came here because I'm here? That I told him I'd be here? What?"

"Naw, of course not." But Zienna could see that Nicholas's jaw was tense. "Why would I think that? You haven't seen him since our dinner."

It wasn't so much what Nicholas said, but the way he said it. He knew. He knew about Wendell showing up at her office.

"Wendell told you he came to see me," Zienna said, feeling a sense of irritation.

"What I'm wondering is why *you* didn't tell me."

This had to be a game for Wendell. Maybe Alexis had hit the nail on the head when she'd said he wanted to cause trouble deliberately because he was jealous. "I should have told you a few days ago, but I figured I'd tell you when I saw you again. It's not a big deal. Wendell said he wanted to apologize for how he blindsided both of us at the restaurant. But he added that you and he had cleared the air, which you and I had already discussed. I didn't want to rehash all of this stuff. But I was going to mention it to you when I saw you."

"Sure," Nicholas said, his tone unreadable. "Makes sense."

Zienna frowned. People around her were kissing and groping, yet Nicholas had gone cold. Was *he* jealous?

"You don't trust me?" Zienna asked. "Is that the bottom line here?"

"I didn't say that. Don't put words in my mouth. I've had a long day, and I'm tired. That's all."

Was he being honest with her? She had done nothing wrong, and she didn't want him suspecting her of inappropriate behavior. She decided that she would quash any issue, right here, right now. "I called you because I wanted to be with you tonight. Anything else you might be thinking, it doesn't make sense that I would call you, now does it?"

"I know." Nicholas took her hand. "I like you. You matter to me. And I guess that makes me feel a bit vulnerable. You're not just some girl I'm passing the time with."

Zienna smiled at him. "Well, that's good to hear. I was beginning to think I was a plaything. Not that I mind." She twirled her finger along the palm of his hand. "You can play with me the way you did Wednesday night...." She wanted to lighten the mood, not feed his paranoia in any way.

"Seriously, Zee—you know I have a fragile heart." He placed her hand on his chest, over his heart. "It's been broken before."

"You're exactly the kind of guy I need," she said, stressing the words. "You're respectful and sweet."

"That's it?"

"No. You're sexy as hell." She extended her leg and rubbed it up and down his. "And since you don't seem to be taking the hint, are you gonna do me tonight?"

Nicholas smiled, and then he drew his bottom lip between his teeth and gave her a look filled with lust. "If you...look closely, you'll see that I'm already hot and bothered."

"Oh." Her eyes ventured to his groin. "*Ohh.* Well, we've got to do something about that." Zienna was ready to take off, but there was the matter of Alexis. She couldn't leave her here with a strange guy, no matter how much her friend claimed she wanted her to do just that.

"Let me check on Alexis," she said to Nicholas, rising. "She's had more than a few, so I want to make sure I get her home safely. My car's at her place, so either you drop us there, or I go with her in a cab and then drive to your house."

"I'll take you." He leaned down, putting his mouth close to her ear. "But I don't know how long I can wait to get you naked, so please, find Alexis fast."

Zienna chuckled. "Okay."

Nicholas held her arm and helped her off the stool, then placed his hand on the small of her back. "I'll go get the car, and I'll see you both out front."

Zienna found Alexis on the dance floor, her body molded to the sexy stranger's. Though she'd just met Brock, she couldn't seem to get enough of him. And Alexis was more than tipsy— she was drunk. Giggling like a giddy teenager, she was groping this guy as though he were the last man on earth.

Zienna tapped her shoulder. "Hey. Alexis."

Her friend angled her head over her shoulder. A smile erupting on her face, she released the object of her desire and threw her arms around Zienna, as though she hadn't seen her in five years. "There you are!"

Zienna smirked. "As if you were looking for me."

"Zienna, this is Brock. Isn't he cute?"

"When did you get so drunk?" The words fell from Zienna's lips. She put the time line together and it didn't make sense, unless Alexis had been constantly throwing them back. Zienna had seen her at the bar only twice.

"I'm very happy," Alexis stressed, then giggled.

"Listen, Nicholas is here, and I'm thinking that you've had enough and so have I, so it's time we both head home."

"Brock can drop me home."

"Yeah." Brock nodded in agreement. "It's not a problem."

Zienna shook her head. She wasn't uptight sexually, and she knew people hooked up all the time for a one-night stand. But Alexis wasn't in her right frame of mind—emotionally, nor physically. Zienna wasn't about to leave her friend in this state with a stranger.

"Thanks, Brock, but she's coming with me."

"B-but—" Alexis sputtered "—I want to go with him. The night's still young!"

"Come over here for a minute," Zienna said sweetly, taking her by the elbow and leading her a few steps away. "Alexis, honey, right now you're not exactly thinking straight. I know you don't realize that, but we've been best friends since what, second grade? I'm always going to look out for you. And I'm not about to leave you with this strange guy. I don't care how cute he is. He could be The Rock—and you know how much I love The Rock—and I wouldn't leave you with him."

"That's because you'd be jealous if he was The Rock," Alexis said with a sly smile.

"Well, that I won't deny. But you get the point. I don't know this guy, and more importantly, you don't know this guy. If he likes you, you two can plan another date. Go out again. And hopefully, next time don't get so drunk."

Zienna knew her friend wanted some fun to forget about Elliott, but this wasn't like her. Zienna hoped to God that Brock hadn't done something stupid, like slip her a pill or put something in her drink.

Of course, it was entirely possible that Brock or Alexis had gone to another bar for more drinks, or even purchased some from a passing cocktail waitress. Maybe Alexis had been drinking steadily, because she wanted to drown her sorrows.

Because as much as she was putting on a brave face about breaking up with Elliott being the right thing, Zienna knew her friend had to still love him. It wasn't easy to just turn off your emotions for someone, not after having been with him for so long.

And though Alexis had had a few random hookups in the past, Zienna was certain that she'd be in for a world of regret tomorrow if she woke up in Brock's bed.

"You're no fun," Alexis told her.

"Yeah, that's right. I'm a party pooper. You can hate me forever, but I'm not leaving without you." Zienna pasted a smile on her face. Then she walked back to the dance floor with Alexis, where she took control and said, "Now, you seem like a nice guy and all, so you can understand why I wouldn't let you take my friend home under these circumstances. But why don't you both exchange numbers and promise to be in touch." She knew she sounded like a chaperone at a high school prom, but she didn't care one bit.

Resigning herself to her fate, Alexis did as Zienna instructed. Then she and Brock shared a long hug and another smooch before Zienna successfully dragged her from the dance floor.

They were walking toward the exit when Zienna saw that Nicholas was still inside, standing with Wendell. Both men were about the same height, with Wendell having the edge by an inch. Both had athletic bodies and both were attractive. But there was something about Wendell, the inexplicable X factor that made him irresistible to women.

"Oh, my God," Alexis said. "You're checking Wendell out!"

Given her drunken state, Alexis had spoken way too loudly. Zienna physically put her fingers on her friend's lips and said, "Hey. Not so loud."

"And you got all huffy with me about Elliott and how he's a nice guy, so the sex shouldn't matter. But I bet I know what you're thinking about right now. Because at the end of the day, it's not just guys who need to get done good. We do, too."

Zienna swallowed. And she finally allowed herself to acknowledge—even though she didn't want to—that that was exactly what was unsettling about Wendell's reappearance in her life. How easy it was going to be to remember their explosive passion.

"There are more important things than sex," Zienna said, a fact that was reinforced as she watched the leggy, artificial beauty pawing Wendell as he stood with Nicholas. "Nothing is more important than a guy who can commit to you."

Wendell turned then, caught her gaze. And as he looked at her, she felt a zap. It was those eyes, damn it. One heated, intense look from those eyes had always been able to seduce her.

And he was giving her the look now.

Sex isn't everything, she thought as she approached Nicholas, Wendell and his tart du jour. She immediately placed her arm around Nicholas's waist and leaned up to snuggle her nose in his neck.

And then, for added effect, she reached up and kissed his jawline, then angled his face downward so that she could kiss him on the mouth. This time she added tongue, another inappropriate public kiss, but one meant to prove a point.

Just in case Wendell *had* been trying to cause trouble for her relationship, she was letting him know that she and Nicholas were absolutely fine, and any plans to destroy their happiness would be futile…whatever his plan could possibly be.

Nicholas was the one to break the kiss, saying, "Wow."

Zienna swatted his behind. "Let's get Alexis home. I can't wait anymore."

"You heard that, Wendell. I gotta bounce. Can't keep my girl waiting."

"Nice to see you again," Zienna muttered, barely giving Wendell a second glance as she took Alexis by the arm and started for the exit. She hoped that Nicholas would feel better about her words and actions, and know that Wendell wasn't a threat. Not in the least.

Zienna got to Nicholas's house about forty minutes later, and she was a little disappointed when he came to the door still dressed in his clothes. He couldn't have gotten home more than fifteen minutes ahead of her, but it was still enough time for him to get undressed. At least take off the dress shirt and socks, but the only thing he had lost was the tie. Worse still, he suddenly looked very tired—not at all like a man who was about to rock her world the way he had on Wednesday night.

"Hey, babe," she said as she stepped into his house, immediately placing her palms on his chest. If he wasn't in the best mood, she was going to get him into it. She understood that he was tired from all the work he was doing at the restaurant, but she needed more of what he had given her the other night.

"Hey." Nicholas put both hands on her arms and rubbed up and down, in a manner that screamed, *Let's just hit the sack. I'm tired.*

But Zienna was having none of that. So she began to pull her dress over her head right there in the foyer, watching with delight as Nicholas's eyes swept over her body. She was wearing another matching bra-and-panty set, this time in black. Reaching behind her, she pulled the clasp of her bra, letting her breasts fall free.

Nicholas said nothing, but she did hear him moan softly.

She stepped toward him now. Taking both his hands in hers,

she placed them on her breasts. She made a mewling sound as she forced his fingers over her nipples. She then leaned up to kiss him, in the hopes of awakening the sexual beast she had seen the other night. The Slayer.

But Nicholas's kiss was his typical gentle one—far from lust-inspired.

"I can't wait to see The Slayer again," Zienna whispered, hoping that would stoke his fire. "Slay me, baby."

And then she began to kiss him with gusto, pressing her breasts against his body, the cotton fabric of his shirt grazing her nipples. She slipped her hands around his waist and dragged her nails down his back, something he enjoyed.

And she thought she was turning him on. Until he took her upper arms in his hands and eased her backward.

"I really, really want to give you what you need—trust me I do. But I'm supertired. It's been a long day, and I know that makes me sound like an old man, but I don't want to disappoint you. Maybe in the morning."

Zienna stared at him in surprise. He had to be kidding.

"I'm sorry," he said.

Oh, no no no. Zienna was having none of this. She had not gotten this worked up, this hot about the idea of getting laid, only for Nicholas to turn her down.

She snaked her arms around his neck and forced her tongue into his mouth. She didn't mind being the aggressor. She twirled the tip of her tongue over his, then suckled it softly. It was something Nicholas had done to her on Wednesday night, and she loved how it had expressed the urgency of his desire for her.

Nicholas's hands went to her breasts, and she sighed with pleasure. "That's it, baby. Yes, touch me like that. Squeeze them harder. Show me The Slayer."

He played with her nipples while he kissed her, but Zienna knew she was losing the battle. Even before he pulled away from her. "I'm sorry." He groaned. "You look amazing, and I'd love nothing more than to bring out The Slayer to satisfy you, but I just can't."

Zienna was mortified. She crossed her arms over her naked breasts. How was this possible? Nicholas was thirty-four, not fifty-four. Couldn't guys easily get it up, even when tired? The offer of sex always got them in the mood.

At least, Wendell had been that way.

"Are you upset?" Nicholas asked.

Zienna quickly scooped up her clothes. "No," she lied. "Why should I be upset?"

She began to dress. Sure, it was normal not to have sex *every* night, and a part of her knew she was being irrational for even thinking this, but she needed to get off.

Wendell had always been ready....

Of course, he'd also been younger then, more virile. Yet the look he'd given her in the club told her that he was still as sexually potent as ever. She couldn't imagine him saying no to her if she was half-naked and trying to get him hot and bothered.

"You're leaving?"

Zienna didn't realize she had stepped closer to the door until Nicholas asked the question. "Sounds like you need a really good night of sleep. It just makes sense."

He frowned. "There's no reason you can't sleep with me. Is there?"

She felt frustrated and even angry with him, and she wasn't exactly sure why. She wanted to leave—punish him for rejecting her.

And then, as she continued to look at him, saw the slump of

fatigue in his shoulders, she came to her senses. It was unfair to expect sex when Nicholas was so exhausted. If he was too tired and didn't perform to the best of his ability, he wouldn't be happy about that.

She stepped toward him. "I'm sorry for being insensitive. I was just looking forward to making love to you." She smiled sheepishly. "Can we at least snuggle?"

"Of course."

She slipped her arm through his. "Good."

11

"Hello, Donald," Zienna said pleasantly as she entered the exam room. "How are you doing this morning?"

It didn't take more than a nanosecond for her to realize her client was unhappy. His lips were pulled into a tight line and the expression in his eyes was cold.

"You told me that I wouldn't have any more pain," he said. It was an accusation.

"You're experiencing more problems with your ankle?"

"Obviously that's why I'm here. We did all that work, and you said I wouldn't have any more problems with it, but I am. You lied to me."

Zienna drew in a breath to calm herself, taking a moment before responding. Donald was already on edge, and she didn't want to make him any more upset. "Actually," she began calmly, "you'll remember I told you that, in addition to the acupuncture and corrective work we did, you needed to do the strength-building exercises I devised. Now, I know you started to feel better, and then canceled the last four weeks of

exercises. What's happening now is you're feeling the results."
She had tried to stress to Donald that the work in repairing his
Achilles' tendon was only half-done. He had made a mistake
other patients often did, and assumed that once he started to
feel better, it meant he was completely healed.

"I don't want to hear any of that!" he snapped. "You lied
to me, and you know it."

Zienna wondered what had happened to make him so irate,
but remembered that during her first session with him, she
had determined that he was holding anger and anxiety in his
body, which also contributed to his pain. She dealt with her
clients holistically—from the inside out, so to speak. Emotional issues had to be dealt with as well, if there was truly
going to be healing.

But Donald's anger was back, and that was going to do
nothing to help him overall.

"Let's see what's going on," Zienna said. "Extend your leg
for me."

"So you want to start that hogwash crap again." Donald
slid off the bed. "I'm done with you. I came here to tell you
that I want my money back. All of it. And if you guys don't
pay, I'm going to sue you."

Zienna was baffled. "You were perfectly happy with your
treatment." He'd been so pleased, he'd hugged her as though
he hadn't want to let her go the last time she saw him, and subsequently had sent her a bouquet of flowers. "As I've explained
to you, we did not get to complete the necessary exercises—"

"I want my money back!" Donald yelled. "I need that cash,
and I need it in five days."

Was that his issue? Some unresolved debt? Or perhaps his
mortgage payment was short this month?

"Donald, you must understand—"

"Five days!"

"I'll talk to Margaret," Zienna said, referring to the clinic's owner and head physiotherapist. "See what we can do."

"Get it done. Before I let everybody know what kind of quack operation you guys are running here."

Then he stomped toward the door and threw it open. Jamie, who must have heard Donald yelling, was standing there, and he pushed her aside, causing her to lose her balance and stumble. But he paid no attention as he continued to march toward the exit.

Jamie, clearly stunned as she steadied herself, volleyed her eyes between Zienna and Donald's retreating form. "What's going on?" she asked once he'd rounded the corner and was out of view.

Zienna waved a dismissive hand. "He's upset. He should be coming back for more treatment, but he doesn't want to do the work."

Jamie stepped into the office. "Are you okay?"

Nodding, Zienna walked toward her. "I'm fine. Unsettled, but fine. What about you—are you hurt?"

"No. But shit, that was crazy."

"Margaret's with a client?" Zienna asked.

"Yes."

"Okay." She would send a message to her voice mail, stating that they needed to have a meeting once she was available. "Thanks, Jamie."

"Can I get you anything?"

"No, I'm fine."

The look in Jamie's eyes said she wasn't convinced, but she walked away nonetheless. Zienna closed the door and went to her desk. She slumped forward, the stress of the incident already spreading across her shoulders.

She didn't like this. She hated conflict, hated disappointing people. But when it came to dissatisfied clients, that really got her down.

She lifted the receiver to send Margaret a message, but decided instead to call Nicholas. She wanted to hear his voice. Vent to him and have him give her words of encouragement. She needed to lean on him right now.

"Hey, baby," she said when he picked up his cell.

"Hi, there. What's up?"

"Are you busy?"

"Pretty much, yeah. What's going on?"

Zienna groaned as she hunched forward again. "I'm having a bad day," she said in a soft voice. "I just had a very pissed-off client who thinks he was duped. Even though he was initially feeling better, he figures that the work I did with him was some kind of hocus-pocus. At least that's the sense I'm getting."

"Hmm, that sucks," Nicholas said distractedly.

"It gets worse. He said he wants his money back. All of it. That I've got five days to get it to him. Or else he'll sue."

"That won't fly."

"Maybe not, but he can still create a huge problem for me and the clinic if he goes forward with a lawsuit. Time, money, all that." Zienna groaned.

"I doubt it'll get that far."

"I still have to talk to Margaret about it, see what she wants to do. Sometimes guys like this are more of a headache than it's worth, and it'll be easier to give him what he wants. Still, he ran up a substantial bill. He was doing well, but he was supposed to continue working on the exercises I devised. He stopped when he was feeling good. That's the problem."

"Yeah. I hear you. No, no, that isn't supposed to be there."

"Pardon me?"

"Sorry. I was talking to the construction guys. Don't worry. I'm sure everything will work out."

"It just put me in a sucky mood," Zienna said.

"No doubt." Again, Nicholas sounded distracted, as if he wasn't truly listening to her. "Listen, sorry, but I've got to run. The guys are redoing the carpeting."

"What, because of that small stain?"

"Yeah."

He was having that area ripped up? "I thought you were just going to have it cleaned."

"It wasn't perfect, and it started bothering me. I want everything right for this Thursday."

"Everything's looking amazing. The grand opening is going to be a huge success," she assured him.

"The biggest food critics are coming. Someone from the *New York Times,* even. The pressure's on."

"The menu's incredible. The decor is stunning. The critics are going to give Reflections on the Bay rave reviews."

"Thanks, babe. I hate to do this, but I've got to run. So I'll talk to you later. Hang in there."

Hang in there.... As though he was giving her a little pat on the back.

And somehow, though she'd called for *his* support, she'd been the one to reassure him.

Zienna couldn't help feeling annoyed as she stared at the receiver in her hand. What kind of support had that been?

Your problem isn't as big as mine, Nicholas may as well have said.

The meeting with Margaret resulted in what Zienna expected. There would be no refund of the fees Donald had paid for services rendered. They would offer him further treatment, the next two sessions without charge. Zienna called Donald to give him the news, and left a voice mail when she didn't reach him. She hoped that would mollify him.

The stress she had felt over the incident still plagued her as she left the clinic at the end of the day. She wanted to go home, get into her oversize tub and take a long bubble bath.

She fished her keys out of her purse as she approached her vehicle, unlocked and opened the door, then got behind the wheel. When she heard knocking on her driver's-side window, she jumped in fright, because she thought she'd been alone in the parking lot.

She looked up, and was stunned to see Wendell standing there.

She froze, not looking away, not rolling the window down, not opening the door.

He gave her a smile, as though his appearance at her car was perfectly normal.

When Zienna did nothing, he again rapped on the window. She opened the door and got out of the car. "You have to stop doing this," she said without preamble.

"I waited until you were done work. That way I knew you'd be free for dinner, or coffee," he added when he saw her scowl.

How long had he been out here, waiting for her to appear? "This is not a good time," she told him.

"Come on," he answered in a jovial tone. "Just one coffee."

"I'm not in the mood."

"Seriously—you can't be afraid to talk to me."

Zienna exhaled sharply and folded her arms. "Wendell, not today. Please."

Something changed in his expression. It went from playful to worried. He seemed to understand that something else was going on. Something that had her upset.

"Hey, what's the matter?" he asked, his eyes narrowing.

"It's just…it's not the time, Wendell."

"I'm not talking about getting something to eat. I'm asking what's bothering you. Because something is."

She looked up at him, and to her surprise, saw genuine concern in his eyes. "I... It's just... I had a client come in today. He was really pissed off. He's threatening legal action if he doesn't get his money back. It's a long story. The end result is I had a very frustrating day."

"Sorry to hear that, Zee," Wendell said.

"Yeah, well, I'll get over it," she said, feigning a nonchalance she didn't feel.

"Of course you will, but right now you're upset. And you have a right to be." He placed his hand on her shoulder, in a supportive gesture. One that jarred her instantly, yet she didn't pull away from him.

"People talk legal action," he went on, "that's serious."

"Yes, it is," she said, relieved that he understood. That was what she'd wanted to hear from Nicholas—that he understood, and that he cared.

"So what's gonna happen? He's already had his treatment, right?"

"Successful treatment," Zienna pointed out.

"Then he can't get his money back. He can make a lot of noise...."

"I hope that's all he's doing. Because if he actually wants to go to court, it'll be messy, ugly. Costly."

"I'm sure he's bluffing. Obviously, he's had his therapy. And he got good results. That's not a basis to sue."

"Do people even need a basis these days? Crazy people launch lawsuits all the time."

"If he *is* crazy, I'd be worried about something else. Do you think this guy could be a threat? And, yes, I mean physically. People are often unhappy when they don't get their way."

Was she worried? The way Donald had pushed Jamie had certainly alarmed Zienna.

"Perhaps I am a little worried. I just didn't like how he acted. And he pushed one of the secretaries out of the way when he was leaving the office. Yes, I'm definitely concerned. I've never seen Donald upset like that before. You never know what a person is capable of."

"Maybe you ought to let the police know. Just a suggestion."

"I'm not sure. I know he's had a rough time with his wife leaving him. I thought we were making headway. I want nothing more than for him to get well."

"That's what I always loved about you," Wendell said, offering her a soft smile. "Your drive and your passion for your work. It wasn't just about a paycheck. Other people would have worked for a professional sports team and had stars in their eyes. But that wasn't you."

The comment touched her. It was nice to know that Wendell had seen her in that way. "Thank you."

"You feel like getting that coffee? We can just chat. I'll be an ear if you need someone to talk to."

In the wake of Nicholas hurrying her off the line without even comforting her, this invitation meant a lot.

Still she said, "I don't know, Wendell. Maybe another time."

"That little café down the street? The one that makes the best deli sandwiches and serves a mean cappuccino. Remember how we used to go there?"

As if she could ever forget… She'd been such a fool for love then.

"I still want to explain some things," Wendell went on. "And it should be pretty clear to you that I'm not going away. But if you need me to sit and listen to you vent about today, I'm happy to do that, too. Just like before."

Four years ago, she had been able to share her joys and sorrows with Wendell, her hopes and dreams. That was one of the reasons it hurt so much when he'd left. She thought they'd had a solid relationship, that they'd wanted the same things. Only for him to tell her he wasn't ready to commit.

"What we had wasn't real," she said, her tone frosty as the reality of his betrayal hit her with full force again.

"What we had *was* real," he insisted. "Just hear me out. Please," he added, with a tone of vulnerability Zienna wasn't used to from the strong, sexy, confident man.

"Fine, Wendell. One coffee. I'll listen to what you have to say."

12

From her vantage point at the café table near the window, Zienna watched Wendell as he stood at the counter placing their order. It was as if the hands of time had turned back four years to when they used to come here as a couple.

Shifting in her seat, she glanced away. She felt on edge, and not just because of the incident with Donald. Wendell was adamant that he talk to her, and she was anxious about what he was going to say.

She'd told him she would have a cappuccino, but nothing to eat because she wasn't very hungry. Yet when Wendell came to the table, he had a tray with two mugs of steaming coffee, and two sandwiches.

"I told you I wasn't hungry," she said,

"It's a turkey pita. You used to love that. And you should eat something."

Zienna didn't bother to argue, instead lifting her cup and saying, "Thank you."

"You're welcome."

She sipped her cappuccino, found it too hot, so set the mug back down and lifted half of her sandwich. She took a bite. The pita tasted like heaven on her tongue.

"What are you thinking?" Wendell asked, after a moment.

She swallowed, then said, "I'm thinking about what you said, and wondering if Donald will cause trouble."

"Hey, if you want, I can go rough him up." Wendell softened the threat with a smile.

"No, that won't be necessary. Didn't you give up your boxing gloves when you left the NFL?" He was known for his tendency to be explosive on the football field. Though he'd played on the team's offense as a running back, he'd often sparred with members from the opposing defense, getting in their faces when he didn't like how they interrupted his play.

"Yeah, but I've still got them at home."

Zienna didn't crack a smile. She didn't want to give him the idea that she was enjoying their time together. "So," she began, "you've been wanting to talk to me."

Wendell nodded. "Yeah."

She took another bite of her pita. She had been stressed out because of Donald, but this was exactly what she needed.

"I want to talk about four years ago. Why I left."

"I know why you left."

"No," he said, holding her gaze, "you don't. You heard what I told you years ago, that I didn't want to be involved. But it's not as simple as that."

Zienna's first inclination was to retort that he had definitely cleared up that matter already with the mention of Pam. Then she'd stalk out of the café and hopefully be done with him forever.

But she was here, sitting with him, and she didn't want to argue. Obviously, it was important to him that he tell her what was on his mind. She might as well listen to him.

"Go ahead," she said softly.

"Obviously, you know about Pam. So you know I was in-volved with someone else when we were together. I'd been with Pam since college. We had a rocky relationship at best. It was up, it was down. Lots of drama. But she was my girl, and a major part of me felt I owed it to her to stay with her. I'd hurt her—I wasn't a saint. But the thing was, I always knew she wasn't the one."

Zienna took another bite of her pita, listening. But it felt as though her heart and the food battled for space in her throat. She wasn't sure why he was telling her this.

"Then I met you," Wendell said. "And things changed. I fell for you."

"You expect me to believe that?" she said, unable to keep silent any longer.

"It's the truth. You and I—we were mad hot together. It was intense. You stimulated me. You inspired me."

"And yet you told me you didn't want to commit." She put her sandwich down, once again not hungry. "You left me and went to Texas to be with someone else."

"I know." Wendell held her gaze. "I can't take back what I did, though God knows I wish I could. No, that's not en-tirely true."

Zienna rolled her eyes. "Great. You really cleared things up for me. I'm so glad we had this conversation."

"That came out wrong. Hear me out. I was planning to break up with Pam. We'd been together a long time, and I wanted to do it in a way that would cause less pain. I couldn't figure out how."

"Why dump your girlfriend when you can have your cake and eat it, too?"

"I tried before." Wendell pressed on, not acknowledging her comment. "And she would threaten to kill herself. Drama like that. One time, she even took a bunch of pills and ended up in the hospital. I had her well-being to think about. I didn't want to push her over the edge. Maybe that sounds wishy-washy to you, but I didn't know how to break her heart." He exhaled loudly. "Then, things changed again, when she told me she was pregnant."

Zienna's heart stopped momentarily as his words registered. The news that he had a child upset her, and yet it shouldn't.

"Wow." She shook her head. "That's some bombshell—four years after the fact. Why didn't you just tell me? Confide in me that you had a girlfriend who was pregnant at the time? I wouldn't have liked it, I'll admit that. But at least I wouldn't have had to spend the years thinking that you'd been my everything, only to learn when I saw you again how deluded I was."

"You thought of me as your everything?" Wendell's voice rose on a hopeful note. And his eyes held hers, this time with the same intensity as in the past.

"Wendell, don't."

"What you felt…it wasn't one-sided." When Zienna made a sound of derision, he pressed on. "I need you to hear this. Pam told me she was pregnant, and I knew then that I had to do the right thing. I didn't know how to tell you, and God knew I didn't want to hurt you more than I would by leaving. So I told you that I wasn't ready to commit. And I went to Texas with Pam for the sake of our child. I didn't want to be like my father, who hadn't been in my life."

Zienna lifted the coffee mug and took a sip, more for something to do than because she needed a drink.

"We had a baby boy," Wendell continued. "Jeremiah." But his tone was tinged with sadness, and his eyes held undeniable pain.

It wasn't so great after all, now was it? Sacrificing your personal happiness for the sake of your child?

"So typical," Zienna muttered.

"Excuse me?"

"You got together for the sake of your child, and then ended up resenting each other because you shouldn't have been together to begin with. And now you're a part-time dad." Zienna summed up an all-too-familiar scenario. The idea of getting married for the sake of any child was always foolish, but people typically had to learn the hard way.

"I wish that was the case," Wendell said softly.

He glanced away, and she saw the rise and fall of his Adam's apple as he swallowed with difficulty. As she continued to look at him, she saw him finger the cross around his neck.

She got a very bad feeling.

Wendell turned back to face her. "My son died." His voice was ripe with emotion. "Last year. He drowned."

"No..." His words pierced Zienna like a dagger. She saw the sadness on his face, in his eyes—and she felt it in her own heart. "Oh, Wendell. I'm so sorry."

His fingers continued to stroke the golden cross around his neck. "This is all I have left of him," he said. "The ashes in this pendant."

Zienna should have put it together sooner. The cross wasn't flat, the way they typically were. It was cylindrical, the type meant to hold a small amount of ashes.

"No," she said, shaking her head. "That's not all you have left of him. You have so much more." She placed a hand over her chest. "He lives in your heart. Nothing can take that away."

Wendell's gaze wandered off again, but only for a moment. "I know you understand this pain. Because you lost your parents."

Zienna's mind drifted to the night she'd told Wendell about losing both her parents at the same time, in a tragic car crash. How she had cried in his arms and he'd comforted her. He had been the rock she needed at the time, sharing her pain, which was still raw six years after the horrific incident.

"Still, what I lost can't compare to losing a child," Zienna said. "I know it's got to be absolutely crushing for you."

Wendell's jaw clenched, as though he was trying to keep himself in check. He succeeded only partially; his eyes began to glisten.

"Damn," he muttered, and steeled his shoulders. He took a moment to bring himself back from the brink of emotions that Zienna knew were devastating. "I loved my son. And now he's gone. Pam and I, we were done right after that. Not because I was angry with her, though she thought I was. Yes, Jeremiah was under her care when he drowned. She forgot to lock the pool gate, he slipped past it.... But these things happen. Blame doesn't help anybody. I guess it was just his time."

Zienna knew the words Wendell was saying were excruciating. How could anyone truly accept the loss of a child?

"I took a year to grieve, get myself together. And I came back here." He paused. "I just... I just wanted you to understand. Understand why I left. I couldn't tell you then."

Zienna's heart thundered. Why was he telling her this? Did he hope on some level that they would get back together? Could that possibly be the case?

"Wendell, I'm dating Nicholas. Your *friend*."

He shrugged nonchalantly. "I get it. A day late and a dollar short." He smiled, but it seemed forced.

She stared at him, her eyes narrowed in confusion, silently asking him what the heck he meant by that comment. But a moment later, she decided she didn't want to know.

She pushed her chair back and stood. She couldn't allow

herself to go there. She couldn't allow herself to think about what Wendell meant, what his motives were, or even the fact that maybe things would have been different for them if not for Pam and her pregnancy. "Wendell, I'm sorry for your loss. I truly, truly am. But if you're suggesting… I don't know what you could be suggesting. All I know is, I've moved on."

That was all she could manage before turning sharply and hurrying out of the café. Stepping outside, she gulped in the warm spring air. Her gut told her that Wendell had dropped all that on her for a reason, a reason she didn't want to contemplate.

Because she was happy now. Happy with Nicholas.

"Zienna!"

The sound of her name on Wendell's lips made her stop. Slowly turn. And damn it, why did he have to look so incredible?

He trotted toward her. "I'm still attracted to you," he told her. "There. I said it. I know I shouldn't be, you're Nicholas's girl. But I can't help it." He paused. "And I had you first."

"Meaning?" Zienna asked, gaping at him. "Meaning that I'm some sort of prize between the two of you? A piece of property?"

"Hell, naw. That's not what I mean at all. But does it bother me to come back to town and find my friend with my former girl? Yeah, it does. I love him like a brother, but I'm just telling you what I feel."

"Things have changed in four years."

"I know. I need to stay away. It's just…I'm not sure I can." Zienna swallowed.

"Don't look at me like that. You can't be surprised. Come on, with how the two of us were together? When I saw you at the restaurant last week… You want to know what I was thinking when I saw you?"

Zienna spun around and took a step. This was too much for her. She couldn't deal with it, because for some stupid reason, her body was still attracted to him.

Wendell's fingers curled around her arm. Turning her to face him, he looked down at her.

"There's no way you and Nicholas can be as hot as we were." His eyes searched hers as if for answers.

Zienna said nothing, neither confirming nor denying his statement.

"Fuck it," he said suddenly, catching her off guard.

But he really took her by surprise when, without warning, his lips came down on hers.

Zienna felt an explosion of heat. Like the end of a fireworks display, with thousands of lights going off at once, popping loudly and creating a big spectacle—that's how the kiss felt.

And for a moment, she was lost. Completely lost in his kiss.

But somehow, she got her common sense back and pushed him away. "Wendell, for God's sake! Have you lost your friggin' mind?"

"I told you that I *know* I should stay away. It doesn't mean I can. Damn, look at you. You must remember how good we were together."

Zienna felt flushed. "What I remember is that your best friend is Nicholas! You're back in town and now you're his business partner. Obviously you are *not* really trying to hit on me. You're not trying to ruin a friendship that dates back longer than you ever knew me."

Somehow, she spoke words of complete reason.

Wendell closed his eyes pensively, then reopened them. He took a step backward. "You're right. You're right. But damn, wrong felt so good."

"This is a game for you," Zienna told him. "That's obvious to me. Some sort of sick game. Some sort of ego thing.

And I—I won't be part of it." She stopped talking, because she knew she was rambling, and she felt stupid. But that's what Wendell did to her. She didn't think straight around him.

"It's not a game."

"Whatever it is," she said sternly, "I don't care. Leave me alone."

She was proud of herself and her firm voice. But as she walked away this time, and Wendell let her go, she was aware that it wasn't anxiety making her heart beat faster.

It was lust.

13

"You're lying." Alexis's eyes were as wide as saucers, and she had a look of twisted glee on her face.

"I'm not," Zienna said, and pressed her cheek against her palm. "That's exactly how it happened."

"You're telling me he kissed you on the street? Just laid one on you?"

Zienna sat across from Alexis in her loft, her legs curled under her on the leather sofa and her elbow propped on the armrest. "He did."

"And?"

"And what?"

Alexis gave her a knowing look. "And how was it?"

"Why do you look so happy about this? Wasn't it you who told me just days ago that I should have been honest with Nicholas, because holding back about Wendell might jeopardize my relationship with him?"

Alexis waved a dismissive hand. "I know what I said. But I also know how much you loved being with Wendell, and that it took you ages to forget him. You tell me he lays one on you—of course I want to know what your reaction was."

"I can't believe you."

"You're avoiding the question," Alexis sang.

"You are enjoying this entirely too much." Zienna eyed her friend suspiciously. Perhaps the wine they were drinking had gone to her head already? "You're supposed to be telling me that Wendell was an ass to do what he did."

"Okay, Wendell was an ass. A pompous, presumptuous ass." Alexis grinned slyly. "But did you like it?"

Zienna opened her mouth, but it took her too long to answer, a point driven home when Alexis clapped her hands together and made a sound of giddy delight. "Oh, my God. You *liked* it."

"Alexis, seriously. How much did you have to drink before I got here? I mean, what's gotten into you? You almost sound as though you're excited at the idea of me and Wendell getting it on, when you were the one to introduce me to Nicholas. Have you forgotten that?"

Alexis sipped her wine, undeterred by Zienna's comment about her drinking too much. "Let's just say I've had a little change of heart. I understand now why it took you three years to get over Wendell."

Zienna stared at her friend, for the first time that evening putting aside her own turbulent emotions and really seeing her. Alexis wore a satisfied smile, and an expression Zienna hadn't seen on her in a long while.

"Is there something going on that you're not telling me?" she asked.

"I went out with Brock," Alexis said dreamily. "We had dinner, and he was fun and sexy and flirtatious, and I went back to his place and… And I spent the night having my world rocked in a way I never thought possible." She grinned from ear to ear.

"You slept with Brock? Already? When did this happen?"

"Last night," Alexis responded, the smile on her face apparently permanent. "My God, now that's the kind of sex I've been looking for. The kind you used to describe having with Wendell."

Zienna felt a little tickle in her stomach, but tried to ignore it. She had come here hoping to have her friend give her a sense of clarity about what had happened today with Wendell, and encourage her to steer clear of her past and embrace her future. Instead, she was getting the exact opposite vibe.

"That's why I *know* you must have felt something when Wendell kissed you," Alexis persisted. "A man who can do you the way you described... Come on. Tell me."

"All right," Zienna said, knowing she needed to get the horrible truth off her chest. "You want to know how it felt? It felt as though I hadn't been kissed in four years." The words tumbled from her lips. And then she felt guilty. "I love Nicholas. I do. Wendell...it's just lust."

"Lust can be very powerful."

"If you let it rule you. I don't intend to."

"But if Wendell doesn't plan to back down—and from what you said, he clearly still has his eyes set on you, so I'm thinking he won't—what are you going to do?"

It was a question Zienna didn't expect from her friend, and it caught her off guard. "What am I going to do? I'm going to pretend it didn't happen."

"Is that even possible?"

"Of course it is." But her words felt like a lie.

"Are you sure about that? Maybe Wendell gave you a taste of something you can't resist."

It wasn't what Alexis said, but how she said it. As if she liked the idea that Wendell could tempt Zienna. Now she knew that her friend had been intoxicated by whatever it was that had happened between her and Brock, which was clearly more powerful than any wine. The woman who had dated Elliott would never have asked her something like this.

"I'm going to forget you even said that," Zienna said.

"But can you forget Wendell's lips on yours?" Alexis gave her a pointed look.

"*You* seem to forget that you introduced me to Nicholas." Zienna was getting slightly annoyed.

"It's more that I remember how much you were into Wendell. You were in deep. And now he's back and apparently still wants you. I know he hurt you, but I can understand why he was conflicted. Pam was pregnant, and he tried to do the right thing. And my God, doesn't your heart break a little, knowing he lost his son?"

"Of course," Zienna said. "When he told me that, I was crushed for him."

"And now you know Wendell didn't dump you just because he was a jerk."

"That's not exactly true."

"If you tell me that you can completely resist him, no problem, I'll *know* you're lying. It comes with being best friends for so many years."

Zienna made a face. "Okay. Here's the thing." There was no point in lying because, as Alexis said, she knew her too well. "When Wendell kissed me, God, it seriously was like fireworks going off. It was…spectacular. I never thought I would still feel such a fierce attraction to him, not after all this time. Especially now that I know about Pam." Zienna paused. "But something about my body craves that man, and I don't know what it is. But then there's Nicholas, a man I've totally fallen for. If I could merge the two of them, I would have the perfect guy. The combination of total sex appeal with that sweet guy who's willing to commit and share his vulnerable side. What would be better than that? But they're two different guys. And it's not like I can date both of them."

"Why not?" Alexis challenged. "You're into Nicholas, that's great. But if you want to explore what could be with Wendell..."

"Alex! Seriously, what's gotten into you?"

"About ten inches of pure heaven!"

Zienna couldn't help it, she cracked a smile. But she was still disturbed by Alexis's suggestion. "I was trying to make the point that you can't always get the perfect combination in one man. I didn't expect you to take what I said and run with it."

"I'm not trying to cause shit. Seriously, I'm not. It's just... I've done some soul-searching, and as I said to you before, I realize we need hot sex just as much as men do. If you can get that with Wendell—"

"Alex!"

"Is that so wrong? Men do it. They date more than one woman at a time and don't feel guilty. One minute Nicholas was rocking your world, but then fell flat when you wanted a repeat. From what you said, Wendell was always consistent."

Thank God, Zienna's iPhone rang, which stopped Alexis's insane rant. Zienna glanced at the screen, saw Nicholas's name and photo flashing there.

"It's Nicholas," she said, and raised the phone to her ear. "Hey, baby."

"What are you up to?"

"Just hanging out with Alex. And missing you."

"How're you feeling?" he asked. "Sorry I was so busy earlier when you called about the matter at work."

"It's okay. I get it."

"I'm leaving the restaurant early tonight. And I was kind of hoping you could come over and spend the night. I can give you a bit of the attention you deserve." His words ended on a suggestive note.

"I'll be there," Zienna told him. "What time?"

"About an hour?"

"See you soon, babe. Love you."

"You're going to see Nicholas?" Alexis asked when she clicked off.

"Yep." Zienna grinned. "He's leaving work early and wants me to come over."

"Good. So he shouldn't be too tired to give you what you need."

"Alex, I've never said that Nicholas didn't satisfy me. Yes, I loved the wilder side of him last week, but I'm perfectly happy with our sex life."

"Happy is one thing. Thrilled beyond your wildest dreams… that's another thing altogether." Alexis's lips spread in a wide grin.

"Since all you can do tonight is talk about sex, why don't you call Brock?" Zienna suggested. "Lucky for you, the night's still young. You should be able to hook up with him and have yourself another hot night. I plan to do the same."

And Zienna hoped that once she was in her man's arms, she would totally forget about the unwanted kiss Wendell had planted on her earlier.

As Zienna pulled into Nicholas's driveway, she thought about Wendell, and more specifically his kiss. Nicholas had spoken to her about being honest with him, and Zienna didn't want to lie, but she certainly wasn't stupid. She couldn't very well tell him that Wendell had kissed her.

She hadn't bothered to ask Alexis's advice on the matter, because she undoubtedly would have told her to keep her

mouth shut. Zienna still couldn't believe that Alexis had suggested she see both men at the same time.

She got out of her car and made her way to Nicholas's front door. Just as she raised her finger to the bell, the door opened.

Nicholas's smile was warm and inviting, and Zienna instantly felt bad for the lie that would be between them. But how could she tell him Wendell had kissed her?

"Hey, you," he said softly, opening his arms to her.

She walked into his embrace and snaked her arms around his waist. "Hey, yourself. You look good. And you smell incredible."

"Mmm." Nicholas lowered his head and slightly pursed his lips, and Zienna gave him the kiss he was asking for. Try as she might, she couldn't stop herself from remembering that Wendell's lips had been on hers hours earlier.

Nicholas released her and closed the door, then asked, "You hungry? I brought home some of that pineapple glazed chicken you like."

"Oh, you did? I actually ate at Alexis's. Pizza."

"I'll keep it in the fridge, in case you get hungry later."

While Nicholas went to the kitchen, Zienna wandered into the living room and sat on his leather sofa. She noticed two DVD cases on the coffee table and lifted them. A romantic comedy and a thriller.

"I was figuring we could chill and watch a movie," Nicholas said as he came into the living room and sat beside her. He pulled her legs onto his lap. "We haven't done that in a while."

"The thriller looks good." She could lie in his arms and cling to him during the scary parts.

"Want some popcorn? Wine?"

She chuckled. "Popcorn and wine. Always a winning combination."

"All right. I'll get it. You put the movie in."

Zienna smiled softly as she watched Nicholas walk away. Alexis could say what she wanted, but Zienna was happy with him. She had a level of comfort with him, the kind that could have them spending the night together without making love, and it not being an issue. Sex was important to them, but it wasn't a basis for their relationship.

Unlike what she'd had with Wendell. With him, it had been all about the sex.

Zienna put the movie into the DVD player, feeling more confident than ever that she could leave Wendell in her rear-view mirror. She wasn't driven solely by sex, and if all she did with Nicholas tonight was cuddle, she would be perfectly okay with that.

In the morning, Zienna was awoken with soft, fluttery kisses at the base of her neck. The next sensation she felt was a hand smoothing over her breast and a finger circling her nipple.

She purred as she woke up, and then opened her eyes, see-ing Nicholas's face across from hers on his pillow. "Good morning."

Easing forward, he planted a kiss on her lips. "Good morn-ing, sleepyhead."

"Uh, I know. I feel like I was hit by a Mack truck." Zi-enna glanced beyond him to the digital clock on the bedside table. It was just after seven. "I don't even remember getting into bed last night."

"You don't? You had a second glass of wine, and could hardly keep your eyes open...."

"And you turned off the movie and said we should call it a night." Now it came to her. Zienna stroked his cheek. "I guess I'd had a longer, more stressful day than I thought."

"I got you to bed…." He kissed her shoulder. "Gave you a kiss on the forehead. And you were out like a light."

"Ever the gentleman," Zienna said.

"Last night, maybe," he stressed. "This morning, I've got a major hard-on."

"Oh?"

"I know we don't have much time…." Nicholas stroked her other nipple, again with his classic gentleness. "We both have to work, and you don't have a change of clothes, so you'll have to make a pit stop at home."

"Actually," Zienna began, arching her breast against his palm, "I have a travel bag in the back of my car. I carry it just in case. For times I'm at Alexis's place…or now."

"Very smart," he said. He kissed her again, more deeply this time, and Zienna arched her back even more, hoping that he would go after her with a little more zeal. Nicholas took the bait, lowering his head to her breast and suckling her nipple. She gripped his head and held it in place, hoping that he would ravage her the way he had done before. But his tongue moved over her nipple with gentle, sensual flicks—certainly enough to put her in the mood, but far less than she craved.

"Mmm," she moaned, and dug her fingers into his back, urging him on. He brought his mouth to her other breast, where he once again suckled softly, tugging at her nipple in a gentle manner. When his right hand began to smooth over her opposite breast, then down her stomach, she knew what was coming next. She knew he would slip his hand between her thighs and fondle her for a little bit. Maybe he would go down on her, or maybe even just make sure she was moist enough and then begin to make love to her.

Once he touched her center, he lifted his head and grinned. "I know what you need." He moved his mouth down her body to the apex of her thighs, where he took her in his mouth. His tongue began to move slowly.

It was sweet and gentle, and yes, Zienna came. But it was a far cry from the animalistic sex she wanted.

Needed.

She climbed on top of him after she climaxed, and rode him hard. And all too soon, Nicholas succumbed to his release.

No Slayer today.

The sex had been pleasant, but far too brief.

And as Nicholas got up and headed into his en suite bathroom, Zienna couldn't help remembering Alexis's words about how women needed hot sex, too.

Zienna had tried to reject that very idea, but she was starting to feel that her friend was right.

Which led her to ponder Alexis's other comment with a sense of unease in the pit of her belly.

Maybe Wendell gave you a taste of something you can't resist.

14

With the grand opening of Nicholas's restaurant looming, Zienna didn't see him or Wendell over the next couple days. Before Wendell had started working for Nicholas, she would have gone to the restaurant to see how everything was coming along, but now she opted to stay away.

She'd told herself that she didn't need the hassle of any further flirtation from Wendell, who was bound to be at Reflections on the Bay, working on the final preparations with Nicholas. But now, as she lay on top of her bed after work on Thursday, contemplating what she would wear for tonight's big launch, she found herself thinking about Alexis's words and admitting to herself the real reason she had stayed away.

If you tell me you can completely resist him no problem, I'll know you're lying.

Alexis was right—she couldn't. The story Wendell had told her about Pam and his child had taken the edge off her anger. And that kiss... Damn it, that kiss had stirred something in her she thought she'd already put to rest.

Suddenly, Zienna had found herself thinking about her past with Wendell, and wondering if maybe everything she'd felt *hadn't* been a lie.

She so didn't want to go there, but she couldn't escape the feelings. The less she saw Wendell, the better. Which was why she was already feeling a helluva lot of anxiety about going to the restaurant's big launch tonight—because she didn't know what to expect when she saw him.

"Why are you doing this?" she asked aloud. "Why are you even allowing your brain to go there?"

It was that kiss, and how it had made her feel. No matter how she tried to dismiss it, she couldn't.

And after that less than thrilling sexual session with Nicholas Tuesday morning, she'd found herself comparing Wendell's prowess in the bedroom to his. Hands down, Wendell was the better lover. Always consistent, always thrilling.

But of course he could be, she told herself. *His football season was over, so he wasn't working. We had nothing but time to screw each other.*

Wendell had had all the time in the world to be at her beck and call, and all the energy to give it to her the way she wanted. So she knew she wasn't being fair to Nicholas by even comparing the two of them sexually.

When it came to the guy who was sensitive, and a real partner...Nicholas won hands down.

You're into Nicholas, that's great. But if you want to explore what could be with Wendell...

Zienna's ringing iPhone tore her attention away from her thoughts, and she stretched her body on the bed so that she could snatch the phone off her night table. Seeing Alexis's number, she quickly pressed the talk button.

"Alex," she said, emitting a little groan. "I have no clue what to wear."

"What are the choices?"

Zienna sat up. "A classic black dress, or something with color? Remember that wrap dress I picked up a couple months ago when we were shopping? The one in shades of mauve, pink and purple?"

"Hmmm. I say go for color."

Both dresses were hanging on the back of her door, and Zienna stared at them now. The black was classic, the tried and true. But the other one showed more flair and vibrancy.

Just like the two men who'd occupied her thoughts this week...

You're into Nicholas, that's great. But if you want to explore what could be with Wendell...

"Earth to Zienna?"

"Sorry, yeah?" Zienna realized she had drifted off.

"I asked if you thought my gold blouse with the pencil skirt would be okay."

"Oh. Sure. The blouse really dresses it up. Combined with your gold stilettos."

"What's wrong?" Alexis asked. "And don't tell me nothing. I can hear it in your voice."

Zienna sighed. "Just tonight. I'm nervous for Nicholas. Anxious."

"Is that all?" her friend pressed.

It should be all, but Zienna was definitely concerned about seeing Wendell, and her reaction to him. Why couldn't she shake him from her system? "That's plenty. Nicholas is under a lot of pressure for tonight to go well."

"I know. And we don't want to be late. My hair's done, my makeup. I'm just gonna put on my clothes and then I'll be right over."

"I'll be ready when you get here."

Zienna ended the call and walked to her door, where she lifted the hanger holding the colorful dress. This was the one she would wear tonight.

Just before seven forty-five, the two friends stepped out of the car. The event had officially started at seven-thirty, but not wanting to get in Nicholas's way by showing up early, Zienna had opted to arrive a little late instead.

There was a sense of excitement in the air, with the buzz of the crowd and sounds of a live jazz quartet. The group was stationed to the right of the front entrance, toward the outdoor seating area. A red carpet stretched at least twenty feet from the door, lined with large helium balloons in red and black, the restaurant's signature colors. Zienna could see some of the red streamers tastefully decorating the patio area, where lines of tiny white lights hanging beneath the awning created an elegant glow.

"Wow, this is something," Alexis commented as they made their way up the red carpet. Two women dressed in classic black sat at a table to one side of the door, were checking off names on the guest list. Zienna and Alexis gave their names, then entered.

The place was filled with about fifty people—food critics and other special guests. It was the grand unveiling of the restaurant for a select clientele, before the doors opened for business on Saturday. Zienna knew that platters of samples of the various appetizers and entrées would be presented at regular intervals, as well as a sampling of the restaurant's wines, champagnes and exotic cocktails.

Alexis took the scene in with wide eyes. "This is amazing."

"I can't believe how different it looks even since last week," Zienna commented. "It's really come together now." All the framed photographs were now placed on the walls, and the dark floors were polished and spotless. Nicholas had opted for a high quality wood laminate, which would be easier to maintain. The carpeted areas in the raised seating section also appeared flawless.

Zienna continued to survey her surroundings, and then her eyes landed on a familiar form. Wide shoulders beneath a black blazer tailored to fit him perfectly. Bald head...

Wendell.

Her breath caught in her throat as he turned. He was dressed in a black blazer, black slacks and a white silk shirt opened at the collar. He had forgone a tie, creating an easy, sophisticated, sexy look.

"Wow," Alexis said. "Wendell looks incredible."

That he did. And Zienna wished he didn't. She wished that whatever carnal part of her body and brain was attracted to him could simply turn off that attraction.

He looked at her from across the room, held her gaze for a moment. Then she saw his eyes take in the rest of her, and a satisfied smile spread across his face.

Zienna jerked her gaze away. She took in the sight of the waiters, dressed impeccably in black pants and white shirts with bow ties, walking around with various trays of food. Zienna knew that Nicholas was due to speak at eight-thirty, and at this point he was probably in the kitchen. Wendell, so far anyway, was out entertaining the guests with his easy charisma.

"I'm going to the kitchen to see my man." Zienna walked briskly, not giving another glance in Wendell's direction. The kitchen was filled with noise and chaos, unlike the serenity in the restaurant's dining room.

When she saw Nicholas, dressed almost identically to Wendell, except that he wore a tie, she smiled. Her man was just as sexy as Wendell was.

"And keep them coming," Nicholas was saying. Then, as though he sensed she was in the kitchen, he turned and looked over his shoulder, offering her a grin. But it was a quick one, not the kind of lingering look Wendell had given her. Not the kind that said *That's my girl. I can't wait to be alone with her.*

Undeterred, Zienna walked toward him. "Hey, baby." She placed a hand on his arm.

"Hey." Nicholas sounded harried.

"It smells delicious in here," she told him, offering encouragement. "And everything looks wonderful. Everyone out there is smiling."

"Thanks."

Zienna eased forward slightly, hoping Nicholas would give her a quick kiss. Instead, he turned back to the stainless steel counter and checked out the plates of bacon cheeseburger balls below. "I hate to rush you out of here, but..."

"No. It's fine. I know I'm in the way." Zienna turned on her heel and walked out of the kitchen, and a quick glance as she was exiting the door told her that Nicholas wasn't even giving her another look.

She told herself that his rejection didn't faze her. Because it wasn't rejection. Why was she even seeing it that way?

It was just that when Wendell had seen her, the way his eyes had drunk in the sight of her...in that one look he had given her, he'd conveyed that he believed she was a woman who was desirable and sexy.

Nicholas...Nicholas had barely noticed her.

Zienna went back out into the dining room, and seeing a waiter passing her with a tray of champagne flutes, she reached out to take one. She downed half of it in one gulp.

"What's the matter?" Alexis narrowed her eyes as she approached her.

Zienna waved a dismissive hand. She and Nicholas were

in a relationship. Nothing was the matter, except that he was busy tending to business. Business that was excruciatingly important to him tonight.

"Zee?"

"Nothing," she said. She felt stupid for being even mildly upset, so she couldn't tell Alexis that she felt rejected.

"Don't look. Here comes Wendell."

Zienna's eyes bulged and her heart slammed against her rib cage. But she didn't turn to look over her shoulder until Alexis greeted Wendell with a big grin and a hug.

"Long time no see, Wendell," she told him.

"I know. I've been away, but now I'm back."

Zienna sipped her champagne. And felt the burn in her body as Wendell's eyes took in every inch of her.

"I'm gonna go track down the guy with champagne," Alexis announced.

"Alex—" Zienna began in protest, but her friend was already walking away.

With her gone, Wendell wasted no time. "Damn. You look...you look divine."

"Thank you." Zienna's tone was clipped.

"You want me to stay away from you, and then you come here dressed like this." He pulled his bottom lip between his teeth. "You do want me to stay away from you, right?"

"I do," Zienna said, though every fiber of her being told her she was a liar. The thing was, she was a human being, not a rabbit, and if she couldn't control her urges, she certainly knew she didn't have to act on them. "And I don't want to have to—"

Zienna's words stopped abruptly when she saw Nicholas emerge from the kitchen. He looked at her and then Wendell, and she saw the assessment in his eyes.

She smiled uneasily as he walked toward them. Ever the

workhorse, he was holding a tray of meatballs. "I'll take one," Zienna said, and lifted one of the toothpicks that held a bacon cheeseburger ball.

"The critic from the *Chicago Tribune* is here," Wendell told Nicholas. "And the one from the *New York Times*. Right now, they're both on the patio. I got a call from the mayor's assistant. He'll be here momentarily."

"Great," Nicholas said.

"I'm greeting and schmoozing," Wendell said, a huge smile dancing on his face. "Zienna, lovely to see you again."

She nodded. "Likewise."

Zienna watched Nicholas and Wendell head farther into the restaurant, away from her. When he was about ten feet away, Nicholas glanced back.

And she was pretty sure he looked pissed off.

The fact was fairly evident to Zienna soon afterward, when Nicholas would pass her and barely acknowledge her. He was busy, yes, but she knew him well enough to know that he was deliberately ignoring her.

Zienna did her best to enjoy the evening and the food. She mingled and chatted with some of the celebrity clientele— players from the city's professional sports teams who were friends of Wendell and Nicholas—as well as the mayor, the critics. Everyone she spoke to seemed to enjoy the food items immensely, something Zienna waited around to tell Nicholas after the last guest had gone.

"I'll only be a minute, Alex," she said, grateful that her friend hadn't complained about the delay. They both had to work in the morning. "I just wanted to talk to Nicholas when things finally died down."

"I'll be at the bar. Those Island Sunsets are good!"

Zienna then headed into the kitchen. She passed the kitchen

staff, who were all helping with the cleanup. Not seeing Nich-olas, she headed to his office.

He was in there, talking with Wendell. He saw her over his friend's shoulder, and must have said something, because Wendell turned to look at her.

"Hey," Zienna said softly. "I was wondering if I could have a moment with my man."

Wendell nodded. To Nicholas he said, "I'll be out front."

When Wendell left the office, Zienna closed the door. Then she approached Nicholas and slipped her arms around his neck. "Finally. Congrats, sweetie. That had to be one of the best restaurant grand openings the city has ever seen."

"Thanks." Nicholas's tone was clipped.

"It's over." She kissed his chin. "You did it." She lowered her voice. "You ready to get out of here and celebrate?'"

"Actually, I'm gonna be here late. Cleaning up, sorting things."

"That's okay. I'll drive Alexis back to my place first, where she parked her car. Then I can meet you at your house."

"It'll have to be another night."

Again, Nicholas's jaw tensed, and Zienna got the sense that something else was wrong. She dropped her arms from around his neck and settled them around his waist. "Are you sure?" she asked, a little disappointed. She was dressed up, she looked good—and so did he. After a night like this, shouldn't they spend the rest of it celebrating in the bedroom? "I'm happy to come back and help you do whatever you need to. Then we can leave together...." Her voice trailed off, but the sug-gestion was clear.

"It's okay. I wouldn't want to cramp your style, anyway."

"Cramp my style?" She blinked, confused. "What does that mean?"

"Just observed stuff tonight. And honestly, when you first

came in here saying you wanted a moment with your man, I wasn't sure if you were talking about me or Wendell."

Zienna withdrew her arms from his waist, as if she'd been scorched. "What?"

"I saw you both. Getting cozy. And the way you were looking at each other."

"Excuse me?"

"You heard me."

"No, I don't think I did. Because what you said is crazy. I can't speak for how Wendell may or may not have looked at me, but I can tell you with one hundred percent certainty that I didn't do anything wrong." And she hadn't. She had shot down Wendell's suggestive comment, despite her lust for him.

"Every time I turned around, you were with him."

"That's a lie." Yes, Wendell had made sure to bring her more food or drink, but he'd done the same for everyone.

"I know what I saw."

"Then you should get your eyes checked." Her heart seemed to have grown exponentially in her chest as she spun around and marched out of the office. She hadn't asked for Wendell to come back into her life. She hadn't asked for him to be working with Nicholas.

And she didn't appreciate Nicholas's jealousy.

Zienna pushed the kitchen door open and stormed into the restaurant. She saw Wendell whip his head in her direction, and she glared at him. If he had only been able to respect her boundaries and her relationship, Nicholas wouldn't have gotten pissed at her.

Zienna then looked toward the bar. Alexis's jaw dropped as their gazes met.

"Shit, Zee, what's the matter?" she asked when Zienna reached her.

"We're going. *Now.*" Zienna grabbed her by the arm and pulled her off the stool.

"Whoa, let me put my drink down," she protested, and as she hastily placed it on the bar, more than a drop swished over the sides.

Zienna strode purposefully out the restaurant, and Alexis was fast on her heels. "What happened, Zee?"

She didn't answer until she got to her car. "Nicholas. He's pissed."

"Uh-oh. So I *was* right."

"Yep, you called it." Alexis had pointed out that Nicholas seemed frosty toward Zienna. "He thinks I've been flirting with Wendell all night."

Zienna slammed the car door, then jammed the key into the ignition. She looked in her rearview mirror, saw Wendell standing in front of the restaurant. Had he come out to talk to her?

She didn't stop the car, but threw it into Reverse and backed out of the parking spot. Her tires squealed as she tore out of the lot.

Alexis gripped the door handle. "Hold on there, Ms. Andretti."

"Do you think I asked for Wendell to come back to town? I didn't ask for any of this."

"What exactly did Nicholas say?"

"He said that every time he looked around, I was with Wendell. Which is a lie. Then some garbage about me checking Wendell out all night."

"Nicholas will calm down. See that he's being an ass."

"Will he? Fuck, if he only knew what really happened. What I said to Wendell."

Alexis faced her. "What happened?"

Zienna blew out a breath, then related what had transpired at the beginning of the night.

"Hmm," Alexis replied. "Well, I'm not surprised. I told you Wendell didn't seem like he was going to back down."

"But I shot him down. I told him to leave me alone. That's what matters. Yet as far as Nicholas is concerned, I may as well have been screwing him in the back room."

"He really does have a jealous streak. I thought that was just an insecure thing when he was first getting to know you."

"Me, too. I thought he just needed to know he could trust me, and that once he did, everything would be okay." And that had been the way it was...until Wendell's bombshell about their past affair. "I don't like this side of him. Not at all."

"I can't say I totally blame him," Alexis ventured softly. "Wendell is...hot. And if there's anyone who can tempt you—"

"Alexis, not now," Zienna snapped. "Please."

"Sorry."

Zienna groaned in frustration, then slapped her fist on the steering wheel. "You know what's crazy? I should be going home with Nicholas tonight. We should be celebrating the successful launch of his new restaurant. He should be so happy, he'd make love to me all night long. Instead he brings up this bullshit and has to ruin everything."

Zienna fumed the rest of the drive to her apartment, and when they got there, she said no to Alexis's offer to come up and hang for a bit.

"I'm not in the mood, Alex. I'm going right to bed."

And that's exactly what Zienna did. She went upstairs, got undressed, did her nighttime ritual and then climbed into bed.

The knock at the door about twenty minutes later startled her. But she got out of bed and went to answer it, assuming that Alexis had come up to check on her. Or maybe Nicholas had shown up to apologize for being a jerk.

She placed her eye at the peephole, then stepped back and gasped.

Because it wasn't Alexis at her door, nor Nicholas. It was Wendell.

15

For several agonizing seconds, Zienna contemplated what to do. She stood frozen, barely even breathing.

"Open the door," Wendell said.

Still she didn't move.

"Come on," he said. "Zee, please let me in."

Zienna's head was spinning. She was conflicted, but found herself turning the lock and then opening the door.

"Hey," Wendell said softly, a small smile gracing his lips. He looked sexy and at ease, with his arm stretched high and resting against the jamb. As though he was a normal fixture at her door at this hour of the night.

"What are you doing here?" Zienna asked.

"I noticed that you left the party alone. Without Nicholas, I mean."

"And do you have any clue why?" she snapped.

"My guess? He probably thinks we're already sleeping together."

"Which is exactly why you shouldn't be here. Your return to town has ruined my life."

"I'm tired of pretending," Wendell said. "Tired of pretending every time I see you that I don't want you."

Zienna swallowed. Wendell shouldn't be here, and he shouldn't have dared to say what he just had. And yet parts of her body were thrumming from a massive sexual rush.

Still, she said, "You're not welcome here."

He lowered his arm and took a step forward, forcing her to take a step back. "You sure about that?"

"Yes." But the word came out weak. Zienna didn't want to be in this position. She didn't want to have to constantly turn down his come-ons. It would be so much easier if he didn't want her, but clearly he did.

"You don't want me here?" It was a question, but the way he spoke made it plain to Zienna that he knew what her answer was. The answer she couldn't deny in her heart.

He took another step, and she took one more step backward. He shifted again, and then closed the door behind him. He turned the lock, and the sound of the click made her swallow again, because she could almost hear her fate being sealed.

This time, when Wendell took a step toward her, Zienna didn't move. Instead, she allowed him to slip his arms around her waist. Allowed him to pull her body against his hard chest. Allowed him to kiss her.

"You shouldn't— Wendell…"

"I shouldn't?" His hand moved down the column of her neck, oh so gently and yet eliciting fiery sensations. "You're not saying that I should stop."

She wanted to tell him to stop. If for no other reason than the smugness in his touch. The way he seemed to know she couldn't resist him.

He brought his lips down on hers, softly. His lips moved

over hers, causing a slow burn. Then his tongue flicked out, trailing the fullness of her bottom lip before he gently grazed the flesh with his teeth.

Zienna couldn't help it; a little sigh escaped her. Both Wendell's hands went around her, gripping her tightly as he deepened the kiss. And she was lost, God help her. Swept up in a tornado of passion.

Wendell's hands groped her body, roamed over her back and down to her behind, then up to her shoulder blades and into her hair. Gently tugging on her hair, he pulled his lips from hers and brought them to her jawline, where he tantalized her skin, suckling from the base of her neck down to the hollow between her breasts.

Zienna's body was gripped with lust. Her thong was moist. She could lie, pretend that his touch was not affecting her in any way. But it was. And she was powerless to do anything about it.

"If I were Nicholas, I would have never let you go home without me. Not after a night like this one. And the way you looked tonight? Hell, no." Wendell trailed his fingers below the area his mouth had just kissed, slipping them into her robe. "That was Nicholas's mistake."

"Why?" Zienna's voice was a mere rasp. She still had a portion of her sanity, and was trying to cling to it. "Why are you doing this? To prove that you can?"

Both Wendell's hands went to the tie on her robe, and Zienna stood, immobilized. If he was about to strip her naked right here, she couldn't stop him.

But all he did was retie the loose knot and then drop his hands back to his sides. He was no longer touching her, and Zienna felt oddly cold.

"It's not about proving that I can. This is not about a quick lay." He extended his hand to her. "Come. Sit and talk with me."

Zienna didn't want to take his hand. She didn't want to talk. If she was going to cross the line with him, she wanted him to simply take her, as he had so many times before. At least that way she could have an excuse in her mind that made sense.

But Wendell continued to offer his hand, and after a few seconds, she placed hers in it. He walked her into the living room as though he had never been out of it. He sat her on the sofa and then settled beside her.

And for several seconds, they simply stared at each other, neither saying a word. Finally, Zienna glanced away.

"I want to know where your head is at," Wendell said. "With what I told you that day at the café. About me and Pam. If you're okay with everything."

Zienna glanced at him, incredulous. She felt her nerve coming back. The anger. "Are you serious? You want to fuck me, but only if you receive absolution from me first?"

"In a way, I guess. Your forgiveness is important to me."

"So your ego can feel good? Doesn't it already?" She tightened her robe around her body, hiding her exposed cleavage. "Obviously, my reaction to you just showed that I'm still attracted to you. Even though I shouldn't be. But forgiveness? Screw you, Wendell. Why should you get everything you want?"

"Hurting you hurt me, too," he said, and he had the gall to sound contrite.

"Don't." Zienna shook her head. "Don't act as though it hurt you to hurt me. God, just tell me you want to fuck me. That I can respect."

"I told you about Pam, I told you about Jeremiah."

"For the record, *Nicholas* told me about Pam. You couldn't very well keep lying after that."

"I know. But I didn't hold back. I told you everything. Something I was already planning to do."

"And you expect that to erase the past?" She didn't want to think about how he had hurt her. Right now, she was horny, and Nicholas had already acted as if she'd cheated on him. If she was going to make it official, she didn't want to talk about four years ago.

"No, but I hoped that you would stop looking at me like that," Wendell said softly. "The way you are right now."

Zienna lowered her gaze to the floor. Inside, her emotions were raging. Anger, hatred and lust all mixed together.

"You expect way too much," she said after a moment.

"Because you love Nicholas?"

"Because you broke my heart!"

Zienna shot to her feet and started to pace. Why was she even letting Wendell stay here right now? Why was she giving him another platform to justify his past behavior?

She looked in his direction, but didn't make eye contact. "I want you to leave."

He got to his feet and stood in front of her, then took her by the shoulders. "Look at me," he commanded. She did. "All the while I was in Texas, I never forgot you. Never. And then I lost my son."

He stopped talking and sucked in a breath. His grief was palpable. Zienna had never seen him looking this vulnerable. He had always been the confident, sexy man who knew how to take what he wanted. And here life had dealt him a blow that would bring any man to his knees.

"I lost my son, and everything changed. In an instant, I learned a major lesson. That life is short. Too short not to go after what you want. I know you're dating Nicholas, but God help me, I want another chance with you."

Zienna's heart was beating a mile a minute. "I was the other woman, no matter how you're painting the situation now. You never told your family or friends about me. I was your dirty secret. Our relationship wasn't real. Unlike what I have with Nicholas."

Wendell shook his head, as if he didn't want to accept her words. "You want Nicholas? Is that what you're telling me?"

Zienna had her strength back. "Yes." She nodded. "I'm sorry about your son and about your relationship with Pam falling apart, but I need you to leave."

"All right, then." Wendell released her suddenly. His lips twisted in a scowl, he started for the door.

Maybe it was the mention of his son that had brought him down emotionally, turned what had started as lust into something altogether different. But Wendell exited the apartment without a backward glance.

Zienna released a breath she didn't know she'd been holding. She stood in the living room, trying to process what had happened.

And then the door suddenly flew open again, and in charged Wendell. He moved toward her with the stealth of a panther. And then he was pulling her into his arms and his velvety, sweet lips were coming down on hers, and he was kissing her with ferocity, with a carnal passion and urgent need she hadn't felt in a very long time.

There was no talk this time. No questions. No conversation about whether or not this was right. Wendell simply lifted her into his arms, and she snaked her legs around his waist, locking them behind him. He carried her to the bedroom, a path he had been taken many times in the past during a relationship that had been sexually explosive.

He crossed the threshold, and when he got to the bed, he lowered her onto it none too gently. His body landed on hers, all hard muscle in all the right places, taking her breath away.

Still kissing her, he slipped his hands inside her robe. He spread the folds wide, exposing her breasts. Only then did he pull his lips from hers and lower his head in search of a nipple. He drew it into his mouth and began to suckle, releasing a groan of delight as he did.

He tweaked and tugged on her other nipple until it was a hardened peak. Then he moved his mouth to that breast, trailed his tongue over it before grazing it with his teeth.

Zienna gasped at the sensation of pleasure that emanated from her nipple and went straight to the core of her femininity.

"God, I missed you," Wendell rasped. He pushed her breasts together and drew both nipples into his mouth at once. He suckled her like a man starved. He gently bit. He laved both nipples with broad strokes of his tongue.

A long and rapturous moan escaped from Zienna's throat. She was already close to orgasm.

"I remember," Wendell said. He kissed the underside of one of her full breasts. "Oh, baby, I remember." While his hands tweaked her nipples, his lips found the hollow between her breasts, and he used the tip of his tongue to create a fiery path from there down to her navel. He paused, flicking his tongue inside her belly button delicately.

His hands went to her hips as his mouth went lower, planting soft kisses over her pubic area, through her thong. And then his lips covered her nub, and the heat from his mouth made her shudder.

Wendell lifted his head and then his body to drag her thong down her thighs, taking his time to feast his eyes on her even as he pulled the delicate fabric over her toes. Then he kissed the inside of her ankle, and began moving his lips higher, kissing her skin all the way up to her thigh.

Zienna hardly breathed.

Almost urgently, Wendell spread her legs wide and settled his upper body between her thighs. Positioned this way, she was totally exposed to him, the light in the room leaving nothing secret. He didn't touch her, just regarded her as if examining a piece of art.

"Seriously, I have missed this pussy."

She watched his eyes roam over her center and become darkened pools of lust. Just the way he was looking at her, she was so aroused she felt she might come.

Gently, Wendell stroked her, and Zienna exhaled a shuddery breath. Then his mouth came down on her and he began to devour her.

And oh, the pleasure. Oh, his touch. Zienna closed her eyes, threw her head back and moaned in delight. Moaned as his tongue found all the right places. Moaned as he added his fingers. He suckled her nectar like a man enjoying his last feast, savoring every inch of her womanhood.

His other hand eagerly sought one of her nipples, adding to the already delicious sensations flowing through her. Zienna locked her thighs around his face as he continued to tantalize her. His movements became gentler, his tongue exquisite.

Zienna came then. Came hard. Wendell didn't let up until every ounce of her orgasm had drained.

His wet lips skimmed her inner thigh. Then he stood and began to undress. Her chest rising and falling rapidly, Zienna watched him take off his shirt, then his pants.

She'd done it. She'd crossed the line with him, and her orgasm had been one of the sweetest ever.

It was too late to feel guilty now.

When Wendell dropped his pants, she saw his massive erection and once again felt the stirrings of desire. She sat up and reached for him, and he stepped toward her. She took his shaft in her hand. As Wendell had done, she simply looked at it, then touched it gently, getting reacquainted with the member that used to rock her world.

She stroked him. Kissed the tip.

Wendell took her face in his hands. Bending down, he kissed her again, his tongue sweeping into her mouth deeply. When he broke the kiss, Zienna was panting.

"Lie down, Zee-Zee," he said, using the nickname he used to call her. "Show me that sweet pussy again. Show me that you're ready for me."

"I am ready." She pulled one leg onto the bed, exposing herself again. She sat, watching, as Wendell put on a condom. She could tell him to stop, that they'd already gone too far.

But she didn't.

Because right now, there was nothing she wanted more than to feel him inside her.

Doing her all night long.

Wendell joined her on the bed, stroked her face gently and gave her a kiss that was hot and tender at the same time. He moved beyond her lips to her neck and her collarbone, creating sensual heat everywhere.

In a fury of heat, Wendell finally pulled her into his arms, went down on his back and grabbed at her legs, to help her straddle his body. He suckled her nipple as she positioned herself over him. And then he was guiding his shaft into her.

Zienna cried out, the feeling of him entering her pure ecstasy. Wendell's growl mixed with her own. He gripped her hips and thrust upward in hard, fast strokes. Zienna pushed downward, making sure he went deep. As they found their rhythm, she arched her back, her moans getting louder.

Wendell played with her nipples. "Look at me, Zee-Zee. Look at me."

She dropped her head forward and looked down at him. And on his face, she saw an expression of exquisite pleasure that matched what she was feeling. He brought his fingers to her mouth, slipped them between her lips. "Yes, baby," he said. "Oh, yes. That's the look I want to see."

Zienna sucked on his fingers as his strokes filled her deeply. This was what she had craved for four long years. What she had missed.

Wendell's hand crept to the back of her head, and he urged her down so that her lips met his. His tongue played in her mouth with the same urgency that his shaft moved inside her.

The sensations became sweeter, dizzying.

"Yes, Zee-Zee," Wendell said against her lips.

And then Zienna came, this orgasm even more earth-shattering than the first.

And all she could think was that if this was so wrong, why the hell did it feel so right?

16

The night had been a dazzling whirlwind, unexpected and exciting, and Zienna had lost herself completely in the experience. But come the morning, merely a few hours after Wendell kissed her on the forehead and told her he had to leave, Zienna awoke in a state of disbelief.

She'd slept with Wendell. She'd let him back into her bed. And she could hardly believe it had actually happened.

Worse, she felt great. Her body still tingled in the most wonderful ways. Wendell had given her exactly the kind of sex she needed. The kind she had hoped for from Nicholas after last night's successful launch.

Instead, Nicholas had snapped at her in a jealous rage, and Zienna had done the exact thing he had feared: had sex with his best friend.

She lay still, staring at the ceiling. Dawn had broken, and her bedroom was beginning to fill with light. It was a new day, and she had no clue what she was going to do.

She was both excited after her night of carnal pleasure, and disgusted with herself. Feelings on either end of the emotional spectrum.

People wanted simplicity. Right versus wrong. Good versus bad. Black or white. But life wasn't simple. It was usually complicated with shades of gray. She understood that all too well now.

Zienna wasn't a cheater. She wasn't the kind of person who looked for attention from other men when she was in a relationship. Yet she had allowed herself to be driven by lust last night.

"Nicholas," she said softly. How would she face Nicholas?

She was angry with him for treating her as though she had betrayed him, when she had in fact rejected Wendell's advances. She could use the excuse she'd heard others produce in similar situations before: if he already thinks I'm cheating, then why shouldn't I? It would be all too easy to blame her actions on Nicholas's outburst, but that wouldn't be the truth.

No, Zienna had to own what she'd done with Wendell. He had made it his mission to seduce her, but at the end of the day, she had allowed herself to be seduced.

Was it possible that Nicholas had known she wouldn't be able to resist his friend? Was there something about how she'd looked at Wendell, even though she'd tried to reject him, that had made it obvious she would end up in bed with him again?

Zienna closed her eyes. Thought once more about the moment she'd seen Wendell through her peephole. The alarm and the tingle of excitement. Then she'd let him in and he'd made that comment about being tired of pretending. Now she couldn't help wondering if he'd been talking about himself or the both of them.

Had the two of them started down this road toward sex the moment they'd laid eyes on each other again?

She knew what Alexis would say. Her friend would talk

about how hard it was to forget a guy who could utterly thrill you in the bedroom. And Zienna couldn't deny that truth. Her body was still feeling the pleasure of Wendell's touch. She'd made love to Nicholas countless times and each of those experiences paled in comparison to what she'd shared with Wendell last night.

But still, she was in a committed relationship with Nicholas. How had she ended up caving to her baser instincts?

Groaning, Zienna rolled over in her bed. It was 6:47 a.m. She reached for her phone. She wanted to send Alexis a text and fill her in on what had happened, and also check to see if Wendell had sent her a message. They'd programmed each other's numbers into their phones last night before he'd left.

Her phone showed that there were three missed calls and five new text messages. Her stomach jumping with excitement, she opened her messages. Two from Alexis. Three from Nicholas. When she checked the call log, she saw that the three missed calls had been from Nicholas, as well.

Her stomach fluttered with a smidgen of disappointment. Which didn't make sense. Wendell had left her bed only a few hours ago. She didn't expect to hear from him already.

But in an instant, she allowed her brain to acknowledge what her heart already knew. She *wanted* to hear from Wendell. A text, something. Something to let her know he was thinking of her after what they'd done.

Zienna had fallen into bed with him, and though it should have been only about lust, her heart was already taking a huge step back in time. Wendell was saying the things now that she'd wished he had said years ago, and it was so hard to think of what they'd done last night as only sex.

Could it possibly be about more?

"Seriously, you are a huge idiot," she told herself. How stupid was she, already getting stars in her eyes where Wendell was concerned? She'd done that before and had been burned. She needed to take what had happened as only sex. Sex she had enjoyed, and nothing more than that.

Because Nicholas... Oh, God. Nicholas.

Drawing in a breath, she opened the messages from him.

I was an ass. I'm sorry. Please forgive me.

You have every reason to hate me, but please, call me.

Zienna, a million times I'm sorry. I was out of line. Call me in the morning. I need to know we're okay. I love you.

I love you.... The words made Zienna's stomach roil. She couldn't call Nicholas and tell him that they were okay. Her night with Wendell had ensured that they were far from okay.

She lay back down for several minutes, silently pondering what she should do. Wondering what she even wanted anymore.

"You don't want Wendell," she told herself sternly. In fact, she should block his number. Because what good would come of him calling her now? Would the two of them get together again? Go for another round of illicit sex with no promises? No, it was better that they not stay in touch. Better that whatever had happened between them be a one-time thing.

She'd needed a taste of him, God only knew why, but she had. She had satisfied that craving, and now she could move forward with Nicholas.

The words sounded great in her head, but Zienna was entirely uncertain. She needed Alexis's perspective. She lifted her phone and typed out a message to her.

OMG, Wendell came by last night. Totally confused. Need to chat!

Then she lay back, not quite ready to get up. Minutes later, the phone rang. She quickly raised it and looked at the screen, expecting to see Alexis's name. Her stomach twisted when she instead saw that Nicholas was calling her.

She let the call go to voice mail.

Nicholas called twice more while Zienna was getting ready for work, and both times she decided not to answer. She had no clue what she would say to him, and needed more time to get her head straight.

She phoned Alexis at seven-thirty, told her she wanted to drop by before work. And when she explained that it was about Wendell, without giving any further details, Alexis told her to hurry up and get to her place. Then Zienna called her clinic and left a voice mail message that she was going to be late, something she didn't normally do. But her first appointment wasn't until ten-thirty, so she knew she would have a little bit of leeway. With Nicholas's restaurant launch being last night, the staff at the clinic would assume she'd been out late, and was perhaps a bit hungover, and hopefully there would be no issue with Margaret.

Zienna hightailed it out of her apartment and got to her friend's just before eight forty-five. Luckily, Alexis's workday as a receptionist for a veterinary clinic didn't begin until ten.

When Zienna got to the door, she pounded on it urgently. Alexis, wearing a blouse and no pants, opened it quickly. "Come in," she told her. "And tell me what Wendell said."

Zienna whizzed into the loft and Alexis closed the door behind her. "Don't keep me in suspense," she said, facing her once more. And then, suddenly, her lips parted in surprise. "Oh my God. He didn't come by to talk, did he?"

In response, Zienna whimpered.

"Follow me to my bedroom. I've got to get my jeans."

Instead of following her, Zienna went to the sofa and plopped down, stretching her body out and using her hands as a pillow. It was becoming real now that last night hadn't been a dream.

"Zee?" Alexis called. She came back out to the living room seconds later, still shimmying into her jeans.

"Zee, what did you do?"

"I don't know," she mumbled.

"Sit up," Alexis commanded. "I need to see your face."

Slowly, Zienna did as instructed.

"Zienna?" Her friend's eyes searched hers, and after a moment, they bulged. "Oh my God! You *did* it!"

"You're the one who told me I should."

"Huh?" Alexis asked, her eyes narrowing.

"You remember. You told me that I should explore things with Wendell and with Nicholas."

"I don't remember saying that exactly, but fine. You actually slept with him? Is that what you're saying?"

Zienna faced her friend. She bit down on her bottom lip as she looked at her, then said, "That's what I'm saying."

"Oh my God!" Alexis exclaimed, louder this time. Then she clamped a hand over her mouth, staring at Zienna with a mix of awe and confusion.

"Well? Does that make me a slut?"

"Tell me how it was." Alexis actually squealed as she sat on the sofa beside her. "Seriously, was it as hot as before? Better?"

"Don't make it sound like I did something great."

"Wasn't it?" Alexis raised an eyebrow.

Zienna closed her eyes, remembering Wendell's lips on all of her body's erogenous zones, bringing her the utmost pleasure. "It was. Shit, it *was* great. Better than before, I think."

"How did it happen?" Alexis demanded. "We left together, and when we got to your place, you told me you were going right to bed."

"And that's exactly what I did. Then about half an hour

after you left, I heard a knock on my door. I thought it was you coming to check on me. Or maybe even Nicholas. But it was Wendell." Zienna gulped in a breath, remembering that moment. The rush of excitement mixed with the feelings of uncertainty.

"Then what?" Alexis asked. "Because you said you told him you weren't interested. Even last night, at the launch."

"Exactly. Which makes what happened all the more baffling." Zienna paused. Leaned forward and cupped her face with her hands. "A part of me was pissed with Nicholas. And not just because he accused me of lusting after Wendell all night. But he hardly even noticed me, and I'd gotten all dressed up in that sexy outfit, hoping for a look from him… something. And then there was Wendell. There was no doubt that *he* noticed me. And even though I didn't want to cross the line with him, knowing that he thought I looked sexy made me feel nice. Desirable. Then he showed up at my door, and he started telling me how amazing I'd looked and that Nicholas was stupid to let me go home alone… Suddenly, he was kissing me, and—and I didn't stop him."

Zienna felt flushed even remembering it now, which didn't make her feel like the best person in the world. She should be racked with guilt. "What's wrong with me?"

"There's nothing wrong with you." Alexis patted her knee. "You're human. You're a woman. And no matter how nice Nicholas is, you're feeling the same kind of frustration I felt with Elliott. We're more alike than you might want to admit. Knowing that you have a good guy isn't always enough."

Zienna shook her head. "No. I love Nicholas. This isn't about needing more," she said. Though maybe it was. Maybe Alexis was spot-on with her assessment. "I mean, I have enough with Nicholas. But for some fucked-up reason, I'm still sexually attracted to Wendell."

"You don't want to admit it, but a guy who can rock your world… Hell, I know I'd keep going back for more. Even making love to Brock the first time, it felt as though something inside of me had finally awakened. Finding that person you connect with sexually, that's a rare thing. And once you have a taste of that, it's hard to forget it."

Zienna heard Alexis's words, but didn't think they totally applied to her. She'd had great sex with Nicholas. So what if Wendell was better in bed? Surely she couldn't be motivated simply by her libido.

Could she?

No, she was certain there was more to it, and after a long moment of silence, it came to her. Finally, she understood.

"Ahh, now I get it," she said, and felt relief at her discovery. "It was about the way he left me. About there being unresolved feelings. At least on my part. He never even said goodbye. Not really. He told me he was leaving, and that was it. I was devastated. You know how crazy I was about him."

"About his cock," Alexis added with a giggle, perhaps to lighten the mood.

Zienna gave her friend a look of reproof. "Last night was about closure, that's what I'm saying."

"If that's what you want to call it."

Zienna frowned again. "So you think all that matters is a person's sex drive, and not a true connection between a man and a woman? You've broken up with Elliott and suddenly your views on love have changed?"

Alexis glanced away, and Zienna saw something in her expression, a slight shift. When she turned back again, she said, "There's something I haven't told you. The night I met Brock?"

"Yeah?"

"Before we went out, I spoke to Elliott. And he confessed

something. I guess he thought it was the reason I'd called off our engagement. But apparently, he cheated on me six months into our relationship. He thought I'd somehow found out."

"What?" Zienna couldn't have been more perplexed.

"Yeah. My nice guy. The one I swore would never cheat. He said that was all it took for him to realize he wanted only me. Talk about cold comfort…"

Alexis's voice trailed off, and Zienna could both see and hear her pain. Elliott's affair, even though it had been nearly two years ago, still hurt her. Which explained Alexis's apparent about-face.

"Why didn't you tell me sooner?" Zienna asked.

"I don't know. I was shocked. Embarrassed. I couldn't deal with it at the time. I just knew that I needed to go out and meet someone else."

"Alex…"

"No, don't give me that look. It's good he told me. Because it made me do some serious thinking. I went out, I met Brock, and I get it. Sex can be a bigger draw than love. Everything that's happening with me and now with you…I know I must sound like a broken record, but I really believe that women don't want to settle sexually any more than men do. Sure, it's not the only thing, but it's a pretty big part."

Zienna shrugged. She'd had conversations with men in college and in the workplace where she'd shot down their notions that sex was the most vital component of a relationship. She wasn't sure she agreed with Alexis. "I didn't jump into bed with Wendell just because of sex. Part of it was because I was pissed with Nicholas. After his accusation, all I could think was he's got a real jealous streak and I don't like it. I thought we were done with that after those issues in the first month. Not to mention I was really disappointed that he barely noticed me last night. I wore that dress for him. All I wanted was one look. A look that said he thought I was ravishing."

"The kind of look Wendell gave you."

"Yeah," Zienna said softly. She shook her head. "It's stupid, isn't it? All we really want is a good guy. At least that's what we say we want. A nice guy who's thoughtful and caring. Then we get him. And we start finding all the flaws."

"Or he secretly screws around on you," Alexis pointed out.

"Alex, I don't know what to say."

"Forget it," she said. "If Elliott had been giving me the kind of sex I needed, I wouldn't have dumped him and I wouldn't have found out about his affair. And if you had the kind of sex with Nicholas that left you thinking about it day and night, you wouldn't be noticing any of his flaws. Tell me I'm wrong. Come on, it was only after Wendell broke up with you that you started to question the big picture. How you'd never met his friends or family, how you spent more time in the bedroom than out...."

"I get it," Zienna said, and frowned. And she couldn't deny Alexis's words. She *had* ignored the important questions four years ago, because she'd been mesmerized by Wendell. But had she been so naive that she'd confused lust for love? She'd always thought she was smarter than that.

"So..." Alexis's voice rose on a high note, and amusement danced in her eyes. "Are you going to see him again?"

"You just reminded me how deluded I was about Wendell four years ago."

"Yeah, but things have clearly changed," Alexis said.

"How so? Because we slept together again?"

"No. Because of what he told you. About Pam, about his son. Zee, I doubt he'd be coming after you again if he didn't have real feelings for you."

Alexis wasn't helping her. Not at all. "Aren't you supposed

to tell me that I *shouldn't* be seeing him again?" Zienna challenged.

"Only if you don't *want* to."

"I…" En route to Alexis's, Zienna had decided she was ready to put Wendell behind her. But now… Did he really still have feelings for her? And did it even matter if he did? "I don't know what I want. Damn, why can't you just tell me that I need to stay away from him?"

Alexis waved dismissive hand. "It's not up to me to tell you that. If I did, I'd be a big hypocrite. Not with what I'm going through in my own life. No, I think it's more important than ever to figure out what you really want. Nicholas has potential. But maybe Wendell does, too…"

"Maybe," Zienna said. "Or maybe all I really wanted to do was let him know what he missed out on by leaving me. What he walked away from." Her perspective was becoming clearer and clearer. "And I did that."

"So you're not going to see him again?" Alexis surmised.

"No. I don't think I will."

Her friend stood. "I'd love nothing more than to hang out all morning, but I can't."

Zienna stood as well, glancing at the wall clock as she did. It was almost twenty after nine. "I know. And I'm already late. Thanks for listening to me."

"So, it was really that good?" Alexis asked in a conspiratorial whisper. "After all these years?"

"Oh my God, it was amazing."

Alexis beamed. "Of course. Damn."

"What?"

"Well…it's gonna be tough to stay away, don't ya think?"

Zienna didn't want to think about tomorrow. "What do I do?" she asked. "About Nicholas? Do I tell him? Do I come clean about this?"

Zienna had never been in this situation before. She would never have labeled herself a cheater. Never the type to stray. Which was what bothered her all the more about how she had so easily let Wendell into her bed.

"Are you out of your mind?" Alexis asked. "When have you ever seen a guy confess his sexual escapades? Not Elliott, and not…" Her words ended on a shrug, but she gave Zienna a pointed look, reminding her that not even Wendell had been honest with her four years ago.

"I know. And I should totally hate him. I don't understand why I…how I let him back into my bed."

"You had an itch, it needed to get scratched." Alexis spoke matter-of-factly. "And quite frankly, I think there's a lot to what you said about wanting Wendell to know what he's missed out on. It's one thing for him to see you looking hot, see you with his friend. It's another for him to have wild sex with you and know that when he chose someone else, he really should've chosen you."

"Exactly!" That logic resonated with Zienna loud and clear. "But still…Nicholas…"

"What he doesn't know won't hurt him." Again, Alexis spoke with a nonchalance she didn't used to have. But learning of Elliott's affair had clearly soured her. Zienna had always figured and hoped that Alexis and Elliott would get back together, but now she wasn't sure that would happen.

"Women sit around pining over guys, hoping they can be faithful. While guys go out and do what they need to do. At the end of the day, you're not married to Nicholas. Once you say 'I do,' that's a whole other story. But technically, you're still single. Sometimes we get so caught up in the fantasy of Mr. Right or Mrs. Right that we jump into relationships without thinking, and then we realize when we're in them that they're not exactly what we want. The way I see it, what happened with Wendell is either meant to make you realize how much you really love Nicholas, or that you and Nicholas aren't supposed to be together."

17

Wendell still hadn't called by late afternoon, and Zienna was becoming increasingly angry.

And not just angry with Wendell, but pissed at herself. She had spent the hours at work checking her cell phone every ten minutes or so, eager to see a missed call or text from Wendell, but there had been nothing from him.

Obviously, he'd wanted a piece of her, and that's all. His words about hoping for another shot with her, how he now knew what he wanted... It was all bullshit. The kind of thing meant to help rid her of her panties.

Even as Zienna walked to her car, she wished she would see Wendell lurking, as he'd done before. Damn it, she needed to talk to him. She wanted to know where his head was at, what he was thinking. If, for example, he was contemplating telling Nicholas about what had happened between them. Or if he wanted to forget it altogether.

She got behind the wheel of her car, slamming the door.

The fact that Wendell hadn't even sent her a one-word text told her exactly where his head was at.

God, she was so stupid! How had she let him get to her again? How? All he'd had to do was show up, say that he wanted her, and that was it.

You wanted to show him what he missed out on, Zienna told herself. *That you were the better woman than Pam.*

But the words didn't quite ring true. Yes, after the fact, she could say that she'd wanted to give him a taste of all he had walked away from. And she certainly had. But she couldn't claim any sort of victory if he had already forgotten her again. So instead, Zienna was the one to feel like crap now, her one night of pleasure turning into her biggest regret.

As she started her car, she thought about the texts Nicholas had sent. He sounded like a completely different person in his texts and voice messages than the one he'd been last night. He was taking all the blame for their spat, and pleading with her for forgiveness.

In part because Zienna wasn't sure what she would say to him, she'd decided that she would call him after work, once she was back home. It was weighing heavily on her mind, whether she should confess her sins, and see if they could move forward.

When she got into her condo unit, she kicked off her heels and slumped against the door. The stress of the last twenty-four hours was clearly getting to her; maybe a hot bath and a good book were in order before she spoke with Nicholas. She was on the fence about what she should tell him, but one leg was firmly on the side of being honest.

Just as she was turning off the faucets in her Jacuzzi tub, she heard knocking on the door. Her stomach fluttered.

Wendell?

Zienna hurried to answer it. She peered through the peephole with a sense of excitement…excitement that soon turned to anxiety when she saw Nicholas standing there.

After closing her eyes for a beat, she opened the door. This was inevitable. Seeing Nicholas, talking to him. Explaining that she'd screwed up.

He swept into her apartment and immediately drew her into his arms. "Oh, baby. I'm sorry. I'm so sorry."

He held her tightly, as though he didn't want to ever let her go. Guilt assailed her. He had been wrong, but she had committed her own sin.

"Nicholas—we should talk."

She tried to pull out of his embrace, but he wouldn't let her. "No. There's nothing to say." He drew his head back to look at her. "Except that you forgive me. Please, tell me you forgive me for being a total jerk. I can't believe I accused you of flirting with Wendell. I know he's your past. I'm sorry."

"Nicholas—"

"Please," he said, and his voice held a vulnerable edge Zienna hadn't heard from him before. "Just tell me you forgive me, and that we can get past this. It's not even twenty-four hours yet, and look at me. The mere thought that you might want to end things… I'm dying here. That's how important you are to me."

Zienna looked up at him. And she did the only thing she could do at that moment. She said, "It's okay. Let's put it behind us."

"Oh, baby." He kissed her. "I love you, Zienna. Please know that, okay? No matter what I say or do. I love you."

He kissed her again, this time slowly and deeply, and she could feel the relief in his body. But soon the kiss changed into something else.

It became more urgent, his tongue trilling over hers as his hands tightened on her back. "Oh, God. Touch me, Zienna. I'm already hard."

A little stunned at how quickly things had turned, Zienna slipped a hand between their bodies and placed it over his erection. And all she could think was that barely more than twelve hours ago, Wendell had been here in her doorway, slipping his hands between her robe....

"Nicholas—"

"No." He took her face in his hands and kissed her with insistence. "I need you. I need you naked. Right now."

"B-but the restaurant—"

"The restaurant is not as important as you. I'm sorry I made you feel like you weren't a priority last night."

And then he lifted her into his arms as though she weighed no more than ten pounds, and rushed with her to the bedroom. He went down on the bed with her, his hands moving to her breasts through her shirt. His lips dropped to her jaw and then her neck, and then he was yanking her shirt open and placing his head between her breasts.

"You're so beautiful," Nicholas rasped, and began to play with both her nipples. "Don't ever leave me." He skimmed his lips over hers. "Don't leave me, baby."

He slipped his hands between her thighs as he spoke, ran his fingers up her leg. Zienna hardly breathed. She felt trapped, stuck in a place of silence. There was no way she could discuss Wendell now. Not with what Nicholas was saying.

He began to stroke her, and she sighed with pleasure. This felt wrong on so many levels. Wendell's scent still lingered on her sheets....

Nicholas's fingers slipped beneath the silky fabric of her panties, and he groaned as he touched her center. He slipped a digit between her folds and then inside. He added a second finger, then a third. Zienna arched her back and moaned.

And that was all it took for Nicholas to become consumed with raging lust. He didn't even tug her panties off, just pulled them to the side as he buried his head between her thighs and began to pleasure her with a tongue that was hot and relentless.

He gripped Zienna's hips as she came, laved her even more with his tongue, as though he was hoping to force another orgasm out of her. His fingers worked at rapid speed, until she could no longer control her cries.

Finally, he pulled off her panties and then guided his shaft into her. He made love to her hard, his sounds animalistic with each plundering thrust.

It wasn't Nicholas. It was The Slayer.

And he had come to claim her.

Just as Wendell had done the night before.

And even though Zienna was caught up in the pleasurable sensations of lovemaking, she was all too aware of a glaring, shameful reality.

For the first time in her life, she had slept with two different men in a twenty-four hour period.

"Hey," Nicholas said, planting a kiss on Zienna's forehead moments after her eyes opened. "Good morning."

"What time is it?"

"After ten," Nicholas told her.

"Oh my God. I slept that long?"

He smiled sheepishly. "Well, we had a very busy night."

That they had. Nicholas had spent much of the time making love to her, almost with a sense of determination. It had been alternately hard and fast and wild, and tender and loving. But if Zienna had ever had questions about his stamina and virility, those questions were clearly answered.

"Thank God it's Saturday," Zienna said. There was no way she could get up and go to work today. She wasn't even sure she could walk. Between Wendell and now Nicholas, she was beyond sore and wouldn't need more sex for a week.

"I've made you a cappuccino." He gestured to the mug on her night table, and it was then that she realized he was lying on top of the covers, not beneath them. "What do you feel like having for breakfast? Crepes? Omelets?"

"All I know is that I don't want to go anywhere. I need to recuperate."

Nicholas chuckled. "Sorry. The Slayer got a bit out of control. But it was great, wasn't it?"

"It was… Wow. That's why I need to stay in bed."

He gave her a kiss on the cheek. "Good thing your boyfriend is a chef. I can make you an amazing breakfast right here."

"Oh, but I think my fridge is empty."

"It is. I already checked. But you tell me what you want, and I'll run out and pick up what I need."

Zienna stroked his arm. "You're so good to me."

"I haven't been. But that's gonna change." He took her hand in his and kissed the back of it. "Crepes or omelets?"

"Since I can make a fairly decent omelet for myself, I'd love crepes. With some strawberries and whipped cream?"

"Of course."

Nicholas got dressed, then scooped up Zienna's keys from her dresser. She stayed in bed until he was gone. Then she quickly lifted her phone and pressed the home button to turn on the screen. She'd made sure to turn the ringer off after her first lovemaking round with Nicholas, just in case Wendell called.

She went to her call log, and saw Wendell's number on her screen. He had phoned her once. And he'd texted her, asking her to call him. No special message telling her that he missed her or that he was thinking about her.

Zienna punched in Alexis's number. But after four rings, the phone went to voice mail.

She didn't bother to leave a message. She would have to try Alexis later, once Nicholas had left for work.

She was about to put the phone down on her night table, but then decided to send Wendell a message.

Things got out of hand between us. Nicholas is here right now. Please don't call or come by. I think it's best we forget about what happened between us. It was fun, but it won't happen again.

Then she set down her phone and drew in a breath, feeling a smidgen of satisfaction that she was the one to reject Wendell this time.

It was shortly after eleven-thirty when Nicholas started getting ready to leave for the restaurant. He'd made Zienna the most delectable crepes topped with a mix of fresh berries, then apologized that he would have to leave and head in to work. It was the day that Reflections on the Bay was opening to the general public, and he needed to be there.

"If it was any other day, I'd blow off work and stay here," he told her as he slipped into his shoes in the foyer. "As it is, I shouldn't be late, but Wendell's gonna be there. He'll hold down the fort till I get there."

"Right." Zienna smiled, hoping the expression came off as easy and nonchalant—and not as if she was hiding a huge secret.

"Anyway, I don't expect a mad rush before noon."

"I'm sorry. You shouldn't have bothered to make me breakfast."

"You're my number one priority," he told her. "Everything else is secondary."

He opened the door and stepped into the hallway, then turned back to face her. "This was nice, wasn't it? Breakfast in bed?"

"It was wonderful."

He reached for her hand. "You know, it can be like this all the time…me spoiling you with my culinary skills for breakfast, dinner." He paused. "I'm thinking that maybe it's time I clear out some closet space, make room for you."

Nicholas's eyes held hers, hopeful. Zienna's lips parted in surprise.

"The last time you slept over, you had a suitcase in the car with extra clothes. I've got a big place. I think it's time to share some of that with you. I mean, we're good, right?"

"Yeah." Zienna forced a smile, but was thinking that this had come out of the blue.

"I'm not saying you have to move in. Not yet. I know you'll have to sell this place first. But there's no reason you can't have a key and some closet space. A spot for makeup and perfume on my bathroom counter…"

Zienna swallowed. "You're really serious."

"Of course I'm serious. I want you in my life, always." Nicholas gave her a quick kiss, stroked her face. "Now, I really have to run. I love you, babe."

"I love you, too."

Nicholas beamed, as though her words gave him the most incredible feeling. Then he trotted toward the stairwell. He never took the elevator, since she lived on the second floor.

Just before he disappeared through the door, he said, "I'll call you later, babe."

Zienna raised a hand to wave. Then she slipped back into her apartment.

For a few minutes after she locked the door, she leaned her back against it, thinking. Nicholas's parting words only made her feel guiltier than his sweet actions already had. He was being the epitome of the doting boyfriend.

Zienna went to her bedroom and called Alexis again, but

still got no answer. It wasn't like her friend to be up and out before noon on a Saturday. She treasured her weekends because it meant she could sleep in. One of the texts Zienna had retrieved this morning had been from Alexis the night before, saying she was going out with Brock again, so it was pretty certain Alexis had had a very late night. If her friend had spent her night the way Zienna had, she was no doubt still in bed. And probably hungover. Zienna decided to head over to her friend's apartment.

She stopped at her favorite coffee shop a mile away from Alexis's place, knowing that her friend would need the caffeine as much as she did. The one cup she'd had with Nicholas was not nearly enough.

Zienna entered the building lobby and hit the buzzer for Alexis's unit. A minute passed with no answer. But luckily, a young woman leaving in jogging gear opened the door, so Zienna was able to slip in without having to buzz again.

Balancing the tray of coffees in one hand, she knocked on the door with the other once she got upstairs. The seconds ticked by. Either Alexis hadn't heard the door or she wasn't there.

Zienna knocked again. Then pounded. Still no Alexis.

Zienna set the tray of coffees on the hallway floor and dug into her purse for her iPhone. If Alexis wasn't home, there was no point in her standing in the hallway any longer. And if she was perhaps still sleeping, hopefully the phone would wake her up. Alexis was a bit of a diva when it came to her sleeping routine. She needed earplugs to block out any noise, and a mask over her eyes to keep out the light. But she kept her phone by her bedside at all times.

The phone rang three times, and a groggy sounding Alexis said, "I hate you."

"I'm at the door," Zienna said sweetly. "Open up."

She disconnected the call, then slipped the phone back into her purse. Several seconds later the door swung open and her friend, wearing a robe and looking seriously pissed, appeared.

"I brought coffee," Zienna said without preamble, stepping past her into the foyer.

"I'm dying here," Alexis said.

"That's why I brought you this." She handed her one of the cups—a caramel-flavored cappuccino, her favorite.

"I just want to crawl into a hole and die," Alexis grumbled, heading into her living room.

"Well, that won't do. Because I need my friend. I need a girlfriend day, when we can talk and I can let off some stress."

One of Alexis's eyebrows shot up as she sat on her sofa. "Did you see Wendell again last night?"

"No. Nicholas."

Alexis's eyes lit up. "Oh?"

"And The Slayer was back." Zienna took a seat beside her. "He was insatiable."

"Then girl, what are you doing here? Even the way you just sat down, I can tell you're sore. You should be home nursing your private parts with a hot water bottle after another night like that."

"He was just so…different. So intense. He said he was afraid I'd dumped him, and the way he went about sex with me… it was like he tried to give me the best night of my life to ensure I would never leave him."

"Sounds amazing."

"It was."

"Then why are you frowning?"

Why, indeed? Nicholas had given her a night she wouldn't soon forget, proving his prowess in the bedroom. And yet…

"I guess it's because I keep thinking about Wendell. Even though I've told myself I shouldn't. I mean, how can he come back into my life at this point? How can I have any residual feelings for him? It's crazy."

Alexis took a sip of coffee before speaking. "Well…you were really into him."

Zienna nodded. A beat passed. "Nicholas said he wants to give me a key to his place. Closet space."

Alexis nearly spit out a mouthful of coffee. She coughed, and had to bang on her chest to help with the liquid that had gone down the wrong way. "Are you serious?"

"It's not like things weren't going well for us. Heck, before Wendell showed up I wasn't doubting anything."

"And now you are?"

"Now, I just…I want to make sure my head is straight. I'm seeing some things I don't like about Nicholas. Obviously he'd be pissed to find out what I did with Wendell. It's the worst time for me to make a decision about taking our relationship to the next level."

"You've got to follow your heart. You talked about closure with Wendell, but it seems more like you've still got unresolved issues."

"I just feel…conflicted."

Alexis suddenly groaned. "God, my head is pounding."

"So, you saw Brock last night," Zienna said, turning the attention away from herself. "How was it?"

"It was sexual nirvana. We're talking hours." Alexis smiled sheepishly. "Truly, an all-night session."

"You mean without a break?"

"A little break here or there. Not much, though."

"How's that possible?"

"He had a little help." Alexis's expression was sly, mischievous. "We both did…."

Zienna's eyes narrowed as she looked at Alexis. And she remembered her feeling that night when they were at the club and Alexis had become so drunk so quickly.

"Please tell me you're not saying what I think you're saying."

Perhaps because of Zienna's tone, Alexis lost her playful expression and her voice took on a defensive edge. "It was no big deal. Just something to make me feel better because I kept blabbering on about Elliot."

"What did he give you?" Zienna was starting to get angry. How could Alexis be so stupid?

"Just a pill."

"What kind of pill?"

"He said it was ecstasy."

"Alexis!" Zienna shot her a look of reproof.

"I know…"

"What were you thinking?" Zienna pressed on. "A guy you barely know—taking *E* from him? For God sake, you're smarter than that."

"I *am* smarter than that. You don't have to worry."

"Right," Zienna replied sarcastically. "He gave you ecstasy the first night at the club, too, didn't he?" Zienna didn't bother to wait for a response. "Smart people don't take pills from guys they just met. Better yet, they don't take drugs at all. You could be lucky to be alive, for all we know."

"I don't need the lectures, Zee. I'm not your sister."

Alexis's words struck her, killing her comeback before she could utter it. Zienna wasn't treating her like her sister, was she? She knew Alexis didn't do drugs—at least she hadn't. But Zienna had lived a nightmare that she didn't like to talk about—having a younger sister who was always looking for the next fix. Tabitha was always looking for something to help escape the pain of losing their parents so tragically. But the truth was, there was no running from it.

"I'm not saying you're stupid," Zienna said. "But your be-havior wasn't very smart."

"Lots of people do ecstasy," Alexis protested.

"Do you hear yourself?" Zienna asked. "Now you're jus-tifying what you did? Taking a pill from some guy in a club the first night you met him?"

"It's not like I haven't seen him again. Obviously, he wasn't out to hurt me. A pill here, a pill there… As long as it's not habit forming it's no big deal."

"It can't believe you just said that."

"Okay, okay," Alexis said testily. "Fine."

"I know you're not my sister," Zienna continued a little more gently. "The problem is that my sister didn't come out of the womb a drug addict. When our parents died, she couldn't handle it. Tabitha started with alcohol to numb her feelings. Then she moved on to weed, and then harder drugs. You know the rest."

Tabitha had eventually—inevitably—overdosed after taking heroin, which had landed her in the hospital fighting for her life. Rehab had followed, but Tabitha had fallen back into a life of drugs. Zienna had tried to get her help, but Tabitha had become angry, angry enough to leave Chicago. Zienna hadn't heard from her since. She assumed Tabitha was still alive, since she hadn't gotten a call from the authorities as Tabitha's next of kin. At least, she prayed her sister was.

"Really, I can take care of myself," Alexis insisted.

"I know you can." Zienna didn't add that she also knew how easy it was for people to go from sanity to insanity, as Tabitha had.

But she didn't want to think about her sister, not with the ten-year anniversary of their parents' death coming up in nine days. Every year when that sad date came around, it was always harder to bear, because she hadn't only lost her parents, she'd lost Tabitha as well. Her sister, younger than her by four years, had cut her out of her life nearly eight years ago, and while Zienna was hopeful, she didn't truly know if she was dead or alive. It was the not knowing that was especially painful, so Zienna had done her best to put a wall around her heart and the memories of her sister, and simply hope that she was somewhere doing well. Maybe with a family of her own by now.

Zienna crossed the room to the window and opened the blinds, and Alexis groaned as she squinted at the assault of light. "Seriously, are you trying to kill me?"

"It's a beautiful day. And I'll be damned if we stay here and spend it sulking." She planted her hands on her hips. "Let's do something. Anything. Forget about men and drama for one afternoon. Let's have a pedicure, or better yet, a massage. Just give me the word and I'll call our favorite spa...."

Alexis's frown began to lighten. "Massage and pedicure?"

"The works—on me, if they can fit us in this afternoon."

"Make the call. You drive a hard bargain," Alexis said.

"That's why you love me." Zienna smiled sweetly as she reached for her phone.

18

Wendell didn't try to reach Zienna all day Saturday, leaving her more conflicted than ever. Alexis was right—she clearly had unresolved feelings for him. And despite her own words telling him to stay away, she wished he would call her.

"It's official," she said to herself Sunday morning, taking a moment to pause during her weekly jog along the lakeshore. "You're insane."

She'd told Wendell to forget what had happened between them, but it was clear she didn't want him to. If he really meant it about caring for her, wouldn't he try to talk to her, regardless of what she said? Would he really give up on her without a fight?

Zienna sipped from her water bottle, then wiped her brow. It was a beautiful day, the sky clear and the sun bright, still not too hot in early May. If only she could enjoy being surrounded by the trees in bloom, the chirping birds and the scenic lake dotted with sailboats.

He got what he wanted, she said to herself as she turned and began a brisk walk along the path heading south. Wendell was a player and he'd played her, end of story. There was no sane reason she should ever let him back into her life now.

But it was one thing to tell yourself something, and another to heartily believe it. Maybe she was suffering from the same thing that plagued addicts—your brain knows she should stay away from drugs and alcohol, but once temptation hits, all reasoning and logic go out the window.

Zienna turned up the music on her iPod and began to jog again.

There were other runners out enjoying the spring weather, and she fell into pace behind a man running at a good clip, which challenged her to go faster than usual. And she was making record time, pushing herself hard. But as she reached the trail near East Cedar Street, her eyes narrowed when she saw someone standing on the edge of the path and looking in her direction.

Her heart began to beat in overdrive.

Oh my God, she thought. *Wendell?*

He took a few steps onto the pavement as she got closer, and then she knew for sure. It *was* him.

Her legs faltered from her steady stride and she began to slow down. Finally, she veered off the path and under the shade of an oak tree, staring at Wendell in surprise while trying to catch her breath.

"I was fully prepared to join you," he said, his smile easy.

Zienna took in his appearance. A loose-fitting black T-shirt and black nylon shorts. Nike sneakers. He certainly was dressed for running.

"You're trying to tell me I coincidentally ran into you?" she asked between labored breaths.

"Hell, naw. I knew you'd be here. Sunday mornings, shortly

after ten, beautiful day... I was hoping this was still your routine."

Zienna said nothing. So he remembered. Big deal.

"You want to keep going, I'll run with you. Just about half
a mile more, right?"

"What do you want, Wendell?"

"I thought that was obvious. I came out here to see you."

"I told you that you need to stay away from me."

"And I fully intended to do so."

Though that was what Zienna claimed she wanted, his
words stung—further proof of her insanity. But she straightened her spine and said, "Okay, then. We understand each
other."

"The hell of it is, I can't stop thinking about you. One minute I feel I can stay away because of Nicholas, then he tells me
you're moving in with him and suddenly all I can think about
is you in his bed...."

Zienna made a face. "That's what he told you?"

"Is it true?"

Wendell's eyes held hers.

"What's true is that you and I crossed a line, one we knew
we shouldn't have crossed. It was a mistake and—"

"Was it?" Wendell challenged.

She paused a beat. "Yes."

He stepped toward her, closing the distance between them.
"Then why is that just looking at you now, I'm hard?"

Zienna swallowed. Damn him, his words were already
arousing her, but she couldn't let him know. "Because you
love sex."

"And I can get it anywhere. I've had lots of sex, Zee."

"You don't need to remind me," she retorted, her stomach
twisting with jealousy.

"I'm making a point here. The point that I can't get you

off my mind." He brought a hand to her face, and the touch of his fingertips on her skin was lighter than she expected. "I don't care how many people can see us. If it were legal, I'd make love to you right here under this tree."

He trailed his fingers down the side of her neck, creating sensations of delight. He stopped just above her cleavage.

Zienna's breathing was heavy, and it had nothing to do with her run. It had everything to do with Wendell, and the words he was saying, and the feelings his touch evoked deep inside her.

And she completely agreed with him. If it were legal, she'd get naked right here, right now, spectators be damned....

"I've had lots of women," he went on, beginning to stroke her skin again. "But you're the one I can't forget."

What was she doing, standing here and letting him touch her like this?

"Come home with me," he continued. "I've got a new place. You'll like it." His finger trailed over the fullness of her breasts exposed above her tank top. "Don't say no, Zee. Please."

"Is it closer than my condo?" she found herself asking. She was dancing in front of the fire, getting too close.

He gestured behind him. "Right on East Cedar, the Gold Coast. Ten-minute walk."

His place...a much better option than hers, in case Nicholas dropped by.

"You're not far from my apartment," she commented.

"You don't know how hard it's been for me to stay away."

Zienna took a step backward. "My bike. It's parked down the trail."

"I'll walk with you to get it."

And as Wendell strolled beside her, Zienna knew she couldn't claim that what she was about to do was impulsive.

It wasn't like the last time, when Wendell had shown up at her door and seduced her.

This time, she was going with him willingly, fully aware of what she was getting into.

Zienna spent a few glorious hours at Wendell's place that afternoon, and went back for more on Tuesday. With Nicholas dividing his time between his two restaurants, he'd only been able to talk to her by phone or text.

And she had filled in his absence with Wendell's presence.

Nicholas made a tentative plan for them to get together on Thursday after work, but just after 9:00 p.m., he called to cancel. "Sorry, babe. There's a problem in the kitchen. The dishwasher malfunctioned. It's a fucking mess."

"Oh, that sucks."

"I can't make it over tonight. Tomorrow, we'll get together for sure. Spend the weekend at my place."

"That'll be great," Zienna told him, trying to sound cheerful.

But when she ended the call, she sent Wendell a text:

I can see you tonight. What time?

Wendell messaged her within minutes, telling her he would be home by midnight. Then he sent a follow-up text.

No panties

Zienna arrived five minutes after midnight. Wendell opened the door wearing only a pair of boxers. He drew her into his arms and kissed her. As his tongue played over hers, his hands slipped beneath her skirt. His palms went higher, smoothing over her bottom.

"Mmm," he moaned. "Just the way I like it."

He gripped her behind as his kiss became deeper. One hand

moved from her ass around to the junction of her thighs, finding her nub and beginning to stroke.

"You're already wet," Wendell rasped. He grazed her lips with his teeth, then suckled her tongue as he slipped two digits inside her. With one arm secured around her back, he urged her upward, and Zienna wrapped her legs around his waist. With his fingers thrusting, he carried her up the first flight of stairs to the smaller bedroom there. He'd meant what he'd said about christening every room.

One touch, one look...that was all it took to get Zienna in the mood where Wendell was concerned. By the time he laid her on the bed, still pleasuring her with his fingers, Zienna's body was already on sensory overload. Wendell moved away from her only to strip off his boxers.

She was slipping the satchel holding her phone over her head when it rang. For a moment, she froze, wondering who was calling.

Wendell stepped toward her, naked and hard. "Let it ring."

He settled beside her, his lips finding her neck as the phone rang three more times. Zienna closed her eyes, figuring it was likely Alexis who had phoned, and she let the sensations of desire consume her.

Slipping his hand beneath her blouse, which she had left mostly undone, Wendell found one of her braless nipples and delicately stroked it. "Why have you put a spell on me?"

"I think it's the other way around." Zienna arched her back.

"I can't stay away from you." He began to slowly move his head lower, toward a breast. "I just can't."

And then his mouth closed over one of her nipples, and his fingers sound her sweet spot once more.

Zienna closed her thighs around his hand. "Oh, baby. I could come already...."

The phone rang, jarring her from her pleasant sensations. It was a different ring this time. Wendell's phone.

"Oh my God," Zienna muttered.

With a grumble, Wendell snatched up his phone from his night table. "Shit, it's Nicholas."

Zienna sat up with alarm. Had he been the one who'd called her?

"Don't answer it," she said.

Wendell hesitated a moment. Then he said, "I'll get rid of him."

Zienna's body was throbbing and her heart was racing as she listened to Wendell answer the call.

"Bad time, my friend," Wendell said without preamble. His eyes went to Zienna. "Yeah, I'm here with a girl. Is she hot?" His heated gaze roamed over her languidly. "Oh yeah, she's smoking."

Zienna drew in a sharp breath. Her man on the line, her lover referencing her, and Nicholas not knowing…

"And she's not gonna want me on the phone, man," Wendell went on. "So I'll hit you up tomorrow."

"He didn't suspect?" Zienna asked when Wendell set his phone back down on his night table.

Wendell's hand caressed her nipple as his lips skimmed her neck. "He suspected nothing." His mouth moved to the nipple he'd been stroking. "I wasn't lying. You are smoking."

He was laving the hardened peak with his tongue when Zienna's phone started to ring again.

"It's Nicholas," she said, knowing it without doubt as she reached for the pouch that held her phone. And yes, his name and photo were flashing on the screen.

"Fuck." Zienna didn't know what to do, only that Wendell had to stop teasing her. She pushed him away. "What do I do?"

"Go ahead and answer it. Tell him you're in bed. That's technically the truth."

Zienna pressed the screen and answered the call. "Hey," she said, feigning her best just-woke-up voice.

"Babe, it's me."

"Mmm. Hi."

"I've done the best I can with the dishwasher for tonight. And I was hoping I could come by."

"Oh. Sorry, sweetie. I already fell asleep, and it's late."

"Yeah, I know. I was hoping you were still up. Ready for The Slayer."

"I'm sorry." Zienna closed her eyes as guilt washed over her. "But tomorrow, right?"

"Of course. Get some rest, then. I love you."

"Love you, too, babe."

Zienna ended the call and sat forward on the bed, her elbows resting against her knees.

"That was awkward," Wendell commented drily.

He sat beside her and placed a hand on her leg, but she shot to her feet before he could take it further than that. "I have to go."

"You're leaving?"

Zienna began to pull her bunched up skirt down from around her waist. Wendell rose to stand in front of her. "Nicholas isn't coming over, is he?"

"No." She started to button her blouse.

"Then why are you leaving?"

"Doesn't that bother you? At all?"

"What bothers me is that I had to listen to you tell Nicholas you love him, when you're naked in my bed."

"Naked in your bed," Zienna retorted. "That sums it up. That's what we do, Wendell. We get naked and we fuck. Why am I even doing this again?"

Hearing Nicholas's voice had been a wake-up call for her. She could no longer pretend that she and Wendell existed in some fantasy world where only the two of them mattered. It suddenly bothered her that Wendell was completely unfazed. Hell, Nicholas was his best friend.

Zienna started out of the ornately decorated bedroom, and Wendell followed her, stark naked. "Come on, Zee. Don't leave."

"So you can screw me without guilt?" She went down the stairs, not looking over her shoulder. "Well, maybe you can do that, same as you did with me when you were dating Pam. But I can't."

"You want us to talk to him together, tell him what's going on? Say the word."

Zienna whirled around as she reached the main level. "No! And don't you dare say anything to him." She averted her gaze from Wendell's magnificent form, which had given her so much pleasure. She looked him steadily in the eye and said, "Promise me."

He shook his head as he regarded her. "In other words, you want to keep him in the dark. And you're still giving me shit about Pam?"

"This isn't the same."

"Really?" Wendell's eyebrows shot up. "How do you figure that?"

"Because...b-because..." Zienna couldn't think. "Because you pursued me. You...you made me think things would be different this time, but it's just the same as before. Both of us sneaking around having sex, not involved in a real relationship."

"You want me to take you out in public? Wine and dine you? Say the word. The reason for the hiding is because I'm trying to be respectful of your situation. This time, the ball's in your court."

"The ball's in *my* court? Then please, stay away from me."

"Look at me and tell me that."

Zienna made a deliberate effort to stare him in the eye. "This was a great week," she said in a softer tone. "But I can't keep doing it."

"I'm all for that." Wendell matched her gentler tone. He stepped toward her. "Let's tell Nick. Break it to him easily. Or you end things with him, wait a couple of months, then we can officially get together."

Zienna stomach twisted. She couldn't even contemplate that. Breaking Nicholas's heart when he didn't deserve it...? Wendell was the one who'd hurt her.

She turned away from him, from that unfamiliar expression of vulnerability on his face. "Get together for how long? Until the next woman who makes you horny?"

"Jesus, Zee, if you think that's all this is..."

She cringed. She *didn't* think that's what this was. Not in her heart. But that had been the problem the first time around. She'd allowed herself to believe that what she and Wendell had had was meaningful and special—and that had led to the greatest heartbreak of her life.

"I can't do this. Wendell, I'm sorry that we complicated things. But I can't hurt Nicholas. And there's no point in pretending that what's happening between us is more than it is. We both know it's sexual. And I'm okay with that."

"You're not hearing a word I'm saying."

Zienna strode to the door. "Please, I've told you what I want."

She couldn't allow herself to think about what Wendell was suggesting, that there could possibly be more between them. Suddenly, it was all too real. And she was once again the woman she'd been at thirty-one, confused and devastated by the one man who'd had the power to hurt her. How could she allow herself to trust a word he was saying?

Her heart was vulnerable again, all because he'd come back into her life, and she needed to protect herself from spiraling out of control.

If she kept up this affair, she would no doubt lose Nicholas, a man who loved her and wanted a future with her. With Wendell, there were simply no guarantees. She couldn't take the risk of losing what she had for what might be.

She put her hand on the doorknob.

"Zienna."

Slowly, she turned. Her throat constricted when she saw the look on Wendell's face. "Don't leave," he pleaded.

The Wendell standing in front of her, naked and vulnerable, had the power to destroy her. Because he was different than he'd been the first time. This Wendell truly seemed to care about her, was saying all the right things. But if she believed him and he turned out to be lying...

Zienna threw open the door and ran outside.

And as she was hurrying toward the gate that bordered the property, she heard Wendell call, "You think I *like* this situation? I fucking *hate* it. But there's one way to resolve it, and I'm ready to take that step."

Zienna spun around. "Don't you do it. If you really care about me—for God's sake, if you care about Nicholas—don't you say anything to him. Don't you dare."

Wendell stood in the open doorway, obviously not caring about his nudity. "You know who you sound like, right?" he asked. "Me."

Zienna swallowed. Then she opened the gate and stepped through it.

"Guess you can understand now, can't you? Understand

what it's like to feel guilty and want to spare a person's feelings. But I'll give you some advice…prolonging things with
Pam only made the situation worse. If you can tell me you really love Nick, I'll turn around and leave you alone. Forever."

"For God's sake, there's someone walking up the street.
Go inside."

"Do you love Nick?"

"Don't tell him," Zienna reiterated, a warning. "I swear,
Wendell, don't say a thing to him. Nothing. If you do, I promise I'll never speak to you again."

She quickly got into her car and started to drive, but she
couldn't escape Wendell's words.

19

The following Saturday, while Nicholas went in to work, Zienna took a trip to downtown Chicago to get a pedicure with Alexis. Last weekend they'd only been able to arrange massages last minute, but Zienna had subsequently booked them for today at Arbre Nail Spa, a salon not far from her apartment.

Since they were coming from opposite directions—Zienna from Nicholas's home in Lincoln Park, and Alexis from her loft in the West Loop—they agreed to meet at the salon.

The place was packed. Several women were getting manicures, and all the pedicure stations at the back of the narrow, long space were filled.

She scanned the waiting area and spotted Alexis sitting with a magazine in hand. Grinning, her friend jumped to her feet. "Hey, Zee."

Zienna went over and hugged her. As they pulled apart, she asked, "It's seventy-five degrees outside. Why on earth are you wearing a turtleneck?"

"A sleeveless turtleneck," Alexis clarified. "You don't like it?"

"It's cute." It was black, and hugged Alexis's breasts. She wore the top with a pair of dark skinny jeans and black wedge-heeled sandals.

Alexis went back to her seat and lifted her purse from the next chair, which she had obviously been saving for Zienna. "A lot of people here today. But they say we'll get in for our one o'clock appointments."

"It'll give us some time to gab," Zienna said, easing onto the chair. "And I love this place. The feel of it, the smell, the ambience. Everything." The pedicure chairs were cream-colored leather, as were the seats in the waiting area and those at the manicure stations. The lightness of the upholstery was offset by the dark wood tables and counters. Zienna especially loved the crystal chandeliers hanging along the length of the room. The place had a sophisticated, modern look to it. "Not to mention my feet feel brand-new when I leave here."

"That's why it's always packed," Alexis commented. "They do a great job, *and* it's the time of year when every girl wants her toes looking good."

Zienna reached for a magazine, the cover of which featured two popular musicians who had just announced their engagement. That's when she overheard "…at this stage of our relationship? What does he expect me to do?"

She was immediately intrigued by the conversation, even before she heard the woman's friend reply, "He knows what you're going to do. Which is absolutely nothing. But what you should to is kick his ass to the curb."

The first woman, who was seated two down from Zienna, made a sound of derision. "I don't think he means it. He can't. Maybe he's just testing me."

"There you go—already making excuses for him. When a guy tells you he wants an open relationship after dating for three years, he's not joking."

Now both Zienna's and Alexis's ears perked up. That was the thing about going to a salon—customers were always full of stories and happy to talk to perfect strangers about their problems.

"Excuse me," Alexis said, leaning forward in her chair. "Did I hear you say that your boyfriend wants you to have an open relationship?"

"Yeah," the woman concurred. "But he can't really be serious. I mean, he can't want me to be out there dating other guys, right?"

Alexis shook her head. "I'm with your friend. If he tells you that, he's not kidding."

"And she's wondering if she should see how it goes," the other woman said, rolling her eyes. "I think all he wants is an excuse to cheat."

The first woman frowned. "What's wrong with men?" she asked. "I thought we were happy. We went out for dinner, and I thought he was going to propose, and instead he tells me this?"

"He knows he can do what he wants, because you let him," her friend said.

"I say take him up on his offer," Alexis said. "Start dating other guys. Why do we let men call the shots?"

"And I say dump him," Zienna countered. "I know it's hard, but there are other guys out there. Your friend is right—your boyfriend just wants an excuse to fool around, and we give guys that free pass. We hand it to them on a platter. We let their bullshit excuses slide, we don't call them on inconsistencies in their stories. And what do we get in the end? Heartache."

As she said the words, she was thinking of Wendell. Thinking of how he had trampled her heart so many years ago. How she had betrayed a good guy for a player.

"But I love him," the woman insisted. "How do I get past that? I've invested three years with him. And maybe this sounds shallow, but he's a doctor. He's got a great job, he's gorgeous…. If I let him go, someone else will snatch him up in a heartbeat."

The woman's friend rolled her eyes again. "What she isn't telling you is that he's really great in bed. That's why she lets him walk all over her."

Alexis said, "Well, it *is* hard to resist the pull of great sex." She faced Zienna. "Isn't it, Zee?"

Zienna shot her a look, then faced the woman at the center of the dilemma. "There's more to life than great sex. Believe me, being good in bed won't make up for him not respecting you."

"She's got this other guy who's totally interested, and she won't even go on a date with him," the woman's friend said. "I think she's nuts."

"I say go on the date," Alexis exclaimed.

"And I say don't complicate the situation," Zienna retorted.

One of the salon workers came over then and called the woman and her friend. The two made their way to the manicure tables.

Alexis turned to Zienna. "What are you going on about? 'Don't complicate the situation'? I thought you had a very different view of things these days."

Her stomach roiling, Zienna tossed the magazine onto the table in front of her. "That's what I haven't told you. I saw Wendell on Thursday night, for the last time."

"What? Why?"

"Because I suddenly realized that was I was doing was wrong. I was being a total hypocrite."

"You're just figuring out what you want."

"At Nicholas's expense?" Zienna shook her head. "No, it isn't right."

"And what about the fact that you clearly still have feelings for Wendell? You're just gonna pretend they don't exist?"

"That's the other thing that hit me. No matter what Wendell is saying now, how can I trust him? Come on, he's a player. Once a player, always a player."

"People grow up," Alexis argued. "They change."

Zienna wanted to believe that more than anything, but the very thought that Wendell might not be in this for the real thing had shattered her Thursday night.

"Nicholas called me," she said in a lowered voice. "Right when I was about to...you know...with Wendell. I didn't answer, then he suddenly called Wendell's place. I don't know... I got this feeling that he suspected we were together."

"Why? You said you didn't answer the call."

"He phoned a second time, a few minutes later, and I knew I had to answer it. He wanted to come over, so I had to lie. And then I felt like shit. I told Wendell I couldn't do it anymore. This isn't for me, this kind of life. Lying and sneaking. It was good while it lasted, but it's over now."

"And what did Wendell say?"

"That we should tell Nicholas the truth."

"See?" Alexis swatted Zienna's leg. "He obviously likes you. He wouldn't suggest that if all he wanted was to screw you."

Zienna put up a hand. "It's done. Nicholas is the guy for me. He's a good guy, and he loves me."

"Yeah, well, you know my thoughts on good guys. They can surprise you with their dark sides."

"I wouldn't call a one-time affair a dark side," Zienna said.

"Whatever. I don't want to talk about Elliott."

"Anyway, things are already moving forward with Nicholas. I'm staying with him this weekend, and he gave me a key.

I'm not moving in or anything, but giving me a key is still a huge step. It tells me how much I can trust him."

"And how was the sex last night?" Alexis asked as if that was the only thing that mattered.

"It was good. It's not going to be the moon and stars all the time. But it's how I like it. Sweet and consistent."

"Is that why you look so excited?" Alexis asked drily.

Zienna took a deep breath to calm her rising anger. "You and I can agree to disagree."

"If you say so."

Zienna snapped, "I really don't need lectures from someone who dumped a perfectly great guy and now is doing drugs with strangers."

Alexis threw her magazine down on the table, a hurt look streaking across her face. But she said nothing, just got up and marched out of the salon.

Zienna sat awkwardly for a moment, hating the fact that they were arguing in public. Arguing at all. Then, not making eye contact with anyone, she got up and followed her friend outside.

"I'm sorry," she said without preamble.

Alexis, who had her arms crossed and was facing the street, angled her head over her shoulder. "Are you?"

Zienna expelled a heavy breath. "Yes, I am. It's just…it feels like you're judging me."

"I'm looking out for you. Because I know you. Sometimes I think I know you better than you know yourself."

"But you're the one who introduced me to Nicholas! And now it seems all you can do is tell me to screw Wendell. That's what doesn't make sense."

Suddenly, Alexis gripped the neck of her shirt and pulled it down. "You want to know why I'm wearing a turtleneck?

This is why. Because sex with Brock is so fucking hot. Look at this hickey."

Zienna did. But she saw something else. Something that looked like...fingerprints?

"What is that?" she asked, concerned.

"A major hickey."

"But the other marks. Did he squeeze your neck so hard he left bruises?"

Alexis's eyes dropped downward as she pulled the turtleneck back up.

"What are you doing?" Zienna asked her. "Did you actually let him do that to you?"

"It was fun," Alexis said. "Exhilarating."

"Oh, my God."

"I felt alive," she insisted. "For the first time in my life."

Zienna looked at her with utter stupefaction. "You say you know me better than I know myself. Well, I know you. And this isn't you, Alex. Doing ecstasy, letting a guy hurt you."

"It's the new me."

Zienna shook her head as she stared at her.

"Stop looking at me like that. As you said, we can agree to disagree."

Zienna threw up her hands, giving up the fight. "Okay. You're right. As long as you know what you're doing—"

"I do."

"Good." She took a breath. "Are we going back inside for our pedies?"

A few seconds passed. Then Alexis turned toward the door. Zienna followed her into the salon, hoping that their disagreement would soon blow over.

But she didn't care what Alexis said. She was afraid for her friend. Her behavior was totally out of character. And this Brock guy was definitely bad news.

Zienna went into work a little earlier on Monday morning so that she could call Donald. She'd left the message with him, offering two free sessions, but hadn't heard back and was starting to get worried that he was truly going to follow through on his threat. She'd come to the conclusion that even if Margaret didn't want to offer him a refund, she would. The idea of a lawsuit—even if she was ultimately vindicated—was not one she wanted to entertain. A lawsuit would be a long, ugly and expensive process. Who knew if Donald would pursue action in court, but Zienna couldn't afford to take the chance.

She found Donald's file, jotted down his phone number, and called him from the privacy of her office.

The phone rang twice before Donald answered it. "Hello?"

"Hello, Donald." Her pulse was racing. "This is Zienna Hughes, your kinesiologist."

"Oh, yes," he said.

He didn't sound unpleasant, which put Zienna's frazzled nerves at ease—somewhat. "I haven't heard from you about the two free sessions the clinic would be pleased to extend to you. I'm just wondering if you'd like to accept the offer."

There was a pause, and Zienna held her breath.

"Actually, I don't think I will," Donald told her.

Zienna's stomach sank. "You won't?"

"No," he said, "but not for the reason you think. I...I started doing the other exercises you suggested. And I've been feeling better."

"You have?" Zienna asked, tentatively hopeful.

"Yes. A lot better, actually."

"Great!" Zienna exclaimed. Relief washed over. "Why didn't you call me back?"

"Honestly? Because I was embarrassed. I was so rude to you the last time I saw you, I just...I just decided to leave it alone."

"I understood your frustration, Donald. I would have welcomed your call."

"That's nice of you to say. You were always very kind to me. You didn't deserve my anger." He sighed softly, sounding contrite. "My ex-wife always did tell me I had a temper. Guess she was right."

Yes, anger had most definitely been a part of Donald's pain issues, but she didn't dare point that out. "Well, I'm happy to hear that you're feeling better, and I'd love for you to come in and continue to work with me. The offer of two free sessions still stands."

A few beats passed before Donald spoke. "I'll come in. But I'll pay. It's only right."

"Don't worry about it." As long as he was past being angry, that was what mattered. He appeared to be thinking rationally, not emotionally. "You weren't entirely satisfied. You had questions. That's fair. You take the free sessions, and we'll go from there. I insist," Zienna added.

"If you're sure."

"I am." And she was hugely relieved. Not having to worry about a lawsuit was a major weight off her shoulders.

"All right, then. And again, I truly am sorry. I hope you can forgive me."

"Absolutely. Now, when can you come in?"

Zienna was on a high after her call with Donald, and she relayed the good news to Margaret before meeting with her first client. Now in the exercise room with Jesse, a pitcher for the Chicago Cubs, she noticed that he seemed glum as he worked on his exercises with her. But her call with Donald had renewed her faith in what she did. Not that it had truly wavered, but today she was even more upbeat and determined to impart optimism in the face of adversity.

"I know it hurts," Zienna began, "but if you want to use your shoulder again, you're going to have to do these exercises."

Jesse looked defeated, as though he didn't have the energy to keep going.

"What's the point? I'll never be good enough to play again."

He had torn a ligament in his right shoulder, but continued to pitch despite the pain, and had subsequently dislocated his shoulder. That injury had ended his season. He'd had surgery, often prescribed for pitchers with this type of injury, and then he'd begun physical therapy to regain his strength and mobility.

"You will play again," Zienna told him. "It's just going to take some work." She added a smile, knowing it was important to be firm but kind. For men like Jesse, their entire lives were wrapped up in their careers. If he couldn't help heal his own injury, he would ultimately not be able to play the game he loved so much. And that would no doubt send him into depression.

Zienna had seen it countless times. But in her work as a kinesiologist, she had also seen the reward of single-minded determination to get past obstacles. And didn't athletes understand determination? They'd had to fight to be good enough, then fight to maintain their place on their teams.

Zienna knew Jesse had it in him.

"Has the KT Tape helped the pain?" The elastic sports tape she had applied to the front of his shoulder not only helped provide joint support, but also pain relief.

"Yeah, it feels better."

"Excellent," Zienna said. "Come on. Stretch out on your side like we did last time. We're going to do the same exercises."

Jesse didn't argue. Despite the look of resignation on his face, he lay on his left side, propped up on his elbow.

"Good," Zienna said. She guided his right arm into position against his hip. "Now, remember to keep that elbow against your side." She handed him the two-pound weight. "Just like before, I want you to do up-and-down pulsating motions with the weight. Nice and easy. Right, just like that."

Jesse did the exercises as she directed.

"That's it," she exclaimed. "Now, it shouldn't be painful. Are you feeling any pain?"

"Not really, no. A bit of burning."

"That's the muscle. Okay, now change the direction of the weight so that it's facing upward. You're going to be as good as new, I promise you."

The exercise room phone rang.

"Jesse, keep that up while I take this call."

She hurried to the phone and answered it. It was Jamie. "Zienna, I'm really sorry to disturb you, but you have an emergency patient."

"What?"

"That client who came in a couple of weeks ago. Wendell Creighton?"

Zienna swallowed. "Yeah?"

"He's in examination room three. And he's in a lot of pain."

"Someone else can see him," Zienna said, perturbed.

"He insists on seeing you. Said he needs to see you immediately."

Oh, God. "Fine. I'll see what I can do."

She hung up the phone and went to her patient. "Jesse, keep going for a bit. I have to check on another patient for just a moment. Okay?"

The athlete grunted. "Okay."

Zienna made her way to the exam room, ready to give Wendell a piece of her mind.

She pulled open the door. He was sitting on the examination bed.

"I swear to God, Wendell," she began without preamble. "You can't keep doing this. You need to respect what—"

She stopped short when she saw the pained expression on his face. His right hand was hugging his left biceps, just below the shoulder. Her professional senses kicked in. "What happened?"

"I got hurt," Wendell said, his voice laced with agony.

Zienna closed the door and started toward him. His left shoulder. "Your rotator cuff again?"

He nodded. "I needed to see you." He paused to breathe in deeply. "Because you're the only one who can help me with this."

He had reinjured his rotator cuff. Not good. She touched the head of the humerus. Wendell winced in pain.

"There's massive swelling. When did this happen?"

"Yesterday."

"Yesterday!" she said with alarm. "And you got no medical attention?"

Wendell shook his head.

"How?" she asked. "How did this happen?"

"Nicholas."

Zienna's draw dropped. "What?"

"No—I don't mean it like that. We were playing football yesterday. Me, Nicholas and a bunch of guys. Nicholas hit me, took me down. I landed the wrong way. It was an accident."

Nicholas had told her he was going to meet friends for some pickup football, something he hadn't done in a long time. He hadn't mentioned Wendell would be one of those friends, and she hadn't asked. She suspected Nicholas had guessed she was with Wendell Thursday night—had he intentionally hit him harder than necessary?

"Nicholas…he hasn't said anything to you…about me?" she asked carefully.

Wendell shook his head. "No. Nothing."

Maybe she was just being paranoid. Wendell winced, and she said, "Damn. You've done some serious damage. Can you move your shoulder?"

"Not much. It hurts like hell."

A repeat injury… This was going to take a lot of physical therapy. And she didn't want to be the one to work with him.

"See, babe—I need you."

"Don't call me babe."

"Sorry."

"You need someone who's good. It doesn't have to be me. I can recommend someone else." She gave him a pointed look. "I meant what I said. You and me—we can't keep seeing each other."

"You're the best kinesiologist I know. I don't want anyone else."

"Did you see your doctor?" Zienna asked.

"No. But last night, it wasn't this bad. I thought I could deal with the pain. Today it's fifty times worse."

"You should have gone to the hospital," Zienna said. "You need immediate medical attention. The kind I can't give you."

"Can't you just take care of me? Give me a steroid shot for the pain? Come on, Zee. You see I'm hurt."

Zienna pursed her lips, thinking. "Let me see your shoulder," she said.

Wendell began unbuttoning his shirt with his good hand, but it was awkward and he was moving slowly. "Could you give me a hand?"

Zienna didn't want to touch him, not at all. But she was a

professional. So she undid four buttons, enough that she could ease his shirt over his shoulder. Her eyes scanned his gold cross pendant, and her stomach tightened, thinking again of what he had lost. How he said that had changed his perspective.

She gently pushed the shirt from his shoulders. As her fingers grazed his skin, she was aware that Wendell's eyes were steadfast on her face.

"This is as swollen as a grapefruit," she said when she saw his shoulder.

"Please, I'm begging you for a shot."

"All right," she said, resigned. She couldn't argue that he didn't need it. She just knew that he needed more help than she could give him. "As long as you promise to go straight to the hospital when you leave here. That tear could be much worse than the first time, and who knows if you'll actually need surgery."

"Look at me."

Damn him. But Zienna did as he requested and met his eyes.

"I don't want to leave," Wendell stated.

Zienna looked at him as though he had grown a second head. "Did you hear what I said? You need immediate medical—"

"I heard you. But I'll tell you this—I don't care how much pain I'm in right now. I would rather be here with you than anywhere else. Even if it means my arm will never heal again."

"Don't be stupid," Zienna told him. "I'm not worth permanent damage to your shoulder."

"What if I say you are?"

She sighed, exasperated. "I meant what I told you the other day. We can't do this anymore."

"And I tried to respect what you said. What's it been, three days? Three days and I can't take it. I don't even care that I got hurt, because it brought me here to you."

"You've completely lost your mind."

"Maybe I have. Because there was a time I thought I'd never find a woman I'd ever want to commit to. I went through so many and none of them excited me, made me want to stay. Until I met you."

"Stop."

"And yes, I was involved with someone else. Someone I felt I owed a lot to."

"I said stop."

"And I tried to make a life with her, if only for the sake of our child. But even before Jeremiah died, I thought of you all the time."

"*Stop*. For God's sake." Zienna pulled his shirt back up over his arms, then turned away.

"Do you know how badly I want to kiss you right now?"

"Wendell, please…" Her heart was thundering.

"But I won't. I won't, because I'm trying to respect your feelings. And I want you to realize that I'm in this for us."

"I can't do this." Zienna started for the door. "I'll send someone else to give you that steroid injection."

"Zee—"

But she was already out the door.

20

Zienna was so on edge after Wendell's visit she could hardly concentrate on her work. She told Margaret she wasn't feeling well, which wasn't a lie, and left early. Then she went home, drank some chamomile tea and tried to sleep.

Wednesday was the ten-year anniversary of her parents' death, and she was feeling more overwhelmed than usual. It was tough dealing with this devastating milestone, and to have her emotions in further turmoil because of her personal life.

At thirty-five, Zienna had hoped she would have already found the man she wanted to wed. Her parents had married in their early twenties, had had her a couple of years later, and spent the rest of their days loving each other. It was almost fitting that they'd died together, because Zienna couldn't imagine either one of them being with someone else.

She wanted what her parents had had—and she'd had every confidence that she'd found that with Nicholas.

Until Wendell had come back into her life.

And, damn him, he was saying the right things. He was

acting like a changed man. And Lord, how that thrilled her on one level. But her heart...her heart couldn't handle the pain of losing him again.

And then there was Nicholas. If she were to do what Wendell suggested and leave Nicholas, how hurt would he be? She knew he'd fallen deeply in love with her.

The entire situation was a mess.

After a few hours of ruminating over her life, she called Nicholas. "Hey, how are you?" she asked.

"Just thinking about you," he told her.

"Good." She sighed. "Can I see you later? I just... I need to see you."

"Sure. You've got the key. Why don't you come over and let yourself in. I've put in a long day, so I can be home around eight."

"I'll see you there," Zienna said. "I love you, sweetheart."

"I love you, too."

When she got to Nicholas's, she curled up in his bed and watched a movie. Exhaustion claimed her at some point, though, because she woke up when she felt lips on her cheek.

"Hey, you," Zienna said, coming awake. She slipped her arms around Nicholas's neck. "I'm so glad you're home."

He gave her a slow, languid kiss on the lips. She moaned softly in protest when he ended it.

"I have to tell you, it's nice to come home and see you here," he said.

She sat up, and he settled beside her on the bed. Zienna dropped her head on his shoulder. "It's nice to wake up in your bed."

"Did you notice the painting in the living room?" he asked.

Zienna lifted her head to look at him. "No."

Nicholas took her hand and tugged her off the bed. "I didn't think you'd miss it."

"I was tired."

"Come on." He walked with her out of the bedroom and into the living room, stopping in front of a large painting on the wall near the back patio doors. "What do you think?"

Before her was a piece she had fallen in love with at the Carl Hammer Gallery, where she and Nicholas had gone a couple months ago. It was a vivid painting of African cats on the plains of the Serengeti. The picture had spoken to her because she'd always dreamed of going on safari. Behind the lions, in the distance, were elephants and zebras at a watering hole.

"You like?" Nicholas asked.

"You got the painting I wanted," she said in awe. "Even though you weren't crazy about it."

"And look down."

Zienna did. "And a zebra print throw rug." This hadn't been here on the weekend. "When?"

"I had them delivered this morning. Now that you'll be moving in, I thought it was time to change some things. Elevate my place from the man cave you've always said it was. Make it more interesting with art and accent pieces." He pointed to a far corner of the living room, where there was a large wood carving of a giraffe. "See the theme? Africa. It's like bringing the safari to our living room until we get to go there."

"Oh, my God." Zienna wandered over to the giraffe. "It's beautiful." How had she missed all this when she'd come in?

Nicholas slipped his arm around her waist and kissed her temple. "You've got a key, but it's not enough. Move in with me."

Zienna's lips parted as she looked up at him. "What?"

"You heard me. There's enough space for both of us here, and it's so clear that I'm missing a woman's touch. I already talked to a Realtor about listing your place, and he thinks—"

"Wait a minute." She stepped away from him. "You talked to a Realtor?"

"I like him. He's got a great reputation. He'll fight to make sure you get the best price for your property. I told him we'd have a meeting this week."

Zienna was flabbergasted. "You discussed selling *my* place with a Realtor, and didn't even talk to me first?"

"Why are you surprised? When I gave you a key, you knew it was a first step toward moving in with me."

"A step, yes. Not a leap off of the Sears Tower in less than a week."

Nicholas gave her a quizzical look. "What's the problem?"

"The problem is the decision needs to be mine. I've taken care of myself for years. I don't expect you to call a Realtor about listing my condo, without even talking to me first."

Nicholas's eyes darkened. "Is that all?"

"You don't understand why that would bother me? You making decisions on my behalf?" Surely he couldn't be that dense. She wasn't going to relinquish control of her life, not to anyone.

"Or maybe there's another reason you don't like the idea—something that's holding you back?" He raised an eyebrow, as though in challenge.

Zienna swallowed. Did he know? Good God, did he know about her and Wendell? Was that where this was coming from? Were his questions some sort of test?

"Listen, I don't want to make a mistake by rushing into anything. That's all I'm saying."

"Moving in with me would be a mistake?"

"That's not what I'm saying. It's just that things are going really well for us, coming along at a good pace. Moving in together is more pressure, that's all."

Nicholas held her gaze, seeming unconvinced. "Your hesitation wouldn't have anything to do with Wendell, would it?"

"What?"

"Has Wendell hit on you?"

Zienna's pulse raced. "Why would you ask me that?"

"Has he?" Nicholas pressed.

"He's your best friend."

Nicholas made a face. "So I thought."

Oh God, did he know? Was that what this was about?

"Nicholas, I don't know where this is coming from—"

"Boundaries, like friendship, don't matter to some people. You think I don't know Wendell's still got eyes for you?"

"Is that why you busted his rotator cuff yesterday?" Zienna asked.

Nicholas's eyes widened as he stared down at her. Then a smirk came onto his face, but it held no mirth. "Of course. He went to you."

"Because I worked with him before, to get his shoulder back into tip-top form. And you hit him so hard that you busted it again. Did you do that on purpose?" she asked, a sick revelation coming together in her mind.

"Is that what he said?"

"*Did* you?"

"No." Nicholas shook his head, his expression saying he was offended by the question. "We were playing football. I tackled him. Same as I've always done. Same as he's done to me. It was just a bad hit. It wasn't deliberate."

Zienna said nothing as she regarded Nicholas, trying to determine if he was telling the truth. There was a part of him that was simmering with jealousy, she could tell. Wendell might be his friend, but whatever rivalry lay between them ran deep.

"Why would I want to hurt him?" Nicholas asked, his tone almost too sweet.

His question seemed to be a loaded one. And the way he was looking at her said he was regarding her carefully, to see exactly what was hidden in her soul.

"I'm not going to do this." Zienna took a few steps backward. "I'm not going to let you bring Wendell into our lives at every turn. This is driving me crazy."

"It's happened before."

"I know, you told me. Wendell screwed your girlfriend when you were in college. What does that have to do with me?"

"It means I know him and you don't," Nicholas said. "Wendell loves games. He loves to chase. I saw women falling all over him, thinking they were in a relationship with him, when he was already screwing someone else. It was so fucking pathetic."

"Why are you telling me this?"

Nicholas took a step toward her. "Wendell has this special power. He can make women believe he's totally into them. Would I be surprised if he'd hit on you? No. Even though I know he's fucked at least three different women in the last couple of weeks."

The words were like a punch in Zienna's gut. "There's nothing between me and Wendell," she said, almost stumbling on the words. Technically, they were true now. "But if you don't believe that, maybe I should just leave."

At that exact moment, Zienna heard her phone ring in the bedroom, and she gratefully broke away to answer it. She heard Nicholas following her, but she didn't turn around. With her back to him, she lifted her iPhone out of her purse. And as she saw the photo flashing on her screen, her thoughts began to spin.

Wendell.

"Are you going to answer that?"

Zienna rejected the call. "It's just Alexis. I'll call her back later."

She turned, faced Nicholas. And then the phone began to ring in her hand. Swallowing, she glanced at the screen again. Wendell.

If she didn't answer it a second time, Nicholas would be suspicious. So she accepted the call and put the phone to her ear. "Hey, Alex," she said, forcing a cheerful voice. "What's up?"

"You're with Nick?" Wendell deduced.

"Yeah, I'm good. I'm with Nicholas for the night. Can I call you tomorrow?"

"What if I told you I was outside his house right now. That I wanted to see you?"

"Really?" Her stomach fluttered. "You're kidding."

"No, but I've been waiting at your place. Are you coming home?"

"Just gonna hang out with Nicholas," she replied, her heart thundering. Nicholas was watching her.

"All night?"

"Yep."

"You know you're killing me, right?"

"Oh, wow. I'm surprised he said that."

"Come on, Zee. Cut the bullshit. Tell Nick already, or let me come over and we'll do it together."

"No," she said sharply. "Definitely not. I would definitely not do that."

"Look…I need you. I went to the hospital. My shoulder's fucked up. And I just…I just want to lie in bed with you tonight."

"I'm sure there's someone else who can help you." Zienna

added a tinge of harshness to her voice, hoping Wendell would pick up on it, but that Nicholas would be oblivious.

"Fuck no, there's no one else. Jesus, Zee. You don't want me to come over there, fine. But make an excuse. Tell him you have to leave."

Nicholas was walking toward her now, slowly. "Tell Alexis you'll talk to her later," he said.

"We'll deal with that tomorrow, Alex. Bye." And as Nicholas reached to take the phone from her hand, Zienna's heart began to pound furiously. She pressed the button to end the call, but wasn't sure it disconnected before he could glance at the screen and see Wendell's face.

She held her breath. Nicholas tossed the phone onto the bed and dipped his head to her neck. "Alex is upset about Elliott," she lied. "He called her again, wants to work things out."

"*We* need to work things out," Nicholas mumbled against her neck. His fingers trailed up her stomach and over her breast. He pushed the fabric of her bra aside to fondle her nipple. "Isn't this better than fighting?" he whispered hotly into against her skin.

Zienna closed her eyes, relieved that he hadn't figured out she'd been talking to Wendell. As her heart began to resume its normal pace, she hoped that Nicholas's touch would get her in the mood. But after a minute, she knew that she was only going through the motions. It wasn't just Wendell's call blocking her from becoming sexually stimulated. It was also her disagreement with Nicholas.

"Nicholas…"

His lips found hers, kissing her with a passion she didn't expect and drowning out her protest. He suckled her tongue while slipping his other hand lower, cupping her through her pants.

She couldn't do this anymore. Having sex with two men.

Maybe she should just come clean about her affair. The burden of her betrayal was heavy on her shoulders, and she didn't want to carry it any longer.

She eased her mouth from his. "Nicholas, I… Can we just talk for a minute?"

He ignored her, his tongue working on her neck as he urged her backward the few steps to the bed.

"Nicholas, I'm serious."

He continued on as though she hadn't spoken, pushing both his hands under her shirt and squeezing her nipples.

"This doesn't feel right," Zienna said. "We were just fighting."

"And now we're making up."

"Seriously, Nicholas, I want you to stop," she told him, in case he felt her words were merely part of the foreplay.

He yanked at her shirt, popping buttons, then slipped his hands into her bra. With single-minded determination, he brought his mouth down onto one of her nipples.

He wasn't listening, so Zienna pushed against his head, hoping he would get the point that she was serious.

And then he sank his teeth into her nipple, hard, causing a sharp pain.

"Nicholas!" she cried out, pushing him away from her now. "For God's sake!"

"Was that too much?" he asked, his tone innocent.

"I told you to stop." She jerked her bra back over her breasts.

"Sorry," he said. "I didn't realize…."

Zienna crossed her arms over her chest. "You didn't realize? How many times does a person have to tell you to stop?"

"What—you're saying I was forcing myself on you?" He looked stunned and devastated.

She paused a beat. "No. Of course not." Zienna scooped

her phone up from the bed. "But you definitely weren't listening to me. I'm starting to think that's a trend."

"What?"

"I just want to go home."

"What the hell is going on with you?" he demanded.

What was going on was that she was confused and overwhelmed. Nicholas was changing in a lot of ways, and not for the better. And with Wendell on her mind, she knew she couldn't go to bed with Nicholas right now.

"We're not in sync tonight. That's how it feels to me. I think it's best that I go home."

"I wasn't listening to you. I'm sorry."

She took a step toward him. "Forget it. I think I'll go see Alex, make sure she's okay." It was only half a lie. She would go to see Alex, but not to check up on her. Zienna wanted to avoid going home in case Wendell was waiting there for her. And she wanted to talk to Alex, unload her burdens on her.

Nicholas stared at her, seemingly unconvinced by her words.

"I'll call you tomorrow, okay?" she added.

After a moment, he placed his hands on her shoulders and said, "Sure."

Though he'd said it pleasantly enough, Zienna got the sense that he was annoyed. But she didn't want to argue, so she stretched up on her toes and kissed him on the cheek.

"Do what you need to do," he said when her lips left his skin. "You're entitled."

So he wasn't happy with her. Zienna chose not to say anything, and instead started out of the bedroom.

Once she'd stepped through the doorway, she turned and said, "We'll talk tomorrow, okay?"

Nicholas stood where she'd left him. "All right."

Zienna wound her way through his living room to the

front door. The moment she opened it, she heard a crash, and flinched.

She looked over her shoulder. Didn't see Nicholas.

But she knew what had happened.

He had just smashed something against his bedroom wall.

21

Zienna didn't bother calling Alexis when she left Nicholas. She expected her friend to be home on a Monday night, though she couldn't be sure she wasn't out on a date or doing something. But even if she drove all the way to the West Loop and didn't find her home, Zienna didn't care. She needed time alone in her car to think, if nothing else.

Nicholas had bitten her. After trying to get her into bed, as though what she wanted wasn't a part of the equation. And that whole deal about contacting a real estate agent without speaking to her first. Zienna didn't understand what was going on with him, but knew she didn't like it.

When she arrived at Alexis's loft, it was minutes to nine. She found an available meter on the street, and once she'd parked her car, glanced up. She could see the windows of Alexis's unit, and the lights were on. Zienna crossed the street and entered the loft complex, then buzzed her apartment.

"I already told you, Brock, not tonight," Alexis said without preamble. She'd answered almost immediately, as though she'd been standing beside her intercom unit.

"Alex, it's me," Zienna said.

A moment of silence passed. Then Alexis said, "Oh."

"I know we haven't really talked since the salon." They had exchanged only a few impersonal texts, along the lines of "Hey, what's up?" Zienna had suggested dinner but Alexis hadn't replied, so she'd figured her friend was still getting over their tiff. "But I need you," Zienna went on. "Please let me up."

A moment later, she heard the buzzer go off and the lock's latch release.

Upstairs, Zienna found the door to Alexis's loft ajar. She pushed it open and then reeled back in shock. "Alexis!" she shrieked. "My God—what happened to you?"

Alexis closed her eyes tightly, and a tear fell down her cheek. "It looks bad, right? I mean, it looks like someone beat the shit out of me."

"That's exactly how it looks." The left side of Alexis's face was swollen, especially around the eye. Her eyelid was swollen to a small slit, the skin horribly discolored, and there was dried blood beneath her eyebrow.

"What happened?" Zienna repeated, her stomach twisting with pain. "Who did this to you?"

"Brock," Alexis said sheepishly, then turned away and walked into her living room.

Zienna followed, after closing and locking the door. "What? Why would he do something like this?"

Alexis sighed softly as she sat down on the sofa and reached for a bag of ice she'd placed in a bowl on her coffee table. Zienna sat beside her friend, unable to fathom what could have happened.

"It wasn't intentional," Alexis said, placing the ice on her swollen eye. "It just happened."

"Something like that doesn't just happen. He assaulted you. Please tell me you called the police."

Alexis shook her head.

"God, Alex." A beat passed. "Then why didn't you call me?"

"Because I knew what you would say. You didn't like him. And...and you were right."

Zienna's shoulders slumped. "Come on, Alex. You know you can talk to me about anything. I'm sorry we had a disagreement, but you have to know I'll always be there for you. Especially when something like this happens. If you'd called me, I would have been here immediately."

"At least you're here now. Why did you come, by the way?" She lowered the bag of ice.

"That totally doesn't matter." Zienna gently touched Alexis's swollen face. "How does it feel?"

"It hurts."

"I don't understand how something like this is an accident."

"We were drinking," Alexis explained. "And...I know you won't like this, but we both had another one of those pills."

"Of course." Zienna shook her head in dismay.

"No, you don't understand. It's not what you think."

"Then explain."

"You saw the bruises on my neck, and you reacted judgmentally. I knew you would. That's why I didn't tell you before, but..." Alexis breathed in deeply. "The first time Brock and I were together, he was...well, different than other guys. A little rough. Nothing too out of line. A little slap in the face. He whacked my ass. Threw me down on the bed hard. I thought, okay, something new. Let's go with it. I mean—it was different than Elliott. More exciting."

"You're telling me this was deliberate? You let him hit you, get rough with you, and he punched you in the face?" Even saying the words set Zienna off. No man should ever touch a woman like this.

"I thought he was just going to slap me. He punched me instead."

"Holy shit."

"It was sex play, but it went too far."

"You're damn right it did. I bet the police would have something different to say."

Zienna noticed that the bruises on the side of Alexis's neck looked brighter, newer. "Turn around and face me," she demanded. "Let me see your neck."

Reluctantly, Alexis did.

"Oh, my God." Zienna covered her mouth with a hand as she saw the visible fingerprints on both sides of Alexis's throat. "Does he fucking strangle you?"

"I can't go to the police with this," Alexis said, fresh tears spilling. "I didn't tell him to stop."

"That is *not* okay. Permission or not, no one deserves what he did to you."

"He had a fantasy of raping me," Alexis said, her words barely audible. She didn't meet Zienna's eyes.

"And you let him do this to you?" What had happened to Alexis? Was it the damn ecstasy she'd been taking? "The way I see it, he plied you with drugs and alcohol so that you would be agreeable to his plans of beating you senseless and getting away with it. If you don't call the police, I will."

"You don't understand." Alexis looked Zienna directly in the eye. "I asked him to do it."

Zienna made a face. "You *asked* him to strangle you and leave marks? To punch you in the face?"

"The rape fantasy wasn't just his. It was mine, too. You know, something to make things a bit more exciting."

"So getting beat up is exciting?" The drugs must have altered Alexis's brain cells.

Her friend sighed. "I guess…I just wanted to feel alive."

"Oh, Alex." Zienna was stunned, but didn't say so. She was certain that as well as wanting to feel alive, Alexis wanted to forget the pain of her breakup with Elliott. She was putting on a brave face, pretending she was over him, but it was all bullshit.

Zienna wrapped her arms around her and hugged her. "Alex, I'm sorry. I'm sorry you had to go through this."

Alexis cried against her shoulder. "I know what you must think of me."

"What I think is that I love you. And I wish I could take your pain away. I don't exactly understand what you're going through, but I'm not judging you. Please know that."

Alexis eased back. "I can't go to work tomorrow. Not like this. Maybe not even for the rest of the week."

"I think you need to get checked out—now. I'm taking you to the hospital."

"God, Zee, I don't know."

"I want to make sure you haven't sustained any injuries that need treatment. I know this is going to be hard, but you have to do it. Okay?"

Alexis drew in a shaky breath. "Okay."

Zienna took Alexis to Rush University Medical Center, where she spent the next four hours with her. First came the wait in emergency, and then the assessment of her injuries and treatment.

Both Zienna and Alexis were relieved to learn that she didn't have any injuries that wouldn't heal. Alexis was in pain, but would get better. Zienna had been concerned about her friend's swollen eye and vision, but it looked worse than it was. Alexis needed a couple stitches along her left brow line, which had been split open with the punch. She was given medication for pain, as well as a prescription for the next several days, then discharged.

The hospital staff had asked her how she'd incurred her injuries, advising her that abuse required them to call the police. "I had to tell them I wanted it," Alexis explained in the car. "Explain that we were drinking and things got out of control. They were suspicious, but eventually they believed my story. I don't want the police bringing Brock in, and this whole thing becoming a big mess. I just never want to see him again."

Zienna nodded. "Fine." Given that there was no reversing what had happened, it made sense that Alexis simply move on. "But if he bothers you or harasses you, you need to tell him that you *will* call the police."

Beside her in the car, Alexis nodded. "I will."

They drove silence for a while, then Alexis said, "Is everything okay with you and Nicholas? You and Wendell? When you buzzed up to my place, you said that you needed me. Then we never got to discuss it."

"Compared to what you went through, it's nothing," Zienna said.

"Tell me. Please. Give me something else to think about."

Zienna sighed softly. "If you want the truth, Nicholas got a little weird with me. I'm just not sure anymore."

"What did he do?"

"He told me he'd contacted a real estate agent to list my property—without discussing it with me first. He said he'd set up an appointment for later this week. Apparently he's decided it's time for me to move in with him, whether or not I agree."

"Wow."

"We had a bit of a spat over that, and he accused me of not wanting to move in with him because of Wendell. He asked if Wendell's hit on me. He wouldn't let it go. He went on about how Wendell's always had this ability to charm women, and is a big player. Said something about Wendell having slept with at least a few women in the past couple of weeks."

"You don't believe that, do you? I mean, you and Wendell have been hitting it so hard, where would he get the energy to be involved with anyone else?"

"Energy was never Wendell's problem," Zienna commented. Her stomach tightened at the idea that she hadn't been the only one in Wendell's bed. She didn't want to believe that, though she knew she was the last person on earth to expect fidelity.

"I don't know, Zee. Sounds like Nicholas is suspicious and wants to scare you off. But who knows."

"He wanted to make love after our argument, and I didn't, but he kept pushing. I told him to stop—more than once—and he ignored me. When I told him again that I wasn't in the mood, he bit my nipple. Hard. Honestly, I got the feeling he did that because he was pissed at me. I don't know. I don't know if I'm making too much of it."

"Hmm." Alexis sounded wary. "I'm concerned about his jealousy. He keeps asking you about Wendell."

"What if he knows?" Zienna asked, glancing at Alexis. "What if somehow, in his gut, he knows?"

"But you said he wants you to sell your place and move in with him. Why would he want that if he thinks you're messing around with Wendell? My guess? He's worried that you and Wendell will end up together, and he's trying to move things ahead with you quickly so that doesn't happen."

"I didn't like the way he bit me. It just felt... It felt like he did it because I was pushing him away."

"Or maybe he was lost in the moment," Alexis said. "Trust me, it happens."

They arrived at Alexis's building just then, so Zienna didn't respond to her last comment. She parked, then helped her friend out of the car. When they got to her door upstairs, Alexis said, "I know you have to work in the morning. You don't have to stay with me."

"I'm calling in sick for work. I'm not leaving your side."

"No, I don't want you to do that."

"You don't want me here?" Zienna countered.

"I didn't say that. I'd love to have you here with me. But I can't expect you to call in sick."

"Well, I'm going to. And don't try to get me to change my mind. I'm taking Wednesday off already, because of the anniversary of my parents' death. I may as well miss tomorrow, too."

Alexis grinned at her as she opened her door. "If you insist."

"I do."

Zienna slipped her arm around her friend's shoulders, and together they made their way inside.

22

The next day, Zienna called Nicholas to tell him what had happened with Alexis. To keep her friend's confidence, she lied, saying that Alexis had an accident at the gym and got hit with a barbell. Nicholas seemed pleasant and loving, their argument thankfully laid to rest. He showed support and concern for Alexis, and even had dinners from his restaurant in The Loop sent over for them so they didn't have to cook. Nicholas called her two more times to check on how things were going, and sent a flurry of texts as well.

Zienna figured everything was fine between them, and chalked up his weird attitude on Monday evening to stress. And perhaps fear. While he didn't know that she had slept with Wendell, if some sixth sense told him to be wary, could she really blame him for being suspicious? She knew she had betrayed him, and could hardly play the outraged innocent girlfriend. In fact, now that she'd told Wendell to stay away for good, she was leaning toward confessing the truth to Nicholas and hoping he'd forgive her.

On Wednesday morning, she was back at home, the anniversary of losing her parents already weighing her down. She called Nicholas just before eleven-thirty to tell him when she would be going to the cemetery. She had mentioned it to him weeks ago, asking him then if he could accompany her, and he'd agreed. Last week—then again last night in a text message—she had reminded him.

"Hey, sweetie," she said when he answered his cell. "I just wanted to tell you that I'm heading to the cemetery around two. That way your lunch rush will be over. I thought you could head back to work before the dinner crowd starts to arrive."

"Oh, baby." Nicholas made a groaning sound. "I'm really sorry. I know I said I'd go with you, but right now is a really bad time. This is going to be a busy day for me, and I have to cover both restaurants. There are some deliveries I have to oversee. And the owners of the Chicago Blackhawks are coming by this afternoon for a lunch meeting. Obviously, I need to be here for that."

Disappointment was like a lead ball in Zienna's stomach. "Oh."

"You're upset with me."

"Well…" she hedged. "I'm disappointed. I thought… I hoped you would come with me. But it's fine. I know how busy things are for you with two restaurants."

"You know I wanted to be there for you," Nicholas said, and he did sound contrite. "If it was any other day…"

Zienna found herself wondering if anything would be different if the anniversary were tomorrow, or next week, or even if they were married.

"Alexis will go with you, right?"

"Yeah," Zienna said softly. Though she wouldn't ask her. Alexis was still recovering, and staying inside until her facial bruises healed. Zienna had wanted Nicholas, her boyfriend, to be with her on this day.

"You're always helping her out. I'm sure she'll be there for you."

"Yeah," Zienna repeated. But a part of her was wondering if Nicholas was choosing not to be there for her because of their disagreement on Monday night. Was he still upset with her on some level?

"Let me know how it goes," he said.

What was there to let him know? It was going to be a bad day, a painful one—which was why she wanted him there for emotional support.

"All right," Zienna said, "I have to go. I have to pick up the flowers before I head to the graveside."

"Do me a favor."

"What?" she asked.

"Promise you'll take Alexis with you to the cemetery. I hate the idea of you facing this day alone."

That's why I asked you, Zienna thought, but didn't say. Instead she replied, "Sure. I will."

Zienna didn't ask Alexis. Instead, she picked up the floral arrangement she'd ordered for her parents, then made her way to the cemetery alone.

Ten years. It was a long time, and yet in so many ways it seemed like yesterday. Maybe it was better that she be here alone for quiet reflection. And to spend time with her parents the only way she could.

Her folks had been married for twenty-five years before that awful day. They'd died way too young, only forty-nine. The only bright side was that they'd been together in the end.

"Hey Mom, hey Dad," Zienna said quietly as she worked the legs of the stand she'd brought into the soil between the

two graves. She pushed them in deep so that the arrangement
would be secure. Then she stood back to look at it, and her
lips curled in a small smile. The flowers had been pricey, but
entirely worth it. Close to one hundred white roses had been
crafted in the shape of a heart. It was fitting for how she'd
felt about her parents, and how they'd felt about each other.

Satisfied, Zienna eased down onto the grass. She was shaded
by the branches of a willow tree, and had a view of a pond
not far off. Graceland Cemetery was beautiful and serene, and
while her heart was aching, she also felt a sense of peace here
because of the elegant landscaping.

"Wow," she said. "It's been ten years. I can't believe it. Ten
years since you've been gone." She pulled her knees to her
chest. "I can't believe I've been here doing it on my own for
so long, without you."

Moments passed before she spoke again. "I've needed you
over the years."

She needed someone. Someone to talk to about life and
love other than Alexis. Her sister would have been the obvious choice—if she hadn't disappeared, unable to cope with
her own grief.

"You both seemed to have it so together when it came to
love. Sure, things weren't perfect. But you adored each other."
Zienna paused. "I guess you've seen the mess I've gotten myself
into. Two men. Maybe you're ashamed of me. But I didn't set
out to do this. I don't know what I'm doing, and I'm the first
to admit it. It's just…I always wanted Wendell. Always. Something inside just told me he was my perfect guy. But he broke
my heart and I had to move on. I didn't know I was going to
meet his friend. And I really think Nicholas is a wonderful
catch—dedicated, hardworking. And he loves me."

She paused again as she pulled some weeds from the grass
over her mother's grave. "But if he loves me as much as he says

he does, shouldn't he be here with me now? On a day that's so important to me? I was with him through all of his struggles getting a second restaurant open. I canceled appointments at my clinic so I could be there for him. Couldn't he leave his restaurant to someone else's care just for today?"

As she said the words, she realized that was what was bothering her. It wasn't just that she'd wanted Nicholas to come with her and he wasn't able to. It was the fact that she had sacrificed for him to see his dream come to fruition, and if he cared for her, why wasn't he here for her now? She wasn't asking for a day-long commitment. Just a couple of hours to be here with her as things got rough. To hold her, let her cry on his shoulder. To show her that she didn't have to be alone anymore.

Instead, she felt more alone than ever.

Zienna stretched out on the grass across both graves, using her hands as a makeshift pillow. And the tears began to fall in earnest. She had been twenty-five when she'd lost her parents. Barely an adult on her own, and definitely not ready to handle all the responsibilities that came with planning a funeral. It had seemed so surreal. So unbelievable that she had lost both parents in one sudden, tragic moment. Tabitha, only twenty-one, had been so lost in her pain that she'd been incapable of helping with any of the planning. Thank God for Aunt Christine and Uncle Ned, her mother's sister and brother-in-law from Ohio, who had come to her rescue. They had helped make all the arrangements. They had been there with her and her sister on that awful rainy day when the two caskets had been lowered into the ground, one beside the other.

Zienna cried like a baby now, remembering all that she had lost, and wishing so desperately that that one moment in time could be erased. It had taken her years to fully grasp that her parents were no longer with her. And yes, as people said, it got easier. But it didn't get better. How could the world be better when her parents were gone?

"Hey."

She heard a voice, and thought she had imagined it.

"Zee."

At the sound of her name, her eyes flew open. As she looked upward, the world suddenly seemed surreal.

Wendell?

He lowered himself onto his haunches in front of her. "Hey," he repeated.

Zienna wasn't imagining him. He was actually here.

Slowly, she sat up and stared at him in awe, her heart thudding.

"Wendell... What... I don't understand."

"I went to the clinic. My doctor said I'll likely need surgery, but I'm hoping I won't. I wanted to see you, talk to you about it. Anyway, Jamie said you weren't there. She told me about the anniversary and that you'd be at the cemetery. It took me a while to find you—this place is huge."

"Jamie just gave you all that information?"

Wendell's eyes held hers as his lips lifted in a small smile. "I can be very convincing."

His words made her think of what Nicholas had said, that Wendell had a way with women. But she pushed that thought from her mind and concentrated on the fact that he was here.

He was here, and Nicholas was not.

Wendell reached forward and wiped at her tears with the pad of his left thumb. She looked at his arm in the sling. "How's your shoulder?"

"It still hurts, but I can move it. The sling's to help keep the pressure off so I don't make it any worse. But don't worry about that right now. How are you holding up?"

"It's a tough day," she told him.

"Yeah." Wendell spoke softly. "I know."

"Why are you here?" she asked.

"I told you I didn't come back for the sex. I came back for you."

The words made her heart lift with joy, even amid her pain.

He moved to sit beside her, then slipped his good arm around her waist. "I've got one good shoulder," he told her. "Feel free to use it. If you want to cry, vent, go ahead. I know how it is to want to talk about the loved ones you've lost, and not everyone gets it. It's only been a little over a year since I lost Jeremiah. And I can tell you, I really hate when people pat you on the back and tell you that you're going to get over it."

"Oh, God. I know."

"There's no getting over something so devastating."

"Absolutely not," Zienna said. "I know how awful it was to lose both my parents at the same time. But nothing compares to losing a child...."

Wendell nodded, then glanced away, and Zienna could tell he was fighting emotion. Instinctively, she slipped both her arms around his waist and leaned her head against his shoulder. The two of them sat there like that, each giving and receiving quiet comfort.

"On this day," Zienna found herself saying, "I always feel so alone. But with you here, I don't feel like that."

"Wow. Nick actually chose work over you?" Wendell shook his head.

"It's a busy day at the restaurant. He says he couldn't get away."

"Yeah, I know. The hockey VIPs." He rolled his eyes. "If he loves you, he should be here for you on a day like this. Shit, man. Someone else could tend to the team owners. Nick should be here tending to you."

Zienna glanced up at Wendell. Yes, Nicholas was the one

who should be here, yet it was Wendell sitting beside her and holding her now.

"What about you and your sister? You talking again?"

Now Zienna's eyes narrowed. "You remember that?"

"I remembered that this year was the ten-year anniversary of your parents' passing. So yeah, I remember what you told me about your sister. I know how hurt you were by losing her from your life. How could I forget that?"

A strange feeling of warmth spread over Zienna. Here she was, at the graves of her parents, who had been deeply in love. And now Wendell was with her, showing her that he undoubtedly cared. Was this a sign? A sign that the two of them were destined to be together?

"Has she come back into your life?" Wendell asked.

Zienna shook her head. "No. She's still in California, or wherever she went. She's completely cut me off. It's been easier for me to block her from my mind altogether. Not talk about her."

Wendell took Zienna's hand in his and squeezed. "Okay. We don't have to talk about her."

"But I appreciate you asking," she said quickly.

"I understand. I'm just sorry you had to lose her, too."

Zienna's eyes filled with tears. He understood. He truly did. She had two feet firmly over the fence now, the feelings she'd had for Wendell in the past creeping back into her heart.

"I don't know what Nick was thinking. All I can say is that when I heard you were here, I came right away. Actually, I called Nick, but they said he was attending to some VIPs at the restaurant, and wasn't with you. Then I came straight here."

Zienna stared into Wendell's eyes. She saw genuine affection as opposed to lust.

"I don't want to think about Nicholas."

"Tell me something good about your parents."

Zienna thought. "Sunday mornings," she said finally, smiling with the memory. "After church, we always stopped at a restaurant for brunch. My mom was thankful that she didn't have to slave over a hot stove for us. She would jokingly say that Sunday was when she got her day pass from jail. We used to have so much fun at those brunches. My dad became a big goofball. He'd joke and tickle me and my sister. We just... we had a lot of fun. We were together, and we were happy. It was always a great day."

As Zienna finished her story, she was smiling. Which, she realized, was exactly what Wendell intended.

She kissed him on the cheek, then snuggled against his body. And they stayed there like that, the two of them holding each other for a long while.

And in his arms, Zienna found a little peace on a day that typically brought her nothing but pain.

23

When Wendell suggested that he follow Zienna home from the cemetery to spend a bit more time with her, she didn't refuse.

"It won't be about getting you into bed," he assured her. "I just don't think you should be alone. I can make you something to eat. Hang out for a bit."

Zienna nodded. "I'd like that."

She had told him that they had to stop seeing each other, but she wasn't going to feel guilty about spending time with him—not today, when he was being the friend she needed. And not when Nicholas hadn't been there for her.

She led the way back to her building. She parked, and while Wendell searched for an available meter, she waited for him on the sidewalk. He found a spot about thirty feet down the block. He jogged back over to her, slipped his arm around her waist, and then the two of them walked into the apartment building together.

They were silent on the way up to her condo, Zienna simply leaning into Wendell's body for comfort. The day had been draining, but his appearance had lightened the heaviness.

"You tell me what you want to eat, I'll make it," Wendell began as they were walking down the hallway.

"I didn't know you were a cook."

"I'm not a chef like Nick, but I can hold my own in the kitchen. Don't forget, I opened up a restaurant in Texas."

"Yeah, that's right." When Nicholas had told her that, she hadn't been interested in hearing the story. Zienna began to unlock her door. "I don't have a lot in the fridge. But I don't expect you to cook for me. We can order—"

She stopped dead in her tracks. Because barely ten feet away, sitting on her sofa, was Nicholas.

"Oh my God," she cried. Her head swam. She was shocked. Mortified. "Nicholas… What are you doing here? How did you get in?"

His face contorted with anger. "So I tell you I can't go with you to the cemetery, and you call Wendell," he said, not answering her question. "You don't even skip a beat."

"That—that's not how it happened," Zienna stammered. "It's not what you think."

"Zee needed someone," Wendell explained. "When I found out you weren't with her, I went to make sure she was okay."

"How fucking sweet of you," Nicholas snapped. "Of course, you never said shit to me about your plan." He was clutching a bouquet of flowers, but now tossed it violently to the ground.

Zienna flinched. Then she placed her purse and keys on her foyer table and turned to Wendell. "Go. Please."

"Not when Nick looks like he's about to have a meltdown. Maybe it's time—"

"No!" She widened her eyes, imploring him not to do what

she feared he was suggesting. "Just go, Wendell." She shoved him out the door. *"Go."*

"You want your boyfriend to stay, let him stay," Nicholas said.

Zienna closed the door, then turned to Nicholas. Her chest was heaving. "I asked you how you got in here."

"You have a key to my place. Why can't I have a key to yours?"

"So you took my keys and made a copy—without asking me?"

"Sure, that's the issue," Nicholas retorted. "Not that you've been screwing my best friend!"

Zienna drew in a deep breath, but it failed to calm her. "Nicholas—"

"Don't lie to me." His nostrils flared. "Don't you fucking lie to me."

Zienna swallowed, but said nothing.

"Women used to talk to me about Wendell's stamina. How he could go hard and fast for hours." Nicholas began walking toward her. "When they'd try to get me to talk to him on their behalf, confused as to why he'd stopped calling them. They didn't get that Wendell always was, first and foremost, motivated by his cock. And having a different pussy on it every day of the week."

Zienna's heart thudded.

"Is that what made you fuck around on me?" Nicholas asked. "You prefer his cock to mine?"

"For God's sake, Nicholas. He went to the clinic about his shoulder. Jamie told him I was at the cemetery. He wanted to be there for me. I guess because he lost his son, he understood how hard this day would be for me." Zienna couldn't meet Nicholas's eyes as she spoke.

"Of course." His tone was saccharine sweet. "That's all it was. It has nothing to do with the fact that you're banging him every chance you get. Not at all."

"Nicholas, can we just sit down?"

"Ah, now I know what it is," he said, snapping his fingers. "All this time, I should have been using an ice cube. Ice cube on the clit. Never knew you would like that so much."

A chill swept over Zienna's body. Then her stomach clenched, and she hardly breathed as she stared at Nicholas. Dread filled her as she took in everything about him. The set of his eyes, the smugness in his expression.

How did he know? Surely Wendell wouldn't have told him...

"What?" Nicholas asked with feigned innocence. "You look surprised."

"Why would you...why would you say that?" She barely got the question out. How would he know that unless Wendell had told him? God help her, had she been a pawn in a game between friends? Was she the fool?

Now Nicholas smirked. "You're not going to deny it?" After a moment, he shrugged. "Though I can tell you, video evidence doesn't lie."

Zienna gasped. If he had just kicked her, she would have been less shocked.

God, no. God, no. Oh, my God.

"I knew something was up," Nicholas said calmly. "I followed Wendell one night. Saw him coming here after midnight. I stayed in my car for four hours, waiting until he came back down. Don't bother telling me you were playing a late night game of Scrabble."

Oh, God.

"Then, of course, there was that night when I told you I

couldn't see you, and I knew, just knew, you'd run off to Wendell. Oh, you remember. The night when I called you and said I'd changed my mind, that I wanted to come over after work. You made up some bullshit story about being asleep. But I was in your apartment. I knew you weren't here. I knew you were with him."

Zienna's knees buckled, but somehow she didn't collapse. Her breathing ragged, she gripped the back of her sofa.

"The next day, I set up a camera in your bedroom. You'd be amazed at how tiny they are these days, how inconspicuous."

"I—I'm sorry," Zienna said.

"You're sorry?" He gave her a disbelieving look.

"I…I was going to tell you. I wanted to tell you Monday night, at your place. But I…I didn't know how."

"Yeah, right."

"I know I was wrong. But you need to know I didn't plan this. I—I don't know how it happened. All I know is there were times I needed you and you weren't there, and he was."

"So that's all it takes for you to fuck around on your boyfriend? Because I was working hard for a future for both of us? Shit, Zee—I've been killing myself with the opening of the new restaurant, and you can't allow me any leeway? You've got to go find someone else to fuck?"

Tears filled Zienna's eyes. "That's not how it was."

"Wendell is my best friend, for God's sake. Why him?"

"I didn't want to hurt you. And I definitely pushed him away as much as I could. I kept saying no."

"Until what—he held a gun to your head and made you screw him?"

Zienna was shaking and crying now. Sobbing like a baby.

At least a minute passed before Nicholas spoke. And when he did, he said something Zienna didn't expect.

"The hell of it is, I still love you."

She looked up at him through her tears, saw that the fight was gone out of his eyes.

"Yeah," he said softly. "I still love you. And you might find this harder to believe. But I forgive you."

Zienna was baffled. "You do?"

He slipped his arms around her and pulled her close. "That's what love does. It makes you want to forgive a person. No matter what they've done to hurt you."

"I don't understand."

"I know I wasn't there for you today," he said. "And I'm sorry. It was an important day for you, a tough day, and I should have been with you at the cemetery. I should have been with you all day, if that's what you wanted. I've been consumed with my work, and neglected you in the process. I failed at being a good boyfriend, so I have to accept the blame for making you vulnerable to temptation. Wendell knew your weakness, and he pounced on it."

Zienna was too shocked to speak.

Nicholas cradled her in his arms, then kissed her temple. "I've never loved anyone as much as I love you," he whispered. "Please don't leave me."

Zienna's mind was spinning, unable to process what she was hearing. After a long moment, she said, "You cut a key to my place without asking. You came in here and...and you hid a camera." Just saying the words made her feel sick. "I don't understand."

Nicholas eased back, took her by the shoulders and stared into her eyes. "Because I had to know. The suspicion was driving me crazy. I'm not saying it was right, but fucking my best friend... Which is the greater of the two evils?" He gave her a pointed look. "Look, it's out in the open now. We can move forward. Put this behind us."

He made it sound so simple. But the issue wasn't only her cheating.

"You got mad at me Monday night when I bit you. But I saw Wendell do that to you. And you liked it."

Zienna spun around. "Oh, God."

"I'm just saying, I want to please you the way you need to be pleased."

Zienna faced him again. "Do you know how violated I feel?"

"I'll burn the video," Nicholas quickly offered. "We can do it together."

"I can't deal with this," Zienna said. "I—I can't."

"I'm telling you we can get through this," he replied.

"Go," Zienna told him. She needed to lie down. She needed to scream. Needed to cry.

"We have to talk this through," Nicholas insisted.

"I can't even look at you right now."

He reached for her. "Come on, baby—"

"Go!" she shouted. "Get out of my apartment!"

The door flung open, startling them both. Zienna looked toward the foyer in fright. Wendell was stalking into the apartment.

"Wendell…" She couldn't take any more surprises. "I told you to leave."

"And I did. I stood outside the door to make sure things were okay in here." His eyes volleyed from her to Nicholas, then back to her. "*Are* you okay?"

"I want to be alone."

Nicholas started toward Wendell. "First you fuck my girl, then you interrupt us when we're working things out?"

"You need to tell the whole truth," Wendell said. "Have you told her the whole truth?"

Something akin to hatred flickered in Nicholas's eyes. "My patience with you is wearing real thin."

Zienna's eyes narrowed. Her heart beat out of control as she listened to Wendell and Nicholas. What was going on here? Wendell straightened his spine. He was letting Nicholas know that he was standing firm, that he wasn't going to back down. "Does she know?" he asked, his tone grave.

"Yes, she knows everything, and I know everything," Nicholas retorted. "And we're trying to work shit out. Now, if you don't fucking leave voluntarily, I'm going to make you."

"Wendell, just go," Zienna said.

Wendell's eyes widened with incredulity. "You're choosing Nicholas? Is that what you're telling me?"

She crossed her arms over her chest. "This isn't helping."

"You need to know the truth. About everything. Not the edited version—"

Out of nowhere, Nicholas punched him in the gut. Wendell keeled forward, groaning.

"Nicholas!" Zienna shrieked.

Wendell straightened and faced him, his chest heaving. He finally reacted, taking a swing with his left arm that landed on Nicholas's jaw. Nicholas's head flew back violently.

"Stop!" Zienna cried. She rushed forward, jumping between the two men, hoping she could calm them down. But Nicholas took a punch, oblivious of her, as his own rage was all that mattered to him. As he swung at Wendell again, he caught her on the side of the face with his elbow.

Zienna cried out in pain and buckled over. She dropped to her knees and tears filled her eyes.

Wendell instantly went to her side. "Zienna, are you okay?"

Nicholas grabbed him by the shirt and hauled him backward. Then he took his place at Zienna's side. "Baby, I'm sorry! Are you okay? I'm so sorry."

Zienna straightened, saying, "Don't touch me. Both of you—you're acting like idiots."

She nursed her jaw. Damn, it hurt. Nicholas looked mortified that he'd hurt her. "You know I didn't do that on purpose. I'm sorry, baby."

She moved away from him. "This is not okay. The way the two of you are behaving... I know I'm at the root of this, but violence?"

Wendell took a step toward her. "No, you're not to blame. That's what I want you to know. You and me...us meeting... it wasn't an accident."

"Shut up, Wendell," Nicholas warned.

Wendell faced him with resolution in his eyes. "This is your chance to tell her, bro. Tell her, or I will."

"Fuck you, Wendell. She chose me."

"Nicholas asked me to flirt with you," Wendell blurted out. "He wanted to test you...to know if you'd be faithful."

Zienna's lips parted as confusion spread through her. She stared into Wendell's eyes—eyes that were unflinching.

"What? What did you say?"

"He didn't trust you. He asked me to flirt with you, see if you reciprocated."

Heat began to spread through Zienna as confusion turned to understanding. She faced Nicholas, who was shaking his head, but he could barely meet her eyes.

"Is that true?" She covered her mouth with her hand.

"He's lying," Nicholas said. "He fucks you, now he's pissed you've chosen me. Of course he's got to make shit up."

"Zienna," Wendell said, his tone pleading. "I know I hurt

you. I treated you badly years ago. And I have absolutely nothing to gain by telling you this now, because I'm giving you another reason to be angry with me. But you need to know the truth. Even if it means I lose you forever."

Zienna started to tremble. "What is the truth? That you seduced me as some sort of joke between two old buddies? Some sort of stupid test?" God, she felt like a moron. A complete and utter idiot. She'd fallen for Wendell's charm again, just like a stupid fool. That knowledge hurt more than his betrayal four years ago.

"That was never what it was about for me," he said. "I didn't care about Nick's trust issues. But I used the opportunity to get close to you again. I should have told—"

"Shut the fuck up!" Nicholas hollered, and launched himself at Wendell again. This time, he used the momentum of his body to throw him into the wall, knocking over a lamp in the process. He rammed Wendell's right shoulder against the wall. Once, twice. Wendell howled in pain.

Zienna vaulted toward Nicholas and began to pound on his back. "Let him go! You're going to destroy his arm!"

Finally, he relented, stepping back. Wendell, though wheezing from pain, brought up his left elbow and cocked Nicholas in the face.

"Both of you! Stop this now!" Zienna was crying. "Just fucking stop!"

As she wiped at her tears, she saw the blood. Nicholas's blood. It was pouring from his nose.

"Are you happy now?" She faced each man in turn. "You've both fucked each other up…all because of some stupid game the two of you were playing? With me as some pawn?"

"You weren't a pawn," Wendell said. "Not to me."

He was nursing his injured shoulder, his face full of pain.

Nicholas was holding his nose to stop the flow of blood. But Zienna couldn't afford them any sympathy. "You two want to kill each other, fine. I won't be here to witness it. Be gone when I get back, or I call the police."

She whirled around, then scooped up the purse she'd put on the foyer table.

"Zienna!" Wendell called after her.

"Go fuck yourself!" she retorted, and charged out the door.

24

Zienna drove straight to Alexis's loft with wobbly hands, crying the entire way there. When she got to the building, she followed a man in past the locked door. He glanced briefly over his shoulder at her, then his eyes widened in alarm and concern.

"Are you okay?" he asked.

Zienna didn't answer him. Instead, she ran to the end of the hallway and took the stairs up to Alexis's floor two at a time.

She pounded on her door. "Alex, it's me." She knew her friend would be home, because she'd been keeping a low profile after the incident with Brock. "Open up!"

Moments later, the door flew open while Zienna was in midknock. The moment Alexis took in her appearance, her eyes nearly bulged out of her head. "Zee, holy shit! You're bleeding!"

She was? Zienna looked down, following Alexis's line of sight, and saw that there was blood spattered on her shirt. Then she stepped forward, and Alexis threw her arms around her, and Zienna started to sob.

★ ★ ★

Zienna spent the next half hour telling Alexis everything. The lies, the deception, the pact between two friends to see if she would cheat. The video, or *videos,* that Nicholas had secretly taken of her in bed with Wendell.

"I'm such a fool," Zienna sobbed. "I trusted Nicholas. I trusted Wendell. And they both deceived me."

"Here," Alexis said, offering the cup of tea Zienna had not yet touched. "Drink."

She took the mug and tasted the tea, which was now lukewarm. Even so, sipping it made her aware of the broken skin on her upper lip, a lip that was now swollen because of Nicholas's elbow.

"I don't want anything," Zienna said. "I just want to crawl into a hole and never come back out."

"You don't mean that."

"Yes, I do. I feel...I feel violated."

"Yeah, that's pretty bad. But him *asking* Wendell to hit on you? What did Nicholas have to say for himself?"

"He said Wendell was lying. Making stuff up to come between us. Not that he needs to... Nicholas has done enough on his own for me to never want to talk to him again. My God, he watched me and Wendell having sex. And he had the nerve to imply that he could learn from what he'd seen to better please me. How sick is that?"

"It is a little creepy."

"And Wendell..." Zienna's chest tightened painfully. "I knew, just *knew* that I shouldn't trust him again." She stifled a sob. "I knew it."

"I'm not so sure," Alexis said gently. "He's the one who told you about this plan. And he also said that he *didn't* go after you because of Nicholas."

"How do I know what's real?" she countered. "How?"

Alexis shrugged. "What does your heart say?"

Zienna considered the question. She thought about Wendell being with her at the cemetery. How caring he had been. How much comfort she had drawn from his presence. That had been real…hadn't it?

But even so, he had deceived her on some level. She needed all the facts before she would know what to believe.

"I don't know," she finally said. "Right now, I'm just… confused. And hurt."

"Hey, it's okay," Alexis told her. "You don't have to know anything right now. It's been a doozy of a day for you. Obviously, whatever plan Nicholas had with Wendell backfired, because they came to blows. I think it's safe to say that both men want you."

"I never wanted to come between their friendship," Zienna said, feeling a fresh bout of pain. "Everything's gotten out of hand. I can't imagine the two of us letting a man come between us."

"It'll blow over," Alexis assured her. "And until it does, feel free to stay here."

"Thank you," Zienna said. Then she curled up in a ball on the sofa and closed her eyes.

She must have drifted off, because she awoke to darkness and the sounds of soft voices. At first, she thought she was dreaming. And then she was certain.

There were two distinct voices in the loft. One belonged to Alexis, while the other was male.

Slowly, Zienna sat up. There was one dimmed lamp on in the living room, and she had a blanket covering her. She got up, following the sounds of the voices to Alexis's bedroom.

If Brock was in there…

She placed her palm on the door, pushing it open. And then she got the shock of her life.

Elliott was sitting on the bed with her friend, his hand resting casually on her thigh.

"Hey," Alexis said, looking in her direction. "Did we wake you?"

"Elliott?" Zienna asked.

"Hey, Zee." He raised a hand in greeting. "I hear you had a rough day."

"I told him it's the ten-year anniversary of your parents' accident," Alexis quickly said, with a slight nod. Zienna understood that she hadn't told Elliott about all her drama with Wendell and Nicholas.

"I'm really sorry," Elliott said. "I know it had to have been a hard anniversary to face."

"Yeah," Zienna agreed. She didn't get too close, hoping that standing in the darkness just outside the bedroom door would keep him from noticing her busted lip. "It's good to see you."

"Alex and I are talking," Elliott explained.

"Seeing if we can work things out," Alexis added.

Zienna's eyes widened slightly. "Oh. Wow." Alexis hadn't told her this news, because she'd been an emotional mess when she'd arrived. "That's great."

"Do you want something to eat?" Alexis asked.

"Actually, I wanted to tell you that I'm going to get going."

"Are you sure?"

"Um-hmm."

Alexis left Elliott sitting on the bed and joined Zienna, closing the door behind her. "You don't have to leave because of him."

"Elliott?" Zienna said in a whisper. "You never said a thing."

"I...I couldn't. Not earlier."

"So, are you getting back together?"

Alexis began to walk away from the bedroom so that Elliott wouldn't overhear them. She drew in a breath as a smile came on her lips. "It's looking promising."

"But...I thought you said he was too boring?"

"Excitement is overrated." She gave Zienna a knowing look. "The truth is, I realize I never stopped loving Elliott. I just thought...I thought I wanted something more."

"I'm happy for you guys," Zienna said.

"It's not a done deal yet."

Maybe not, but the light was back in Alexis's eyes. Zienna had no doubt that they would resolve things.

Maybe she'd simply needed this time to truly discover what she needed.

"But he understands why I broke his heart, and he knows about Brock. And he loves me despite it."

"That is definitely the best news I've heard all day."

Alexis beamed. "You really don't have to go. Elliott's not going to stay the night."

"It's okay. I'll just head home. Give you both some privacy for as long as you need it." She winked. "Tell Elliott I'll see him next time."

"Okay." Alexis hugged her. "Call me if you need me."

"I will."

Just as Zienna was about to turn into the drive at her building, she saw a black Infiniti SUV parked on the street. Her stomach fluttered. Then she eyed the license plate to be sure.

Nicholas...

And he was parked facing the driveway so he would see her returning.

By the time Zienna turned into the lot, Nicholas was jumping out of his car. He rushed over to her vehicle and tapped on the back window.

Zienna debated hitting the gas, but instead stopped the car. He came to the driver's side and motioned for her to put the window down.

Reluctantly, she rolled down the window. "You shouldn't be here, Nicholas."

"So you don't want to talk to me? Hear my side of things?"

Zienna sighed. "What you did— What you and Wendell did—"

"He's trying to stir up trouble," Nicholas said. "Why would it even make sense for me to suggest that he hit on you? For God's sake, we're not in college anymore."

Zienna simply stared at him, not sure what to believe. Then someone pulled up behind her and hit the horn, trying to pass.

"Let me get in the car with you," Nicholas said.

Zienna hit the power button to unlock all the doors, and Nicholas jumped in. She began to drive before he had properly closed the door.

"I didn't want to wait in your apartment," he said. "I wanted to respect…what you said."

Zienna didn't respond, just parked her car. They walked in silence, making their way upstairs to her unit.

Only when she opened her apartment door and went inside did Nicholas speak again. "I tried to clean up."

"I see." The blood that had dripped onto the floor was gone, the broken lamp as well, and the flowers Nicholas had trashed had also been cleaned up. But it would be a long time before Zienna could erase the ugly scene from her memory.

"Your lip," Nicholas said, looking at her. "God, Zee, I'm sorry."

"You should be," she quipped. Then she walked into her living room where she plopped down on the sofa.

Nicholas sat on the armchair across from her. "Wendell and I have had a complicated relationship. More than once when we were in college, we dated the same girl. I'm not talking about the girlfriend who cheated on me with him. I'm talking about other girls. Ones we didn't care about. And sometimes, we went to bed with the same girl at the same time. College stuff. You know. When you're young and there are no repercussions."

"I have no clue what you're trying to tell me."

"I'm trying to explain…explain where I think Wendell was coming from. Maybe he thought that what was okay in the past would be okay now."

Zienna gaped at him. "So you're saying that Wendell was just following your old tradition of sharing women by sleeping with me?"

"Maybe. I don't know. I've been trying to figure out for the last few hours why he would say what he did."

"He said you *told* him to flirt with me."

"Which is a lie. Wendell is trying to stir up shit."

"Which is it?" Zienna asked skeptically. "Was he simply following your old tradition, or is he deliberately lying?"

Nicholas got up from his seat and sat beside her. "It's obvious now that he still wanted you. You were involved before, and maybe he thought it would be cool if you guys hooked up again."

"And what—he thought you would give him his blessing?" Zienna said in disbelief.

"As crazy as that sounds, yeah. Although maybe I put the idea in his head."

"So you're admitting it?" Zienna's chest heaved.

"I said something to him about 'didn't you look good,' and he said yeah, that you still had it going on." Nicholas shrugged. "I don't know. Maybe he misconstrued things."

Zienna wanted to slap him. "Essentially, you're telling me that I'm like a piece of property to you. That you maybe inadvertently gave Wendell the okay to *sample* me?"

"What I'm saying is that I fucked up. I know I did. Whether I said something to Wendell and he ran with it, or just the fact that when I knew about the two of you I should have told you. I know I was wrong. I didn't behave rationally."

"Understatement of the decade."

"So you screw around with Wendell before you know what his motives are, and I forgive you. But I screw up, and you're ready to dump me?"

Zienna said nothing. Nicholas's words hit her hard. Was she being unfair?

"Honestly, Zienna. We were in a relationship. Almost six months. I was talking about having a future with you. And what did you do? You started an affair with my best friend."

Zienna swallowed. "I never said I was innocent in all this."

Nicholas raised an eyebrow. "From where I'm sitting, you're sure acting that way." He paused. "I know I was wrong. I own that. But what about you? You don't think you hurt me?"

"I…I didn't say that."

"You didn't have to."

A few moments of silence passed. "I'm confused, Nicholas. I'm not saying it's over—but I sure as hell don't like that side of you I saw tonight. That sneaky, controlling side."

"I was the only one who was sneaky?" he countered.

Again, his words made her consider her own actions and how she was coming across. "I know," she said after a moment. "You think I don't realize that, because of my actions, two men who claimed to be best friends came to blows tonight? I know I'm not blameless. Maybe this will sound stupid, or naive, but I never wanted to come between you and Wendell."

"I can't stay friends with someone who would disrespect me by getting involved with you. Sandra...that was college, and she didn't mean to me what you do. Not even close. So don't blame yourself for the loss of our friendship. Wendell's the one to blame. I told you that he and I always seemed to be in competition. Whether it was on the football field or with women. Sometimes rivalries between friends cause them to do really stupid things."

"Still, maybe I need to take a step back from the situation and let you two work things out."

Nicholas looked crestfallen. "I thought you loved me."

Zienna faced him. "That was before I knew that I was some sort of prize in your game of one-upmanship."

"So you're not going to forgive me. I can forgive your infidelity, but you can't forgive me."

"I...I just need time. And so do you. I don't care what you say, one day you might regret that a girl came between you and Wendell. All I'm saying is that you both need to figure out your friendship. Take a few days to work it out. And I need a few days to collect my thoughts. I'm not saying that we won't work it out. I just need a breather. We all do."

Nicholas faced her, and she saw the resignation that came into his eyes. He didn't look pissed off. Instead, he nodded.

Then he gently ran a hand along her cheek. "Okay. I hear what you're saying, and it makes sense. I know that we both scared you. It was a lot of drama."

Zienna reached up and touched Nicholas's face, examining the injury he'd suffered. He had a small Band-Aid on the bridge of his nose, and his cheek was swollen. "I can't feel any worse for what happened tonight," she said softly. "I know I'm to blame for this. If I didn't fall into bed with him…"

"All we can do right now is forgive each other. Forgive each other and move on. The worst is behind us."

25

Zienna spent the next few days examining her life and what she wanted. She was both relieved and disappointed that she hadn't heard from Wendell. Perhaps it was for the best, though the fact that he hadn't reached out made it clear to her that he'd been playing some sort of sick game.

On the other hand, she continued to talk things out with Nicholas, and he assured her he would do whatever he needed to earn back her trust. He even encouraged her to change the locks on her apartment so he wouldn't be able to gain access. He had taken down the hidden camera before he left her place the night they'd tried to clear the air, making her feel marginally better.

In her conversation with Nicholas, she learned that Wendell hadn't been back to work at the restaurant. And he hadn't returned any of Nicholas's calls. "The way I see it," Nicholas had said, "this proves that he simply came back to cause trouble."

"Yeah," Zienna had agreed, though her heart was hurting. "It seems you're right."

She hadn't been able to tell Nicholas that she was grieving the loss of Wendell again. And she certainly couldn't tell him what she'd come to realize was true—that she had fallen in love with him once more.

And as the fourth day after the ugly incident rolled around, Zienna agreed to have dinner with Nicholas at his place.

He had made a valid point. He had forgiven her. Shouldn't she at least try to forgive him?

Zienna was driving to Nicholas's place when she called Alexis, letting her know what was going on, and that she'd made the decision to forgive Nicholas.

"Are you sure about this?" her friend asked.

"Yes." Zienna swallowed. "Yes, I'm sure. I thought about everything, and it's clear this whole ugly situation is my fault. I was the cheater. If I hadn't gotten involved with Wendell, none of this would have happened."

"I get that you have to own your part in this. I totally get it. But I guess what I'm really asking is do you want things to work out with Nicholas? Or is your heart still with Wendell?"

"I haven't even heard from Wendell. Which tells you where *his* heart is."

"So you're reconciling with Nicholas by default?"

"Gee, thanks, Alex."

"I'm not trying to upset you. I'm trying to make you think. Because Nicholas deserves a woman who can give him her whole heart. And after you got involved with Wendell, it seems obvious—at least to me—that Wendell always had your heart and easily reclaimed it."

"It's just not that simple," Zienna said. "At the end of the day, Wendell is a player. I can't lose sight of that."

"Yet when you were involved with him, I'd really never seen you happier."

Zienna felt annoyed. She wanted Alexis's support. "Elliott has forgiven you, and the two of you are working things out. You have your good guy back. I thought you of all people would understand my decision."

"Elliott and I never stopped loving each other," Alexis pointed out. "I…did my own thing, and it ultimately made me realize I already had the perfect guy. If you search in your heart, do you believe Nicholas is your perfect guy?"

"Why can't you just support my decision?"

"Because I think you're not making a decision you want," Alexis said. "Just one by default."

Zienna groaned. Alexis was her best friend, and at the end of the day, she didn't want her to sugarcoat anything. But her comments were making things all the more complicated for Zienna. Two months ago, Alexis had been Nicholas's biggest supporter. And she knew that Zienna's relationship with Nicholas had been derailed only because of the resurgence of Wendell in her life.

"The way I see it," Zienna began, "if Nicholas is generous enough to forgive me, then I would be fool to do anything other than accept his forgiveness. I could take more time to figure out where my heart is at, but you know what? Following my heart has only gotten me into problems. No, I'm done with that. Nicholas is a good man who was pushed to extremes because he loves me. And Wendell…well, he hasn't shown me that he's anything other than a guy who can make me come consistently. I got distracted by that. And I'm ashamed of myself."

"Are you sure that's how you feel?" Alexis asked. "Are you sure that's what you want?"

Suddenly, Zienna was sure. "Yes. Yes, I'm sure. As they say, don't look a gift horse in the mouth. I think I've found the right guy for me."

"Well, if you're certain," Alexis began, "then you know you have my absolute support."

"Thanks, Alex. That means a lot."

"Love you, Zee."

"I love you, too."

Zienna pulled into the driveway of Nicholas's large home. Her shoulders felt lighter, now that she'd made her decision.

She couldn't expect that she and Nicholas would pick up where they'd left off, and that everything would be instantly wonderful between them. But they would work at it, and she was sure they would get there.

Zienna went to the door and rang the bell. She could use her key, but decided against it. She wanted a fresh start, a clean slate, and not to act as though everything was the way it used to be.

About a minute passed and there was no response. Zienna rang the bell again, and also knocked on the door.

Had she heard something? She put her ear against the panel to better hear. There it was again. The sound of something loud, like a bang.

"Nicholas?" she called. "Nicholas, are you okay?"

Getting no response, she quickly got her keys out, opened the door and rushed inside, surveying the immediate area. She didn't see Nicholas.

But then she heard a moan, loud and distinct.

Dropping her purse and keys, Zienna hurried in the direction of the sound. Nicholas was in the living room, curled in a ball on the hardwood floor, a pool of blood seeping from his body.

"Oh my God!" She ran toward him. "Nicholas! Nicholas!"

He tried to roll onto his back, and it was then that she saw the knife stuck in his gut.

Zienna began to scream. "Nicholas! Baby! What happened! Who did this?"

His eyes were rolling backward. But he made a concerted effort to hold her gaze as ragged breaths escaped him.

"Wendell," he said. "Wendell."

And then his eyelids fluttered shut.

His answer chilled her to the core. She stared at Nicholas, at the knife handle and all the blood, and was paralyzed by his words.

Wendell...

"Nicholas?" she said. Her heart spasmed when he didn't respond. She tapped his face. "Wake up, Nicholas. Don't you fall asleep. I'm going to call 911. You stay with me, you hear?"

He didn't respond, and Zienna scrambled to the nearby phone on the end table beside the sofa. She punched in the digits with shaking fingers.

"911 operator. What's your emergency?"

"My boyfriend—he's been stabbed!" Zienna burst into tears. Saying the words made the situation all the more real.

"Ma'am, is he conscious?"

"I think—he was. I don't know. He's not talking to me anymore. There's so much blood!"

"What's your address?"

"Nine-ninety Kingsbury," Zienna began, then realized she was giving her home address. "No, sorry. I'm in Lincoln Park."

She gave the correct address, adding, "Please hurry!" Then she dropped the phone and went back to Nicholas. The knife was stuck in his gut, and she wanted nothing more than to pull it out. But she knew that doing so could cause him to bleed out.

"It's okay, baby," Zienna said. "The ambulance is on its way."

Carefully, she curled up against him, cradling her fingers over his. His warm blood covered her hand, and she gasped.

How could this have happened? And why? She didn't understand. And had Nicholas meant that Wendell was the one who'd hurt him, or had he merely uttered his friend's name?

Zienna didn't want to believe that Wendell could have done something so heinous.

But she also knew that things between them could turn violent. And in the days since the fight at her apartment, the situation had not diffused.

If Nicholas meant what Zienna feared, the situation had in fact escalated.

And now he lay on the floor of his living room, possibly bleeding to death.

"Hold on, baby. Please, hold on."

In the aftermath of the chaos of Nicholas being rushed to Northwestern Memorial Hospital, Zienna was a complete mess. Fifteen minutes into her angst-filled wait, two detectives—a male and a female—came to speak to her about what had happened.

"I don't know," she told them, too distraught to answer any questions. "I got to his house and I found him like that. He was alone, bleeding, lying on the ground. I saw no one."

"And he said nothing to you?" the female detective asked.

Zienna paused briefly. *Wendell...* Then she shook her head. "No." She wanted to make sure that Nicholas was indeed implicating Wendell before she gave that information to the police. "He said nothing I could make any sense of."

Then she went back to waiting. Both for word from the

trauma doctors, and also for Alexis to arrive. Zienna had called her the moment after she'd seen Nicholas wheeled off through the emergency doors.

Finally, she saw Alexis hurry in through the doors of the waiting room. Overwhelmed with emotion, Zienna leaped to her feet, threw her arms around her and began to sob.

"It's okay," Alexis cooed. She ran her hand over Zienna's hair. "Nicholas is going to be fine. I'm sure of it."

Zienna pulled back and looked at her, shaking her head. "I don't know, Alex. It's bad. They think the knife penetrated his spleen. There was a lot of blood. Internal bleeding. He's still in surgery."

Alexis took both her hands, ignoring the blood, and squeezed them. "We're not going to give up, okay? We're not going to think the worst will happen."

Zienna drew in a shaky breath. "Okay."

Alexis urged her down onto the seat she'd vacated, and then sat beside her. In a lowered voice she asked, "What was it you said about Wendell possibly being involved?"

The very idea made Zienna's stomach tighten painfully. "I'm not sure," she said quietly. "I asked Nicholas who hurt him, and he said Wendell's name. And then he passed out. I don't know if he was coherent when he said his name or if...or if he wanted me to call him to let him know what happened."

"Yes," Alexis said emphatically. "I'm sure that's it."

For a moment, Zienna was mollified. Then her eyes filled with tears. "But that fight...it was so ugly. There was so much hatred. And when I found Nicholas, the house wasn't ransacked or anything. Obviously, that means the person who did this to him was someone he knew. Someone he let in."

Alexis squeezed her hand harder. "You're overthinking it. Let's wait until Nicholas is out of surgery. We'll find out what happened then."

By the time Nicholas was out of surgery and able to see Zienna the next day, things only got worse. Because he confirmed her worst fear.

"It was Wendell," he said, and there was no confusion in his voice, in his eyes. "Wendell tried to kill me."

26

Zienna sat at Nicholas's bedside in his hospital room, worrying her bottom lip as he told her the story. Wendell had come over to have it out with him about his relationship with Zienna. They'd gotten into an argument, one that quickly turned into a brawl. Then Wendell, enraged, had grabbed a knife from the kitchen and stabbed Nicholas in the gut.

It was all so hard to believe. So hard to understand.

"I guess it's like Cain and Abel," Nicholas said, his voice weak postsurgery. "Jealousy is ugly, Zee. It can lead people to do the unthinkable."

"I'm so sorry, baby," Zienna told him. It was a mantra she'd been repeating since Nicholas had awakened and asked to see her.

"It's not your fault."

"You know that's not true, Nicholas. If it hadn't been for me getting involved with Wendell, none of this would have happened."

She had fallen for Wendell again—gotten between two

friends—and this was the result. Emotion clogged her throat. "You could have died."

"The doctors saved most of my spleen, and I didn't die. Hey." He linked fingers with hers. "It's okay, baby."

Zienna fought her tears. She had cried so much already. "It's not. None of this is okay. How can I forgive myself for causing this mess?"

"You're here now," Nicholas said, his lips lifting in a soft grin. "That's what matters."

"And I'm not going to leave you." Zienna squeezed his hand. "I want you to know that, okay?" The decision she had made before going to Nicholas's house for dinner was only solidified. "Everything that's happened has made me realize that I got myself in too deep. And I'm so incredibly sorry."

Nicholas raised their joined hands and rubbed the back of hers against his cheek. "It was almost worth it. To know you're here with me now, no more confusion about Wendell. It's almost worth being stabbed."

"Don't say that." Zienna didn't want to feel that what had happened had any benefit. But it had helped her to make up her mind. Obviously, the Wendell she had known was not the real man at all.

Violence? Attempted murder? And because of her? Zienna couldn't believe it.

But her mind ventured back to the day Wendell had come to see her outside her clinic, and she'd told him about the irate client who'd demanded his money back or else.

If you want, I can go rough him up.

Wendell had smiled, as though joking, but maybe he did have a dark side she wasn't aware of.

"What are you thinking, baby?" Nicholas asked, interrupting her thoughts.

"Oh." She faced him. "Just that I'm so happy you're okay."

"Will you stay with me tonight?" Nicholas asked. "You could sleep here. They can bring in a cot for you. I told the nurse you were my fiancée and that I wanted you here."

Fiancée… The word caused the slightest feeling of anxiety within Zienna. She had made her decision—she was choosing Nicholas and a life with him—and yet she was bothered that he was still trying to control things.

Of course she didn't feel happy. How could she, when Nicholas had almost died at Wendell's hands? Cain and Abel, Nicholas had said. Jealousy between two friends who were once as close as brothers had led to attempted murder.

There was a cloud of guilt hanging over Zienna's head, no matter how many times Alexis told her that none of this was her fault. "If they got into this kind of dispute," she had said, "their friendship wasn't that strong. It was bound to happen eventually."

And maybe Alexis was right, because Nicholas had alluded to the sometimes turbulent relationship he'd had with Wendell over the years. The competition between the two men.

The thing was, Zienna wanted closure. She wanted to understand. Hear it from the horse's mouth, as it were. She wanted to yell and scream at Wendell until she understood. Not just why he would attack Nicholas, but why he had hurt her again.

But Zienna also knew that nothing good would come of talking to him. It was time to simply let go and turn her back on Wendell forever.

"Sure," she said, smiling as she stared into Nicholas's eyes. "I'll have to get a couple things done first, but yes, I'll stay here with you tonight."

The police came to interview Nicholas later that morning, and they also had more questions for Zienna. In light of Nicholas telling them about the love triangle between him, Wendell and Zienna, the detectives wanted to know more from her. What was the nature of her relationship with Wendell? Had he ever threatened Nicholas? And did she have any knowledge of what had happened the night Nicholas was stabbed?

"I honestly have no clue what happened that night," Zienna told them. "I wasn't there when the incident played out. And I hadn't heard from Wendell in days. He hadn't called to threaten me or to threaten Nicholas. I can only tell you that I did see the fight between the two of them days earlier at my place. Yes, they both threw punches at each other, but no, I didn't think it would escalate to this."

The female detective, D'Alessandro, then had a private meeting with Zienna to talk about the more sensitive facts. Zienna assumed that her male partner had let Detective D'Alessandro conduct the interview because Zienna might feel more comfortable confiding in a woman about the complex sexual relationship she'd had with two men.

No matter how nonjudgmental the detective seemed, Zienna was hugely embarrassed to have to acknowledge that she had cheated. Professionally, the police only wanted to track down Wendell. But personally, the woman—who sported a wedding ring—had to think ill of her.

But Zienna supposed no one could make her feel worse about herself than she already did. She'd been torn between two men, and one had almost paid the ultimate price for her sins with his life.

Zienna was thirty-five and embroiled in a love triangle. When her parents were thirty-five, they'd already been married for eleven years. All Zienna had ever wanted was what her parents had had. A love that would last a lifetime. It had taken heartache and drama, but she knew now that she wanted Nicholas.

Once again, she didn't make it in to the clinic. She called to cancel all her appointments for the next couple days in order to be with Nicholas. But she did pop home to get a quick bite, shower and change her clothes.

She couldn't have been more surprised when, just before she headed out the door to return to the hospital, her cell phone rang and Wendell's photo and name started flashing on her screen. Her heart began to accelerate.

After days of nothing from him, why was he calling her now? And should she answer?

The phone stopped ringing, and she let out a breath she didn't know she'd been holding. She slipped into her shoes and grabbed her keys.

The phone began to ring again.

This time Zienna didn't think, didn't hesitate. She pressed the answer button and put the phone to her ear. "Hello?"

"Zee."

One word, but her entire body shook from the magnitude of the emotion in his voice. Anguish, desperation and relief mixed together.

"Thank you for answering," Wendell said. "You don't have to talk. I just want you to know that I didn't do what Nicholas is saying I did. I didn't try to kill him."

"You shouldn't be calling me," Zienna told him.

"Zienna, are you hearing me? I didn't stab Nicholas. He asked me to come to his place Sunday evening so we could talk. I did. And I thought we resolved things. Then the next morning I'm getting a message from the police that they want to talk to me? I go to the restaurant and I'm hearing from everyone that Nicholas said I *stabbed* him?"

"I found him," Zienna said angrily. "I found him lying on the living room floor in a pool of blood."

"And I don't know how that happened. I only know that I didn't do it."

"As if you're going to admit to it," she scoffed.

"You really think I'd stab Nicholas?" Wendell asked, sounding dejected.

"Have you talked to the police?" Zienna asked.

"Right. So they can arrest my ass?"

"If you're innocent, why aren't you making your case with them instead of me? I know they went by your place to find you, and you haven't been there."

"Nicholas is saying I tried to *murder* him. They'll lock me up first, ask questions later."

"I don't have time for any games, Wendell. My man nearly died!"

"*Your man* is a liar!"

"You're the liar," Zienna retorted. And yet she didn't totally believe her words. In fact, Wendell's denial gave her heart a little bit of hope. She couldn't have slept with a monster, could she have? Surely she hadn't been so wrong about him....

And yet how could she refute the facts? Nicholas was in the hospital. And he certainly had his wits about him. It couldn't be argued that he'd mistaken what he'd said.

"Nicholas isn't in a coma," Zienna began. "His mind isn't altered because of the medication. He's coherent. In fact, he's quite rational. And he knew what he was talking about when he said you attacked him. He was absolutely clear."

"Then that's even worse than I thought," Wendell said.

"Why?"

"Because it means he's deliberately lying. It means he set me up."

Zienna called Alexis. It was the only thing she could do. She was already confused beyond measure, and Wendell's assertion that Nicholas was lying made her mind an even bigger mess of uncertainty.

Obviously, Nicholas was the one in the hospital. The one who had been stabbed. The trauma he'd suffered to his spleen could have been fatal if not for Zienna finding him when she did.

She had witnessed the rage between Wendell and Nicholas with her own eyes. Did Wendell really expect her to believe he wasn't behind what had happened? Her heart told her he wasn't capable of something so heinous, but her brain said no one else had a reason to attack Nicholas. The stabbing had been up close. Personal.

Zienna tried Alexis a second time when she didn't reach her, but her friend wasn't answering her cell. It was her first day back at work since her visit to the E.R., and she no doubt didn't want to take any personal calls during office hours. So Zienna returned to the hospital, ate a sandwich in the cafeteria, knowing she needed sustenance, then went back upstairs to Nicholas.

When he saw her enter the room, a smile instantly formed on his lips and he stretched out his hand to her.

"I'm glad you're back," he said.

"How do you feel?"

"Like I've been hit by a truck." He groaned in discomfort. "The police say they haven't been able to reach Wendell. Guess he's on the run. I want you to be careful, okay?"

"Of course."

"If he contacts you, call the police immediately. I want to know that you're safe."

Zienna hesitated a beat, then nodded. "All right."

"Because I'd be devastated if anything happened to you."

He's deliberately lying. He set me up....

"You don't really think Wendell would hurt me, do you?" she asked.

"I'm here, aren't I? I never thought he'd try to kill me. And he's gotta be pissed with you." Nicholas squeezed her hand. "I still see him coming at me with the knife. The pure rage in his eyes. I never thought he'd do it. I even said to him, 'Bro, what are you doing? We're best friends.' But there was no getting through to him. He plunged the knife into my gut and told me that he wanted me to die." Nicholas closed his eyes and drew in a shuddery breath, and when he opened them, tears were streaming down his face. "Please, babe. Don't let him deceive you. If you hear from him, call the police. Until he's behind bars, I won't feel that you're safe. Promise me."

Zienna nodded and wiped at his tears. "Okay, sweetie. I hear you. I get it."

"Good. Because I would die if anything happened to you."

"You don't mean that," Zienna said.

"I do," Nicholas said emphatically. "I absolutely do. If Wendell takes you away from me again, I'm as good as dead."

She offered him a smile, hoping he didn't realize she hadn't given him the promise he had asked for.

27

"What does your gut say?" Alexis asked Zienna the next eve
ning. She was with her in the hospital cafeteria. Zienna had
gone home only briefly that day, after Nicholas's parents and
sister had arrived from Kansas City. Once they'd been brought
up to speed and she'd had an awkward first meeting with
them, she had allowed them time to be alone with Nicholas.
But she hadn't wanted to be gone for long, because Nicholas
wanted her close to him all the time.

"My gut?" Could Zienna even trust her gut? "Well, I don't
expect Wendell to say, 'Hey, yeah. I did it.' But the facts don't
lie. Nicholas is in the hospital after a vicious attack."

"And yet Wendell was adamant that he had nothing to do
with it."

"Like I said, I don't expect him to admit that he tried to
kill his friend."

Alexis shook her head. "I don't know. I can't see it. I think
it's entirely possible Nicholas suffered some sort of memory

loss. Maybe he's remembering the fight at your place, not what actually happened that night."

"I'd love to believe that," Zienna said. "No one wants to believe that more than I do. But Nicholas wasn't confused. I—I have to accept what he's saying."

"Because you feel guilty?"

"Excuse me?"

"Nicholas was attacked, and you've barely left his side since. You're back to being the doting girlfriend. And I just wonder, is that because you *want* to be with him, or because you feel guilty?"

"I always wanted to be with him," Zienna said a little testily. "From the time we started dating, I thought he was the man for me. I let Wendell come back and sway my mind. You know that, Alex. Shit."

"And I also know how you were when you were with Wendell. It's like…you had a glow about you. A vibrant spirit. I know that sounds corny, but it's the only way to describe it."

"I was enjoying the excitement of an affair," Zienna said in a lowered voice. "The same kind of excitement you wanted when you got involved with Brock. But look where it got you. And look where my need for a thrill got me. In between two men, with one of them nearly being killed."

Alexis gave her a pointed look. "You know it's not the same thing. Not at all. I was running from Elliott because I thought I needed something else. You ran to Wendell because he was the man you always wanted. That's why I think you're allowing your guilt to make you settle for Nicholas. Because even if you're not with Wendell, you shouldn't be with Nicholas. That's my opinion, as someone who's known you almost your entire life."

"Maybe the truth is that I've just had to grow up real fast.

I'm thirty-five, and nearly had my boyfriend killed because of my affair."

"One minute you say you think Wendell is telling the truth, now you're changing your mind?"

"I'm confused," Zienna snapped. "Is that allowed? Obviously, I don't want to think Wendell could do something like this. But what I'm trying to say is that something like this changes you in an instant. I was uncertain about Nicholas before, but now...now I am sure."

"Are you?" Alexis countered.

"Yes, and I don't appreciate you acting as if you know me better than I know myself."

A beat passed. "Look, I was just trying to give you something to think about. I wasn't trying to be Debbie Downer."

"Good. Because I don't need any more stress over this. Sure, I feel guilty. But I've also made my decision to be with Nicholas."

"I guess I'd just like to see you looking happier about that decision."

"Nicholas was stabbed. He would have died had I not arrived when I did. I found him in a pool of blood and I've never been more afraid in my life. Sorry if I don't feel like breaking out the champagne."

Alexis raised her hands in surrender. "Okay. I'm sorry. I know I'm not making things any easier for you. I'm just... I can't help wondering if Nicholas is wrong, that's all."

"I'm done." Zienna pushed back her chair and stood. "I'm going back upstairs."

"I know, I know. All right, zipping my mouth shut."

"Nicholas's family said they would leave about eight-thirty, so he's probably wondering where I am." Zienna lifted her purse, not meeting Alexis's gaze. "I'll talk to you later."

She didn't bother to give her friend a hug. She just started out of the cafeteria, not looking back.

Alexis's skepticism was the last thing she needed right now. The absolute last thing. Zienna was emotionally drained as it was.

She got to the room, ready to lie down on the cot next to Nicholas and close her eyes. It had been a long day of waiting for further test results, to make sure Nicholas was healing as the doctors hoped, and that there were no complications. And it had been trying, as she'd had to watch Nicholas go through bouts of pain as the medication wore off. Of course Zienna would be by his side. Where else would she be?

She opened the door.

"...times do I have to tell you?" Nicholas asked, sounding irritated. Then he stopped, his eyes immediately volleying toward her. Detectives D'Alessandro and Ford, who were sitting in chairs by Nicholas's bed, also looked in her direction.

"Oh, I'm sorry," Zienna said. "I didn't mean to interrupt."

"The detectives had more questions for me," Nicholas explained. "I'm not sure how long this will take. But you know what? Why don't you go home tonight?"

The detectives were here at this hour? Zienna thought that was strange, but only said, "You want me to go home?"

"It's almost nine. And you told me you have to go back to work tomorrow. So yeah, go home. Get a good night's sleep, and we'll talk later."

"Have you guys found Wendell?" Zienna asked the officers.

"We'll talk about that tomorrow," Nicholas said, before either of them could speak. "I'll fill you in. Okay?"

Zienna eyed him warily. "Okay."

"I'll take a kiss before you go, though."

Zienna approached his bedside and bent to give him a quick

kiss on the lips, feeling awkward doing so in front of the cops. "Is everything okay?" she asked as she eased back.

"Everything's fine. But I'm in some pain and the nurse is going to give me that medication that will knock me out. There's no need for you to be here for the night."

Zienna hadn't expected this. "If you're sure."

"I am." Nicholas stroked her arm. "We can talk in the morning. If I'm up early, I'll give you a call, okay?"

"Okay."

Zienna nodded at the two detectives and left the room. But she couldn't help wondering why they were there again, and at such a late hour.

Zienna was almost home when she realized she needed groceries, so she turned around and headed to Food 4 Less. She bought bread, eggs, milk and other staples—items she hadn't had time to pick up in the days since Nicholas's attack.

She got the shopping done as quickly as possible and returned to her car with her hands full. Just as she finished putting the items in the backseat, she saw a flash of movement in her peripheral vision. She was too stunned to scream. And the next thing she knew, a hand was coming down on her mouth.

"Don't scream," a voice warned her. "Don't struggle."

Wendell! Zienna's heart kicked into triple speed. She shoved her elbow backward, trying to hit him in his belly. She succeeded, but it didn't have much effect. He didn't release his hold on her.

"I told you, Zee, don't struggle. I'm not going to hurt you."

She didn't listen. She strained against him, trying to get away. And after a few seconds, she was surprised that he released her.

She spun around and looked at him, her chest heaving.

"You wanted me to let you go," Wendell began, "I did.

Like I said, I'm not here to hurt you. I'm here to talk to you. To make you understand."

"My God, Wendell, are you out of your mind? Are you following me?"

"I was waiting for you at your apartment. When I saw you make a U-turn and drive away, I followed you. I thought you were heading back to the hospital, and I wanted to talk to you before you did."

"And now you attack me in a parking lot?"

"Attack?"

"Accost. Whatever."

"I had to see you." He took a few steps toward her. "Because I knew that the moment you looked at me, you wouldn't believe that I tried to kill Nicholas."

Zienna took a couple of steps back. "You thought wrong."

"I didn't stab Nicholas. I wanted you, yes. But not like that. Never like that."

Zienna stared at Wendell, her chest rising and falling with each ragged breath. She wanted to scream. Scream for help. For someone to call the police. Instead, she regarded him carefully. "Why would you expect me to believe you?"

"Because I'm telling the truth. And because you know in your heart that I'm not capable of what Nicholas said I did."

"My heart? My heart's clueless! *I'm* clueless. I have no idea who you really are!" Zienna raised her voice louder than she wanted to, but she was infuriated.

"Yes, you do. You know who I am."

Wendell took another tentative step toward her, and this time she didn't move. If he got too close or tried to hurt her in any way, she would scream bloody murder. Someone in the parking lot would surely help her.

"Look at me," Wendell said. "Look in my eyes. Look in my eyes and tell me that you don't believe me."

Zienna did no such thing. Instead she reached for her car door, knowing she needed to get away. She shouldn't be out here like this. She remembered Nicholas's warning not to trust Wendell, and to call the police if he contacted her.

Wendell rested his butt against the driver's side door, blocking her path. *"Look at me."* He spoke with more urgency this time, and she finally did as he asked. "If I'm guilty of anything, I'm guilty of pursuing you when I knew it was wrong. Of luring you into an affair when you were involved with my best friend. I'm guilty of being selfish. That's why I've stayed away since the fight at your place. You told me to go, and I did. And I realized how big of an ass I'd been. How much pain I've caused. I figured...I figured I owed it to Nick to let him work things out with you. That if you wanted me, you would reach out to me. But you didn't, and I'd already confused the issue enough, so I stayed away. Nick asked me to come by Sunday night to make peace. So that's what I did. Obviously, you'd made your choice, and I loved you enough to let you go. And I loved Nick enough to be happy for him."

"It was so easy for you," Zienna said, mocking him. "Just like the first time."

"You're not getting me, are you? It damn near killed me to walk away this time...because this time I *knew*. This time I was sure about you." He blew out a huff of air. "The first night I saw you again...and with my friend...I knew that I'd made the biggest mistake of my life when I left that day four years ago. And all I've been trying to do since I got back is make that right. When Nick asked me to flirt with you, I thought he was crazy—but I told him I'd do it, no problem. Because I wanted another chance with you. Not so I could report back to him. You know what I told him when he asked me if you'd flirted with me? I told him no, you hadn't. I didn't want to play the game he was controlling. I only wanted you.

I know the situation sucks. But I would never stab Nick because of this. And for him to tell the police that I did… What is *he* capable of?"

Zienna had heard enough. "You're not actually saying what I think you're saying?"

"That he's deliberately lying to get me into trouble?" Wendell replied. "Yes, that's exactly what I'm saying. At first I thought he was confused. Now I know he's not. He's always seen me as a threat, Zee. Always. He loves you, and he's not going to lose you to me. So he orchestrated the best plan to get me out of the picture for good."

"You're out of your mind," Zienna said.

"An attempted murder charge? Nick knows that even if I don't go to jail, you'll never want to be with me again if you believe I'm capable of murder. I bet he's drumming into your head the gory play-by-play of what he alleges happened, isn't he?"

Zienna stiffened. "What you're saying, it doesn't make sense."

"It makes more sense to you that I went to Nick's house, grabbed a knife and stabbed him?"

"You claim you'd made peace with Nicholas on Sunday night. If that was the case—if you were *letting* him have me, as you say—then why would he feel threatened? Why would he need to make up something like this to get you out of the picture?"

"I guess because he couldn't trust that you would stay with him. He had to make sure."

Zienna scoffed at the suggestion. But the truth was, she didn't know what to think. She was royally confused. And everything about Wendell's denial made her heart sing—which downright terrified her.

Because it made her think of Alexis's comments about

whether or not she was sticking with Nicholas for the right reasons, or out of guilt.

"My right shoulder's busted, remember?" Wendell went on. "Nick's doing, by the way. You think if we were in a fight I'd have the strength to stab him with my weak arm?"

Zienna said nothing, but his words were like a bolt of electricity zapping her. She hadn't considered that before, but what he was saying made sense....

Still, she said, "Maybe your shoulder's not as hurt as you claim."

"I'm scheduled for surgery next week."

"That doesn't... How do I know anything you say is true?"

"I love you," Wendell said, the words low and earnest, and washing over her like a warm breeze. "That's the simple truth of it. Do you think I'm lying?"

Zienna said nothing. She could hardly breathe. For years she had waited for Wendell to say those three meaningful words to her. For him to speak them, now it felt as if she was being pushed into a pit of despair.

"I love you. But if you didn't want to be with me, I wouldn't force it. If I didn't see the look on your face that I do even now, I would leave you alone. And that's what Nicholas was afraid of. Do you think he didn't see what I see? He was following us for weeks, knew that we were screwing around. What kind of game do you think he's playing? Do you think that's normal? Or do you think that maybe, just maybe, there's a hint of possibility that he is accusing me because he knows this is the only way to successfully keep us apart?"

"Wendell, stop." But Zienna spoke weakly. For in her heart she wanted to believe him. That much she knew without doubt. She wanted to believe him with every fiber of her being.

But she'd already destroyed his friendship with Nicholas, and she'd be damned if she'd hurt Nicholas any further.

"I'm not going to stop," Wendell said. "Not until I know you get it."

"For me to believe what you're saying, you're basically making the claim that Nicholas stabbed himself."

"If that's what it took, that's what he did."

"I can't hear any more of this."

"When Sandra and I had that affair in college, Nick left a suicide note and disappeared for five days. It was his way of punishing her. Punishing us."

The words were like a sledgehammer to the gut. But in the next instant, Zienna dismissed them. She couldn't hear more of Wendell's accusations. She couldn't accept that about Nicholas.

So she blurted out, "Nicholas and I are engaged."

"What?"

Zienna steeled her jaw, though her heart was beating out of control. "You heard me."

Wendell reached for her. "I can't accept that. Never."

The soft brush of his fingers against her cheek made her turn her head away and gasp. Because his touch still evoked something in her. Something inexplicable.

"You can't marry Nicholas."

Tears filled her eyes. "I should be calling the police, but I won't. Just go. Go, and leave us alone."

"Zee, you can't marry Nicholas. Think about it. If he's lying about me stabbing him, for the sole purpose of getting me in trouble, you don't think he's capable of hurting you?"

"Go!" And now the tears did come down her cheeks. "Go now!"

She faced Wendell then, saw in his eyes that the fight was gone. He nodded, his face grim. "By the way, I talked to the police. They're not arresting me."

"What?" The word came out as a gasp.

"I wanted to know you believed me first, before I told you that part."

And then he turned and walked away, leaving Zienna speechless.

It hurt her to see him like that. Hurt her to see him in pain because of her rejection. But what did he really expect of her? She had already caused too much pain and drama as it was.

For some reason, she felt compelled to call out to him. "This is the road of less drama, Wendell. It's the safe road. But it's the one I need to be on."

She was thinking of Alexis, and her friend's epiphany where it came to Elliott. That the excitement she had wanted with Brock had not been worth the pain.

And that's all Wendell had ever been to Zienna—excitement and heartache.

"Do what you need to do," Wendell called over his shoulder. "I'll never stand in the way of what you really want."

"Thank you," she said, grateful that he was giving her what she was asking for.

He didn't turn back, and Zienna quickly got into her car. But as she started to drive, she began to cry. And the tears that streamed down her face didn't seem like the kind that came when a person was content saying goodbye.

They were the kind of tears that came when a person's heart was breaking.

28

"Nicholas, I don't understand." Zienna stared at him through narrowed eyes. "Why won't the police arrest Wendell?"

"They say there's not enough physical evidence," he replied, sounding irritated. "No prints on the knife. Obviously, Wendell was wearing gloves, but I didn't remember that. Shit, I'd just gone through a major trauma."

"B-but you saw him. You know he was the one who attacked you."

"My word against his—something to that effect. Without hard evidence, they can't make a case. So he gets away with it. As usual. Just like a guy who has a silver spoon up his ass. He can never do any wrong."

"That doesn't make any sense to me. You're the one in hospital. You and Wendell had that fight at my—"

"You think I like this any more than you do?" Nicholas snapped. "I don't. But I can't change it."

Five days had passed since Nicholas's surgery, and he was

finally being released that morning. The police had come to question him four times. And they had called again this morning, asking that he come in to the station.

"What doesn't make sense is why they keep asking you questions about the attack, if they're not going to arrest Wendell."

"My guess?" Nicholas asked, taking a moment to face her as he packed his small suitcase. "They probably think I'm confused about what happened to me."

Zienna had wanted to reject everything Wendell had said to her, but yesterday, when the detectives had come to question Nicholas again, she had tried to listen outside the door. She'd heard the same questions being asked over and over again, almost as though the police expected Nicholas to change his answers.

Where was he when he got stabbed? Was he on his knees? Was he standing? Was Wendell wearing gloves? Did Wendell stab him with his right or left hand?

Nicholas had been understandably irritated with the officers, and he was in a pissy mood this morning, as well.

"It's okay, baby," Zienna told him. "If Wendell did this to you—"

"*If?*" Nicholas cut her off, giving her a look of pure venom. "What do you mean, *if?*"

"I—I didn't mean it that way. I just meant that you know he's guilty, and therefore he won't be able to run from what he did forever. That's all I meant."

"Have you heard from him?"

Zienna made a face as she looked at Nicholas, whose own face was contorted in anger. "No." She shook her head. "Why would you even ask me that?"

"Oh, that's priceless."

"Meaning?"

"How many times did you lie to me when I asked if you were seeing Wendell?"

"That was before the attack. For God's sake, I told you I made my decision. That I cut him off. Honestly, how could you ever think that I would want to be with him or even talk to him, after what he did to you?"

Nicholas didn't answer, and a long silence ensued. After a while, he heaved a sigh and said, "The stress is getting to me, that's all. Unless you've been stabbed and left for dead, you don't know what that does to someone."

Zienna moved close to him and put her arms around his waist. "And maybe...maybe the police have a point. Maybe you suffered short-term memory loss when you were stabbed. Maybe the stress of what happened has confused you and it was really someone else who attacked you."

Nicholas jerked away from her and looked down at her with disgust. "If you don't believe me, you can leave right now."

"Nicholas—"

"Get out."

"What?"

He threw out a hand and instantly wrapped it around her neck. "I said if you don't believe me, you can get out of here." His words were slow, lethal. He pressed his lips to her ear and said, "I've put up with enough from you. You're the fucking reason I'm in here. Do you get it? This is your fault."

She reached for his hand, pulling at his fingers. "Nicholas..."

"Did you prefer the taste of Wendell's cock in your mouth?"

Nicholas asked, as calmly as one would ask a child if she wanted a lollipop. "You can tell me."

"Stop!" Zienna managed to wheeze.

Nicholas pushed her away violently, squeezing her larynx as he did so. Zienna gasped in a breath as tears filled her eyes. She rubbed her injured neck as she tried to regain control.

After a minute, Nicholas said, "All right, let's finish packing."

Still coughing, Zienna stared at him in disbelief. And for the first time, she didn't recognize him.

She saw a monster.

"I'm stressed," Nicholas said, his tone softening. "I'm sorry."

"In all the years my parents were together," Zienna began slowly, "I never once saw my father lay a hand on my mother."

"I'm sorry. It won't happen again."

"I wanted what they had," Zienna went on. "I thought…I thought I would have that with you."

"And you do have that with me."

"Because you almost died, I blocked out all the disturbing things I'd discovered about you. How you weren't there for me the day I told you about the guy from the clinic harassing me."

"What are you going on about?"

"You weren't there for me. I was having a bad day, and I needed a shoulder to cry on, and you weren't available. And you weren't around on the anniversary of my parents' death."

"We've discussed this. I neglected you. I promised not to do it again."

"You called a Realtor to list my place without asking me! My father never controlled my mother. Never. And I don't know what's worse, that or the fact that you videotaped me having sex with Wendell."

"Are you gonna start playing the saint card again?"

"I was willing to forget all of that, because I felt guilty about what happened to you." She heard Alexis's voice in her head, asking if she was staying with Nicholas out of guilt or because she loved him. "But you just showed me a side—"

"I'm recovering from a stab wound."

"—a side I can't forget. Nor forgive. You're not the right man for me."

He stalked toward her. "What are you saying?"

Zienna straightened her spine. She wasn't going to back down, not now.

This was it. It was over. He'd knocked off the rose-colored glasses when he'd put his hand on her.

"You're not the man for me."

He slapped her. Slapped her so hard her head jerked brutally to the right. She cried out and went flying.

And then he was on top of her, banging her head against the hard floor, and slapping and punching her until somehow, mercifully, the assault relented. Zienna opened her eyes to see members of the nursing staff pulling him off her.

"You cheat on me, you do this to me, then you're gonna leave me?"

He was like an enraged tiger, out of control.

"Mr. Aubrey," a male nurse said. "You need to calm down!"

"Get off of me!"

Two security guards came charging into the room, and with five people on Nicholas, they finally got him to the ground. All the while, he raged. Raged about how he hated her, that he wished she were dead because of how she had hurt him.

Zienna watched in horror, not recognizing the man he had become.

But she remembered Wendell's words—words she had wanted to refute at the time.

If he's lying about me stabbing him for the sole purpose of getting me in trouble, you don't think he's capable of hurting you?

Zienna had her answer.

She had the answer to everything.

29

In the days that followed, Nicholas was arrested. And not just because he had attacked Zienna in the hospital. The police also charged him with the commission of a crime in stabbing himself, then filing a false police report naming Wendell as the perpetrator.

There had been too many holes in Nicholas's story, the biggest one being the angle of the wound. Investigators had quickly determined that it was self-inflicted.

Zienna had stayed in the hospital overnight, being treated for her own injuries. She'd suffered a mild concussion when Nicholas rammed her head against the floor, and his hands and fists had resulted in a black eye, a busted lip and a laceration on her cheek that required four stitches.

Three days after she'd been released from hospital, she still looked absolutely wretched.

"How are you feeling?" Alexis asked. They were at Zienna's apartment, and Alex had refused to leave her side. She'd taken time off of work, claiming a family emergency. Because, after all, Zienna was like family to her.

"The truth?" Zienna looked at the half-eaten plate of fries and scrambled eggs Alexis had prepared for her. "What I feel the most is shock. I feel like my life became a soap opera over the last week and a half. The physical wounds will heal, but I'm not sure about the emotional scars."

"You'll get through it," Alexis assured her, nodding. "Just be grateful you saw this side of Nicholas now. That you didn't— God forbid—marry him and then discover how insane he is." She shuddered. "I can't even imagine it."

"Count your blessings, right?" Zienna said, and she forced herself to smile, because she didn't want to feel sorry for herself. "My parents always used to say that no matter how bad things got, you still needed to count your blessings."

"You're alive. When I think of what could have happened… you being here is a huge blessing." Alexis paused. "But I am so sorry I ever introduced him to you."

"Oh, God. Don't go blaming yourself." And then Zienna thought of Wendell. "If not for Nicholas, I might not have reconnected with Wendell."

Desperately worried, Wendell had come to visit her in the hospital once he'd learned of the attack. Though Zienna had been happy to see him, she'd asked him for a couple days to clear her head and get past the incident. He had given her three, calling this morning to ask if he could come by so they could talk.

Alexis smiled. "Yeah. Wendell. See, your face lit up when you said his name."

Zienna was through denying his effect on her. There was no longer the need. "He should be here within half an hour," she said, glancing at her wall clock.

"That means you're kicking me out?"

Zienna smiled sweetly. "If you don't mind."

Alexis placed a hand over her heart. "I'm wounded."

"I'm sure Elliott will help you get over it." The engagement was back on, and Alexis was wearing his ring again. They were now planning a Christmas wedding.

Alexis cleared the plates from the table and washed them, then gave Zienna a kiss on the cheek before leaving. "I love you," she told her.

"I love you, too."

Fifteen minutes after Alexis left, Zienna's intercom sounded. Drawing in a deep breath, she went to answer it.

"Hello?"

"It's me," Wendell said.

Zienna buzzed him in, and a few minutes later he was knocking on her door. Butterflies danced in her stomach as she opened it.

She stared up at him, and he stared down at her.

"Hey," he said, a little sigh escaping him.

"Hey, yourself."

"At least you're looking better than you did in the hospital." Gingerly, he touched her cheek. "But damn, did Nick ever do a number on you."

Zienna stepped back. "Come in."

Wendell followed her to the living room, where she took a seat on the sofa. He sat in the armchair opposite her.

For a long minute, neither of them spoke, just stared. The craziness of the past few days and weeks had taken its toll.

"Can't believe it," Wendell finally said. "Nick's facing jail time. You think you know someone…"

"He said something to me once. That jealousy can drive a person to do the unthinkable. He was referring to you, but I think he was really talking about himself. Because never in a million years would I think him capable of stabbing himself and blaming you. And the way he attacked me..." She shivered, remembering.

"He was completely irrational," Wendell said. "Out of his mind with jealousy."

Zienna knew that Wendell was right, that Nicholas had clearly been emotionally unstable. Yet she said, "Sometimes I can't help thinking that I pushed him to this. That if not for what I did, he'd still be a rational guy, the one who was capable of starting two restaurants from the ground up."

"It's not your fault," Wendell said.

"How can we not hold ourselves accountable?" she asked him.

"I can't. Not completely. I only know that Nick was already messed up. He had that jealousy, that rage inside of him before either of us came into his life. He was just able to hide it really well."

"It feels...if we get together, it would be at the expense of someone else's pain." Zienna looked down, her voice cracking. That was the heart of her problem. She loved Wendell; she knew that without a doubt. But her behavior had devastated Nicholas, and could she ever be with Wendell without remembering that?

"No." He shook his head. "If we get together, it's because we were always destined to be. From four years ago, when I fell for you but was too weak to make the decision to leave Pam. I mean, Nick knew. He knew we were bound to fall for each other. Probably from the instant he saw our eyes connect that first night at his restaurant. That's likely why he asked me to hit on you, thinking he'd be able to control the situation if he was part of it in some warped way."

"I never meant to hurt him," Zienna said, and wiped at a tear.

Wendell got up from the armchair and sat beside her. Angling to face her, he gently cupped her cheek with his left hand.

Zienna's heart fluttered. Fluttered with a sensation of love.

"Of course you didn't. Neither did I. It wasn't about hurting him. And if he never mentioned that whole thing about me flirting with you, things probably wouldn't have played out the way they did. I would have waited for your relationship with Nicholas to naturally run its course." Wendell sighed. "But it is what it is. And we're here now. And I'm really hoping... I just want to know that the cloud of Nicholas won't hang over us forever. That you and I will be okay."

Zienna's stomach fluttered this time. Damn, it always did when it came to Wendell. Whether he was suggesting that they meet for sex, or telling her that he was leaving, she always felt a reaction to him. Either sheer happiness or abject pain.

And that told her something.

Alexis had made the point that Zienna had gone back to Wendell because she'd always wanted him, not for the thrill of an affair. And it was a simple as that. She had heard the truth in Alexis's words and knew that her friend was right, even though at the time she hadn't wanted to accept it.

"Will we?" Wendell asked her. "Will we be okay?"

"Can we?" Zienna countered.

"I look in your eyes, Zee, and I see that you love me. I *feel* it. Why should we have to throw that away because of the external circumstances?"

"It's...it's just the guilt."

"We finally got here, Zee. Finally got to the point where we can be together. I admit it wasn't easy. It was messy. And Nicholas got hurt. But we got hurt, too."

Zienna looked at Wendell's shoulder, still in a sling until his surgery in two days. She had created a mess. All three of them had. But did she and Wendell have to suffer forever for that?

Zienna had learned that there really was no such thing as black or white, this or that, right or wrong. There were shades of gray in every aspect of life.

No, this hadn't been easy. It had been difficult, and painful, but at the end of the day, she was here and Wendell was here. The two of them were still reaching out to each other because they loved each other.

"Maybe we had to go through this pain to know for sure that we're meant to be. Because I know, Zee. I know."

His words made her heart sing, but the cloud of Nicholas, as he'd said, was still there. Yet Zienna could see the rays of sunshine beginning to burst through.

"At least now there's no one else we can hurt." She offered a small smile.

"No," Wendell agreed. "Because I will never hurt you again. I promise, Zienna. I will never hurt you. If you allow me, I'll spend the rest of my days loving you. Don't...don't let Nicholas rob us of that. If you do, then he wins. He wins."

Zienna inhaled a deep breath as she stared into Wendell's eyes. She didn't have to search to see the truth.

This man loved her. It was as obvious to her as how much she loved him.

"You're right," she said after a moment. "Nicholas tried to manipulate the situation, to manipulate me. I told him I'd never once seen my father try to control my mother. And I'm not going to let Nicholas control me now. He'd want nothing more than for us to be apart. I own what I did. Like you said, I wish I'd gotten involved with you after my relationship with Nicholas ran its course. But my God, Wendell." She stroked his face. "I've always loved you. Always. And after everything it took for us to get to this point, you sitting with me and no one between us..." She shook her head. "No. I'm not gonna let you go. I can't."

And as Wendell gazed into her eyes, Zienna saw something she didn't expect. A tear rolled down his cheek.

"There's nothing I want more than to marry you, have babies with you." He took the cross around his neck between his fingers. "I've never wanted that with anyone else. A normal life. A family. To grow old with someone."

"Oh, Wendell." Zienna began to cry softly. "Is this real? Is what I've waited for so long really happening?"

He wiped at her tears, then brushed away his own. "Not just you, Zee. Me, too. I've only ever wanted this with you. But I'd still give it up right now if I thought that would make you a happier person."

Zienna didn't just hear the words. She was touched by their significance. And she felt, for the first time since her parents had left her, the true, unconditional love she had been searching for.

"That's the difference between you and Nicholas," she said. "His love was selfish. But your love…your love fills all the holes inside of me. I want what you want. A life together, children. Forever."

He kissed her then, a slow, heat-filled kiss that warmed every part of her. A kiss that started to melt the cold memory of all the pain they had endured.

A kiss that told her she and her heart finally had a home.

★ ★ ★ ★ ★